CU00900990

TO AN HONORARY DEGREE

TO AN HONORARY DEGREE

Lois Simpson

The Book Guild Ltd.
Sussex, England

The Book Guild Limited
Temple House
25 High Street
Lewes, Sussex

First published 1991
© Lois Simpson 1991

Set in Baskerville

Typesetting by Dataset
St Leonards-on-Sea, Sussex

Printed in Great Britain by
Antony Rowe Ltd
Chippenham, Wiltshire

British Library Cataloguing in Publication Data

Simpson, Lois
To an honorary degree
I. Title
823. 914 [F]

ISBN 0 86332 629 3

1

A shaft of sunlight fell upon a table in a college library. Only one person was sitting there, head bent over a large book, surrounded by a sea of sheets of paper over which were extensive notes and calculations. Anna was engrossed in the thing she most enjoyed doing, discovering new facts in the world of mathematical science. It was expected that she would get a first class degree.

On a cricket pitch bathed in the sunshine of a June afternoon, the fielder on the square leg boundary stood, hands on hips, slowly chewing a piece of grass. He turned his face to the sun, closed his eyes momentarily and exulted in the joy of being there. He was expected to get a third class degree.

Finals had finished the week before and most students were caught up in the whirlwind of social activities which characterised those precious days between sitting the examinations and receiving the results. The weather was warm, the swimming pool crowded and every inch of the grass seemed to be covered with sun-worshipping bodies. There were just two more weeks of term, of being undergraduates, of being free from responsibility.

It was nearly seven o'clock when Richard walked into the library. Anna was still there but she had packed up her books and was reading a newspaper. She smiled at him as he walked across.

'I'm going to take you out to eat.'

'I thought that you were broke.'

'Not quite broke, only nearly broke; I've enough for two packets of chips. I've got something important that I want to talk to you about.'

It had only been seven months ago that she had first met this student and although they were in different faculties, seemed to have a few interests in common and had dissimilar backgrounds they had continued to see each other regularly since then.

Anna Moors was twenty. She could not remember her father who had been killed in a car crash when she was two. Shortly afterwards her mother had resumed her teaching career and until Anna was old enough to start school she had spent the days with Mrs Hoggs, who lived next door. This kindly, elderly woman had been the key person in those early years. She had taken Anna to feed the ducks on the pond; she had let her make jam tarts and, best of all, she had let her strum on the piano and make as much noise as she liked. It was one of the saddest moments in Anna's life when she had heard that her mother had been appointed to a deputy headship of a school in London and that they would be leaving Mrs Hoggs and their little terrace house in Garside. Anna was eight then.

From the quiet of a Yorkshire village she moved to the uproar of a large city. She had known nearly everyone in Garside and they had certainly all known her. Now she knew nobody. Instead of the cosy cottage in the middle of the stone terrace with its small walled back garden, they now lived in a fifth floor flat which had only a tiny balcony and a window box. From her bedroom Anna could see for miles but it was a view of roof tops and chimneys. At first she had hated it but as the years went by she had become accustomed to the life and more appreciative of the convenience of where they lived. Mrs Moors was happier. She enjoyed the reponsibility of the new post, the ease of living in a modern flat, the access to more culture and her involvement with the local Baptist Church. Her working hours fitted in well with Anna's and when she did have to stay late at school Anna would come up and wait for her in the staff room. In the holidays they would go and visit Mrs Moors' two aunts who lived in Brighton and once they went back to Garside to see Mrs Hoggs. In later years they went abroad.

Anna's intellectual ability was apparent at a very early age. She loved school and was always asking for work to do

6

at home. In the evenings while Mrs Moors marked books Anna did calculations. Life worked out well together. At the age of ten Anna transferred to the grammar school. Her mother heard unofficially on the teaching grapevine that Anna's marks in the 11 plus examination were the highest known and her I.Q. testing confirmed that she was a child with quite exceptional ability. Her native intelligence was matched by her protestant work ethic resulting in her taking her O and A levels a year early.

It was during the first year in the sixth form that Anna realised that her mother was not well. Six months later Mrs Moors had a radical mastectomy and although the successful operation and subsequent radiotheraphy treatment conveyed from the medical profession an impression of cure, there was an inevitable anxiety about the future. Anna abandoned her plans to sit the Cambridge entrance examination the following autumn and accepted, instead, the immediate offer of a place at London University to read physics. She would be able to continue to live at home and to commute daily. Mrs Moors did try to persuade Anna to change her mind. She herself felt quite well again and was back teaching full time; yet she had to confess that she was glad to have Anna around. Each led a somewhat lonely life having few friends and interests outside their work and the church.

University life was everything that Anna could have wished for and perhaps even more than that. The physics department was not a large one and there were few women students reading this subject. After being at a girls' school she found the challenge of working with male students something new. She was shy and they teased her but they had to admit to a sneaking regard for her ability. Occasionally she played netball and she was an active member of the student Christian Union but the rest of her time was spent on her studies. Early in the second year her work attracted the attention of the Head of Department and he encouraged her to think in terms of research after her final examinations. She knew then that an academic life was all that she had ever wanted and the possibility of studying for a higher degree was the ultimate incentive, if one had been needed, for aiming at first class honours. In

7

her final year she played no netball but she did go to a Christian Union week-end in the November.

Richard Trevanion had never belonged to the Christian Union because he said when he came to university he needed a break from religion. However, when his room mate spoke of the weekend retreat being so undersubscribed that it might have to be cancelled, he allowed himself to be talked into going for what he was told would be a pleasant, inexpensive weekend in the Cotswolds. He was in his final year reading geography but he also, with much greater success, played rugby and cricket for the university and was likely to represent his country in one of these sports in the years ahead. Although the rugby season was in full swing he had no match that particular weekend and he always loved being in the country, even in November. On the Friday evening, at dinner he sat next to Anna Moors and so began a relationship between two people, which few, least of all themselves, would have predicted.

Every vacation, for part of it at least, Richard returned to his beloved Cornwall. It was nearing Christmas and he was looking from the bus window as he travelled home. When the wind was in the north, it blew straight down the valley. The coniferous trees which flanked the steep eastern slope bent low in its wake and waves ran the gauntlet against the river current. The rectory stood high on the western side nestling in the hillside below the church. Normally it was sheltered for the wind which predominates is a gentle, moist sou'westerly which brings an early spring to the valley. Soon after Christmas there are primroses in the hedge bottoms and daffodils may be in bud by mid February. But when the north wind is funnelled through the narrow straights, the flower buds snap off and the cruel cold of winter returns until this wind is spent.

As the bus wound its way up the valley road Richard noticed the trees leaning with the wind. He knew that it would be howling round the rectory and that the sitting room fire would smoke that night. When the bus turned the corner into the village he saw his father walking down the road to meet him. The rector's overcoat collar was turned up against the wind but he was bare headed. A country parson's stipend did not stretch to running the ancient car for other than essential journeys. On Sundays the close dovetailing of service time in three parishes was dependent upon the car being operational. This situation was rarely put at risk by unnecessarily overtaxing the old car's stamina, and so, even when the weather was as blustery as it was on that day, the rector would walk. He argued that he could not speak with people when he was cooped up inside a car, but if he rode his bicycle, or better still walked, his parishioners found him to be more accessible for the telling of their troubles or just the casual exchange of a daily greeting.

Richard had two cases and a rucksack in the boot of the bus. The driver got out with him to unlock the door and they unloaded the luggage on to the pavement.

'Thanks for coming, Dad.'

'It's a pleasure Richard; it's good to see you. Mum is waiting at home; she is baking.'

It was not far to walk to the rectory and easier with two pairs of hands to carry the luggage. They went in through the back door. Mrs Trevanion had just finished making pasties and rubbing her floured hands on her apron, she hurried from the kitchen to hug him. The feeling never left Richard; no matter how many times he went away, it always felt good to be home. The kettle was boiling on the Aga ready for a cup of tea. It was probably the most boiled kettle in the parish for many parishioners' problems were talked through, and often resolved, in the rectory kitchen while they waited for the rector to return home.

Tom Trevanion had married early in life. He had been ordained, wed and priested within just twelve months and after a further two years as a curate in the Midlands he had moved back, with his young wife and baby son to his native Cornwall, there to remain for the rest of his ministry. He had no ambition to rise within the church hierarchy and, apart from taking his turn as rural dean within his part of the diocese, he continued as a parish priest serving a rural community. As the years went by and the number of men offering themselves for ordination decreased it was inevitable that he would have the responsibility of additional churches. He began his life at Laneast as rector of that

9

parish but fifteen years later he had two more parishes and five ancient buildings to maintain.

The rectory was Georgian and well built. It was large but so was the family, so the spaciousness was an essential if a mixed blessing. In winter it could be cold but the church-warden who farmed nearby let the boys gather timber from his woodlands, and when they were older let them borrow his tractor and trailer to bring it home. Summer months were spent stacking wood to dry; winter days were for sawing, at first by hand and then in later years with a noisy, but far less tedious chain saw.

The garden extended to a little over two acres. All the family had to help to keep it in any degree of order, but it was the source of all their vegetables and soft fruit and the rector kept some chickens in the orchard. They could hardly be described as a commercial proposition but they added atmosphere to the place and each rejoiced in a biblical name from the Old Testament. They also provided eggs for the house somewhat intermittently. It was always possible to adjust the demands of the parish to accommodate the needs of the house and garden. Wet days were for prolific sermon creating, letter writing and parish visiting, and this pattern suited the parishioners too for on fine days they also had important tasks to be undertaken outdoors. Much rain falls in Cornwall so the spiritual side of the parish was never neglected.

Like all families this family had its tensions. The rectory family might be expected to epitomize loving Christian living, but the boys argued and fought with each other and on occasions the parents got angry with them and voices were raised. And because they were as other families there was never a barrier between this one and the other families in the village. Perhaps the obligation upon the rectory children to attend church services was higher and from an early age the boys dutifully trooped into the front pew with their mother. But it was not unknown for them to fidget incessantly during the service, to sigh pointedly with boredom in the sermon and upon one Easter Day when a note had been left in the pews indicating that the offering would be given to the rector, to have a loud and excited discussion about the money that might come their way and the use to which it might be put. The arrival of twin daughters nine years after Richard was a great joy to the rectory. At first the babies slept in their pram at the back of the church but as they got older and more restless this practice had to be varied, and then there were arguments between Hugh and Richard as to who was going to hold the crying sister. Finally, Mrs Trevanion decided that it would be easier to abandon temporarily family church going until increased age made it more compatible with orderly worship.

All the children had been to the village school and after they were eleven had gone by bus to the secondary school ten miles away. In many respects this had been hardest for the eldest son Matthew. His innate intelligence distanced him to some extent from his peer group but the latter interpreted this as snobbishness. Matthew was continually ragged on the school bus which was to make the gap between them even wider. By the time that the next brother, Hugh, started travelling the novelty of the goading was wearing off and when the amiable, sport loving and hence popular Richard became a daily passenger, the breach was finally healed. All the boys had left school when Jane and Kate started at secondary school but they had no problems for few could be less prim and parsonic than the rector's twin daughters.

They would soon be coming in from that school bus. Now thirteen, they were noisy, giggly, argumentative and very enthusiastic about their divergent interests. Richard was their favourite brother. He was more fun than the rather retiring Matthew and more approachable than Hugh whom the twins found to be somewhat arrogant. Richard was different. As babies he had never minded pushing them out in their pram. It was he who had taught them to ride a two-wheeler bicycle, had taken them fishing late at night and when he could drive had never minded collecting them from various evening activities in the precious family car. But it was not all one way; he enjoyed their company. Matthew and Hugh were academics. They studied hard and achieved considerable success in their chosen careers. Both had won open scholarships to Oxford. Richard was the sportsman. He liked being outside. Study was a necessity about which he never enthused, and entrance to a less famous university to read a subject which was rarely over subscribed reflected a need for him to have the opportunity to continue to play representative sport. Richard had played rugby for Cornwall boys and in summer he played cricket although with slightly less success. He was always doing something and inevitably it was the sort of thing which his sisters thought they could do too. They did draw the line at playing rugby but for cricket they had considerable affinity. Numerous chalked wickets on the east wall of the rectory reflected the hours spent by Richard and his friends in developing their batting skills and the need for fielders to guard the boundary in front of the study window created a role for the girls beyond that of just being tolerated. In the fullness of time they were allowed a go with the bat and finally earned the right to bowl.

If our history makes us what we are then Richard and Anna could be expected to have quite different attributes. Life for Richard, although materially somewhat impoverished, was rich in emotional endowment and had been a relatively easy ride so far. He had had much fun, love, support and security from his family. They lived in a beautiful part of Cornwall and even if they could never afford to go away for holidays it did not matter when the moors and sea were so near. Richard had been on a school trip to France but he had paid most of this himself by doing the paper round on his bicycle every morning before school. It had taken him nearly a year to save up, but then he had so many birthdays for which to buy presents and Richard was always over generous. He rarely had any money because he was not very good at saving so the gradual amassing of the French trip account was a tremendous personal achievement. It could have been argued that he would suffer with the middle child syndrome having two scholastically successful older brothers and two potentially equally able younger sisters. It was interesting that of all the women students in the university he should select for friendship the one most equal to his siblings and the one most unlike himself. Yet Richard genuinely rejoiced in all their achievements and balanced these with his own success in the field of sport. Of all the rectory children he had the most engaging personality and if he inherited from his father a lack of ambition, from his mother he had acquired a special warmth and skill in personal relationships.

Anna's father had left his small family well provided for and with her mother's salary they had always lived comfortably. Although they gave some money to good causes and especially their church, they had the luxuries of good holidays, a reasonably extensive wardrobe and expensive, quickly prepared foods. They could not be described as extravagant but they did not ever have to worry about paying their way. The rough and tumble of family life had been denied Anna. She had always seemed older than her years and she had shared with her mother the adult responsibility of their life together. It could be viewed as an upbringing not rich in emotional blessings and Anna early compensated for her unrecognised loneliness by diligent studying and because this was something which brought its rewards and which she enjoyed.

Anna had never had a boy friend as such, in fact she had very few friends of either sex, for exceptionally high Intelligence Quotients can create barriers in relationships. So, when charming, warm, affable Richard had sat next to her one November evening in the Cotswolds she had been ill at ease, uncomfortable and almost embarrassed. He had not seemed to notice and had chatted on quite happily about Cornwall and rugby, cricket and Christ and Anna had found it getting easier and easier to talk with him and this weekend was more pleasurable than any of the previous ones which she had attended. When later she was to ask Richard why he had sat next to her in the first place and then spent most of the weekend with her, he had laughed and said that it must have been Divine Intervention. Richard had noticed that she had seemed to be on her own, but then he did not know many of the students who had come for the weekend so he was glad to share her company. He liked her seeming innocence, he felt sorry that she had missed out on so many things which he knew to have been important for him and was to come to admire greatly her integrity. Anna never spoke ill of anyone. Of her intellect he was more in awe.

Back in college, between playing rugby and doing a little geography he arranged to see more of Anna. She rationed the time with him so that it did not intrude upon her tight work schedule, but this might have been beneficial to him because he was organised into doing more studying. He felt about her as he had felt about no other girl but it was not a particularly serious friendship.

So it was over a packet of chips and a piece of cod that Richard raised his important matter. Term was nearly over, degree results would soon be out. It was likely that Anna would be taking up her research very soon and he would be in Cornwall doing his farming job until he started his year on the Education course. Suddenly he had felt that they were going to drift apart with no plans for the future.

'How about getting engaged?' he asked.

'To be married?'

'Yes. I'm sort of proposing to you.'

He had made his suggestion almost half in jest. To his amazement Anna agreed. Although he had meant what he said he was so convinced that she would reject it that he almost felt panic strickened by her acceptance.

'But we can't think about getting married for some time yet, Richard. We don't know for certain what we shall be doing next year; we've little money and – well – I've got to think about mother also and how she would manage if she were ill again.'

Richard felt quite relieved to hear this but he hoped that it was not obvious.

Anna did not know why she had said that she would marry Richard Trevanion. She did not think that she loved him, yet she thought he would be relatively easy to live with. She had not anticipated his proposal or even considered marriage, yet she knew if she were to marry anyone it could be him; she did not want to give up her academic career and she knew that with him she would not have to do so. They were, however, both talking about a life together which would begin sometime well into the future.

In an immaculately tidy, centrally heated, suburban flat over a meal of cheese salad and yoghurt Anna told her mother that she was getting engaged to a geography student from Cornwall. Her mother was astounded. She had had no inkling that Anna was involved with anything other than her studies and she immediately queried the wisdom of getting engaged only two weeks after finals. But her greatest anxiety, which she expressed with considerable sorrow, was to do with the interference which this might have upon an otherwise brilliant career. It did not help her to know that Richard was not particularly academic and a sportsman and not even the information that he was a parson's son planning to go into teaching eased her troubled mind. Perhaps the thing that hurt her most was that she just did not know anything about this relationship and that it had been going on for several months without her realising that it existed.

The fact that there was unlikely to be a wedding for at least three years did give her some comfort. For Stella Moors marriage and a career had not been compatible, so inevitably she thought the same would hold true for her daughter. She did not believe that a student of such exceptional ability should be sidetracked into marriage at such a crucial stage in her academic life. Secretly, she hoped that the long wait might cool the relationship and later Anna was to guess that this might be so. It was not that her mother did not want her to marry, it was just that at the age of twenty she considered Anna far too young to be even contemplating it.

The limbo life between taking examinations and receiving the results ended with the release of the unofficial pass list. Of course Anna had a first class degree and her professor told her confidentially that she had obtained the highest marks in the university and she would be awarded the principal research scholarship to enable her to work for a doctorate. To his astonishment Richard had obtained a lower second class degree, but as his professor told him in confidence a little later, he had been a marginal candidate and it had been the high marks of one answer on the agricultural geography of the south west which had pulled him out of the third class division. He was, of course awarded his university colours for cricket. Anna's mother took them both out to dinner to celebrate. She was absolutely thrilled by Anna's results and felt quite warm towards Richard who appeared not to have interfered with the academic's progress. About the proposed engagement she said very little. Next day Richard caught the coach back to Cornwall and Anna and her mother went for a holiday cruise along the Rhine.

It was after supper on the first evening at home that Richard told the family of his engagement. If they were surprised his parents did not make it blatantly obvious. They too had known nothing about this friendship and were new to the experience of having an offspring contemplating matrimony, particularly as it was their third child who first was to embark upon this course. They asked much about Anna and hoped that Richard would bring her to stay in the near future. They did ask when the wedding might be and seemed to think that it was wise to delay this for a year or two until their careers were a little more securely established. Jane and Kate immediately proposed that they would be bridesmaids and they assumed that, regardless of anyone else's wishes they would be playing a significant part in a grand wedding.

During the early part of the summer vacation Anna and Richard corresponded. Anna wrote frequently, but letter writing was no problem for her. Richard tried to write regularly but this had never been his forte and he was working long hours on one of the farms in the village. Two weeks before she began her research project Anna came to the rectory to stay. She had yet to meet all the family, although she and Richard had spent an evening with Hugh when he had been in London. At first she found life at the rectory a little like being at Clapham Junction station, but she gradually adjusted to the toing and froing, to the fact that people and times had to be flexible, and realised that it was quite organised chaos. She fell in love with Cornwall; it evoked memories of Garside and she liked the way neighbours greeted her because she was 'Richard's maid'. She remembered that at Garside people had said 'How do' when they passed each other in the street; here they said 'All right'. Nobody seemed to expect an answer but there were many ways of intoning that phrase in reply which no doubt conveyed a range of possible descriptions of how individuals were. They did a lot of walking on the moors, went swimming in the sea and had very little time on their own because the twins usually tagged along as well. When Mrs Trevanion did suggest to Jane and Kate that they might be overdoing their welcome both Richard and Anna said that they did not mind. They also picked, sliced and salted runner beans and stacked the inevitable supply of winter wood.

On the Thursday evening of the second week Anna had a telephone call from her mother. She was ringing from the hospital to which she had been admitted earlier that day for some tests to be carried out. Anna was immediately alarmed; she was only too aware of the implications of the investigations to a woman with her mother's medical history. Her mother seemed to be calm and said that she would not have rung had she not expected Anna to be in touch with her at home. Anna said that she would return home immediately; her mother said that she should do no such thing. But, the following morning Anna did go back. She went straight to the hospital and learned that her mother had begun to have some painful symptoms which were being investigated. The next day she was told that her mother would need to have some exploratory surgery and this was planned for the following Monday, the day she was to begin her life as a research student in the Department of Physical Sciences. It was more usual for Richard to ring her but this time she initiated the call because she felt a real need to speak with him. After hearing his warm, caring voice she felt better and promised to be in touch with him as soon as there was any news. They agreed that the best thing for her to do on Monday morning was to start work.

Anna saw her mother at visiting times on Saturday and Sunday. Even in hospital Mrs Moors was preparing lessons for the following term and Anna took in the various books that she needed. They talked about the research project and the fact that it was going to start that week seemed to bring great joy to Mrs Moors. However, when Monday morning dawned Anna knew that going to work was not going to be the best thing that she could do. She had never felt less like studying nor ever quite so consumed with anxiety. No hospital visiting was allowed on operation day but she had been told that she could telephone after four o'clock for news of her mother. She went into college and did some routine tasks, then left early in the afternoon for home. A little after three o'clock the telephone rang. It was the hospital. They were very sorry but they had some bad news. For some reason which, at that moment, was inexplicable, Mrs Moors had collapsed on the operating table and was critically ill. Anna said that she would come immediately. She ran down the four flights of stairs and hailed a taxi. When she got to the hospital the surgeon explained that during the beginning stages of the operation Mrs Moors had had a cardiac arrest and although she had been revived her condition remained extremely serious and she was in the Intensive Care Unit. Anna was welcome to stay at the hospital for the night.

When she reflected back upon that moment Anna recalled feeling numb and very calm. She could think clearly and was able to plan immediately those whom she must contact. She walked from the ward down the corridor to the telephone kiosk and as she turned the corner she saw Richard coming towards her. He had been to the flat and when she had not been there had come straight to the hospital. As he put his arms around her he said quite simply,

'I thought you might need me.'

Then the tears came and he held her close to him.

Mrs Moors did not recover consciousness and died just before midnight. The post mortem examination subsequently carried out was to reveal that she had an extensive occurrence of secondaries to her original cancer and that had she survived the operation she would not have lived for very long. Richard took Anna back to her flat and stayed with her for the following week. He did the shopping and cooking and helped her with all the arrangements that had to be made. His mother and father travelled up from Cornwall for the funeral, but apart from Mrs Moors' two aunts and a cousin, the rest of the mourners were from their church and from the school.

Richard was due to start at college, so he suggested to Anna that she went back to Cornwall with his parents for a few days. She declined, saying that she had already missed so much time that it would be better for her to get on with the research. Her need to fulfil her mother's ambitions seemed to Richard now to be even greater, and not for the first time he wondered if there was going to be room in that life for him.

2

Although Anna had done her first degree in physics she chose, in her research, to do a project involving more practical experimentation and moved towards the field of crystallography. This fitted well with the research area of her supervisor, the professor and head of the department. In the eminence of his later scientific life he had little time for student supervision and it was rare for any student below a post-doctoral level to be so honoured. However, he had early noticed Anna's ability and recognised in her a scientist of the greatest potential. Initially, Anna's project was to gain her a doctorate but it was also the beginning of a research collaboration destined to be of enormous scientific significance and long standing.

The laboratory shared by the research students was large, reasonably well equipped and pleasantly situated on the south side of the college building. Each of the four students had a small cubicle off the main room which acted as a relatively quiet retreat for studying and writing. One of these was slightly more spacious and it had been the one allocated to Anna, not so much because she was the professor's student, but more because she was the only woman in the group.

When Anna returned after her mother's death she sensed the unease amongst her colleagues. They said how sorry they were, but then did not seem to have anything else to say. One of them Anna had known from her undergraduate days; the other two came from different universities and they had only been briefly introduced upon that first and fateful day. While she had been away it was apparent that a dialogue had developed between them and she was outside this. She knew it would be up to her to ease her way into their working relationship. To some extent she was privileged in that she was the professor's student, but equally she was something of a threat in that her intellect was already legendary. Her second start at being the research student was less difficult than her first of a fortnight previously, but it was not easy. Work now became even more of a compulsive force in Anna's life. She walked in the shadow of her loss knowing now, more than ever before, how symbiotic had been the relationship between her and her mother. She contained her grief and mourned her loss by working excessively hard, even by her standards. If ever a child was to realise a parent's personal unfulfilled ambitions it was to be this one and it was a heavy cross which she chose to carry.

Anna had inherited the flat from her mother and also the proceeds of a fairly substantial life insurance policy. After her husband had been killed Mrs Moors had insured her own life so that if ever Anna were to become an orphan she would always have an income. The wisdom of that action was such that Anna's scholarship was now well supplemented and she could concentrate on her research without ever having to worry about finances.

As an undergraduate, Richard had been something of an academic nonentity and it was as a sportsman that he had achieved fame. The situation changed in his year at the Institute of Education. His prowess on the sports field, together with his relaxed manner and his enthusiasm in the class room, enabled him to establish early in his first teaching practice, a rapport with youngsters which was to be the hallmark of his teaching career. He was what could glibly be described as 'a born teacher.' Teaching geography was for him far more enjoyable than studying it had been, and the ample opportunities in this school for coaching games provided pleasant breaks from the classroom. In the autumn of his teacher training year he was selected for senior county rugby trials, a feat which did even more to ensure his popularity in school. He shared a flat with three other students and had been fortunate in that this first teaching practice was within daily cycling distance. As usual, he managed on a financial shoe string and lived happily. Life for Richard felt good.

He knew Anna well enough to recognise her need to adjust at her own pace. If he thought that she was giving too much time to her work he did not say so. For their relationship to have any permanency he knew that he must wait until Anna was ready to give more of herself to it. Occasionally he felt guilty because he was enjoying his life so much and yet he was aware of another person's loneliness and her sorrow. She chose to deal with this by working rather than by sharing it with him or, apparently, with any one else. When he tentatively had suggested that she did otherwise he had met a rebuff and did not try again. Most Sundays he went to Anna's flat for the day. If she was busy he would cook the dinner, although it was something that they usually did together and could do amicably. Anna liked to go to her church once on Sunday and he would go with her, although he felt far less comfortable there than in an Anglican one and in particular his own village church with his father conducting the service. Anna once bought some tickets for a concert because she knew that Richard had no money for luxuries and she always provided special food when he was coming over because she suspected that he existed on only a moderate diet. And so might have continued a pattern of life for a considerable period of time had not Anna done something which appeared to be totally out of keeping with her character.

It was pouring with rain and quite late one Tuesday evening in November. Richard had just finished marking a batch of fifth year essays and had gone into the kitchen to make himself a drink. He was going to have a bath and go to bed early because next day he had an important rugby match. He heard the door bell ring and he heard John going to answer it. John came back into the kitchen.

'You have a visitor.'

'At this time of night? Who on earth wants to call at this hour?'

'It's Anna.'

'Yes it's me calling at this time of night,' said Anna coming into the room.

John lifted his eyebrows, gave Richard a knowing wink and with a grin withdrew closing the door behind him.

Richard gave Anna a kiss and took off her coat which was soaked with the heavy rain. Her skirt and jumper were wet also. It was so unlike Anna to get caught in the rain or to be out walking without wearing a proper raincoat. He suggested that she had the bath which he had planned for himself to warm herself up and he gave her his track suit to wear while they dried her clothes on the radiator. While she was in the bath he made another mug of cocoa, borrowed some of John's biscuits and put some more money in the meter for the gas fire. And all the time he was pondering about this very unexpected visit.

Anna knelt on the floor in front of the fire and cupped the mug of cocoa in her hands. She looked up at Richard sitting in the only armchair in the room and said quietly:

'I think we should get married very soon.'

Richard stared at her. His head began to reel. Marriage had become a low priority in his future planning, in fact he had sometimes thought that Anna might break off the engagement now that she was so engrossed in her academic work.

'Very soon? How soon? When?'

'As soon as possible.' She continued to look at him and she sensed his alarm. 'You do still want to marry me?'

Then he relaxed and the panic was over. He was overwhelmed with a feeling of warmth for her and he knelt down on the floor beside her and took her into his arms. In his track suit she looked like one of the third form girls he taught, but here was a young woman asking him to make her his wife and as soon as possible. He had nothing material to offer her as his wife; he had not yet had enough money to buy her an engagement ring.

But Anna had thought it all through with the precision of analysis credited only to the scientist. It seemed illogical for her to live alone in her well furnished flat on her more than adequate income while he struggled along, albeit happily, on a pittance. If they were married they could live much more comfortably together and the distance that he had to travel to work each day would only be marginally greater.

'But those are not the best reasons for marrying, Anna.'

Anna was looking into her mug and she did not raise her eyes. She had always found it easier to deal with facts rather than feelings.

'If I am to share my life with anyone then it is to be with you. I suppose that is saying that I do love you.'

Anna stayed for what little remained of that night. She slept in Richard's bed and he in the armchair in the living room. She was late into the laboratory next morning and he played a poor game of rugby in the afternoon. But during that night, for the first time, they had talked someway through the problem areas of different careers, different religions and perhaps different life aspirations. The compromises that were agreed were that they would continue to live near to the university and Anna's laboratory, they would marry in an Anglican church and they would not plan to have a family in the immediate future.

Instead of going for a drink with the team after the match Richard cycled into town before the shops closed. He went into a jewellers and with the proviso that it could be changed if it did not fit, he spent nearly all the money he possessed on an engagement ring. On he cycled to the university expecting to find Anna making up time after her late start that day. The other students had gone home but she was sitting at the bench writing up some notes. With a competent genuflect which only the son of a clergyman could achieve he took her left hand and asked:

'Would the future Mrs Trevanion care to accept a small token of her husband-to-be's affection?'

Then he slipped a slightly too large ring on to her fourth finger.

The rectory telephone rang late in the evening. Richard, wanting to speak to with his father, waited until it was his usual bed time to be sure that he was in. Mrs Trevanion was in the bath but she could hear her husband speaking on the extension in their bedroom.

'Well it's all very sudden, Richard. Why the unexpected change of plans?'

There was a lengthy pause, obviously while he was listening to the reasons. Mrs Trevanion decided that she had better be getting out of the bath and finding out what was happening. She dried herself quickly and hurried into the bedroom.

'It's Richard ringing from a call box but he had run out of

money and I didn't think to ask him for his number before the pips went. He wants to get married at Christmas.'

'This Christmas?'

'Apparently so.'

'Why the rush?'

'I don't know; he said something about it being more convenient all round and then he was cut off.'

The telephone rang again.

Richard had found another coin.

'Give me your number and I will ring you back,' said his father.

Mrs Trevanion put on her dressing gown and went downstairs to listen on the telephone in the study. By the time they had dialled back to Richard they were over the initial surprise. After having reared a family of five they were really well versed in the art of adapting to the unpredicted. The main reason for Richard's phone call was a request to his father that he marry them in his own parish church one day in Christmas week.

'If this is to be, I shall need to see you in the same way as I do any couple whom I am to marry.'

'Shall we come home this weekend?'

'That would be nice,' came Mrs Trevanion's voice on the study extension.

So it was that the following Friday evening Anna and Richard met at Paddington station and caught the evening train to the west country. Mrs Trevanion met them at the station and there seemed to be an extra warmth in her hug as she greeted them both.

'Dad has a meeting, but he shouldn't be late.'

In fact Mr Trevanion was home before them and had put the kettle on. Next morning he saw Anna and Richard quite formally in his study. They talked about the responsibility of matrimony, the fact that they were not members of the same religious denomination and the implications that this might have for any children born of the union. Finally, he agreed to marry them on the Tuesday after Christmas.

It left just five weeks to organise what the young couple hoped would be a quiet wedding and which, if previous weddings in the village were anything to go by, would be anything but quiet. Anna had only her mother's two aunts

25

who would expect to be invited but there was an extensive network of Trevanion relatives, most of whom lived in Cornwall and all of whom enjoyed family celebrations. Anna asked Matthew to give her away. After Richard she thought that she felt closest to his studious elder brother and he said that he was honoured by her request. The ever diplomatic Richard invited Hugh to be his best man and Jane and Kate, who had always planned to be bridesmaids, once more offered their services.

'It is a quiet wedding,' said their mother, 'don't be so pushing.'

'It doesn't sound very quiet to me,' retorted Jane, 'and anyway what is a quiet wedding?'

'Anna's mother only died last September, so as a mark of respect there has to be some limit on the amount of celebrating.'

But Anna wanted them to be bridesmaids and said that she would like to buy their dresses for the occasion. It was planned that they would have a small family reception at the rectory after the marriage service.

☆ ☆ ☆

'I publish the banns of marriage between Richard James Trevanion, bachelor of this parish and Anna Elizabeth Moors, spinster of the parish of St Saviours. . .'

The congregation stirred. Richard felt eyes turning upon him. He continued to look at his father at the chancel steps.

'. . . if any of you know cause, or just impediment, why these two people should not be joined together in holy matrimony, ye are to declare it.'

The congregation had been caught completely unawares. Few had suspected an unofficial engagement; none of them had anticipated a wedding. They knew, of course, that Richard had a girl, but this was nothing unusual since he had had several girls even in his short life. Although some members of the congregation that morning did try to block out uncharitable thoughts while in the present of the Almighty, the reading of the banns could not fail but to evoke some speculation about the possible necessity of such a rapidity of events. After all Anna had first been down to the rectory only that summer and they all knew that she had gone back early because her mother had been taken ill. Now, within three months there was going to be a wedding. There were some who were to say that it was hardly decent so soon after the funeral, and a few who were to go even further and comment upon their surprise at the rector allowing it. But the information had brightened up considerably the morning's worship and as they shook hands with the rector in the porch after the service nearly everyone, with varying degrees of sincerity, said how pleased they were to know about the young couple.

It could be predicted that a December wedding in Cornwall would dawn wet and windy. Richard rarely noticed the weather having been raised in this climate, but Anna was very aware of the rain beating on the bedroom window when she woke up. She lay in bed reflecting on the day ahead. At times she felt alone in the world and no matter how warm and welcoming were the Trevanion family, she did not feel that she was part of them. She wondered if she ever would. Her thoughts turned to Richard and not for the first time she had qualms about the wisdom of bringing forward their wedding plans. Perhaps she was being selfish in shackling him with matrimony when he would have been quite contented to wait until their careers were more firmly established. Hers was very clearly identified with the university research department and this fact in itself would tie Richard to seeking jobs within that area.

There was a knock on her door and Richard came in with a cup of tea.

'I'm told that it is very unlucky for the bride and groom to meet before the ceremony on their wedding day.'

'Ours must be a different sort of marriage.'

'Yes, I suppose it is. . . or is it?' He sat down on the bed. Then he got up, closed the bedroom door and lay down on the bed beside her.

'I suppose that it is even more unlucky for the groom to share his bride's bed on the wedding morning.'

He leaned over and kissed her. Anna was apprehensive.

'Somebody will come in,' she said.

27

'So what?'

'But this is the rectory.'

'That doesn't mean the lusts of the flesh should be banned.' He smiled at her. 'All right, I'll wait just a few hours longer.'

He kissed her gently and she knew that he understood.

'If you really are superstitious,' Anna retorted, 'they say in Yorkshire that a wet wedding day makes for a fine marriage.'

She did not feel like eating any breakfast and nobody said that it would be good for her to have something. The ceremony was at 11 o'clock. There was no sign of the rain easing up. Mrs Trevanion suggested that the family got changed in good time and there was discussion about whether or not they should use the car. Anna said that she would still prefer to walk over to the church as they had planned so they allocated her and Matthew the large multi-coloured umbrella. They sorted out several ancient umbrellas and with much laughter tried to match them with outfits. There was not one for Richard and Hugh who were told that they were young and fit enough to run so as to avoid getting too wet.

Mrs Trevanion came up to Anna's room as she was changing. Although Anna was wearing a simple cream dress and a small hat with which she would hardly need any help in putting on, she appreciated the sensitivity of this motherly person in recognising that some assurance would be welcome. Anna, usually so calm, so organised and so sure of herself, was on this particular morning feeling very nervous and much in need of support.

'Richard and Hugh have gone across early and Tom, of course has been in church for some time. He always likes to be there well before the service begins and when it is a member of his own family getting married. . . well I suppose that he anticipates a last minute hitch!'

The flow of chatter calmed Anna. Jane and Kate came in to say that they were ready and then added that Richard would be quite nice to live with, but did she know that he was incredibly untidy.

'And now you tell me,' said Anna but she was smiling and feeling much more confident.

28

Mrs Trevanion kissed her and then took her down to the sitting room to wait with Matthew until five minutes to eleven. It was time for Mrs Trevanion to leave and she walked across with the twins, all of them picking their way between the puddles and trying not to splash their dresses.

'If we open the window,' said Matthew 'we might be able to hear the organ playing.'

He pushed up the nearest window.

'Yes, I can hear Handel's Water Music. . . that seems a particularly inspired choice for a wet day.'

Matthew laughed.

'Mrs Pearse hasn't a large repertoire and most weddings have a portion of Handel whether the day is wet or fine.'

He closed the window, put some more coal on the fire and checked his watch again.

'I think that we should leave in another two minutes.' He paused and then he added, 'When I was a child and had to be quiet for the two minutes' silence I used to think that this was a very long period of time. You must be feeling like that now.' Anna smiled and nodded.

'I wonder why it is that wedding days cause so many nervous moments?'

Matthew glanced at his watch again.

'Right Anna, come on. My young brother issued his strict instructions this morning; Hugh is not to mislay the ring and I have to get you there on time and not to let you get wet. If we are late Mrs Pearse would have to repeat the Water Music and that Richard may not be able to bear.'

Anna had to laugh.

'Do you think that we shall be able to run under this umbrella?'

Matthew opened the front door and stepped outside to put up the umbrella. He turned and held an arm ready for the bride. Anna walked along the hallway, pausing to pick up a prayer book and posy of Christmas roses from the table. She took his arm.

'Ready?'

'Yes.'

'Let's go.'

The church porch was wet despite the caretaker's frantic mopping between guests. Jane and Kate were standing one on either side of the door and each with a broad grin on her face.

'It's packed – all the village is here – every pew is full. It's only like this on Christmas Eve; quiet weddings seem better attended than most.'

Mr Trevanion, as he did at all marriages which he conducted, was waiting at the church door to greet the bride. He spoke a few reassuring words and, as usual, mentioned that the bridegroom had arrived and all was well. Then he turned and from the door nodded to Mrs Pearse. She had already focussed her little organ mirror on the west door in preparation for this signal. She set her stops and the congregation stood as she began to play the opening bars of the Arrival of the Queen of Sheba which she fancied was one of her personal triumphs on the organ. The rector walked slowly in front of Anna and Matthew while Jane and Kate, now looking very demure, followed behind. Richard half turned to watch the small procession of five people whom he loved dearly, and for a moment he was overcome with emotion. As Anna drew alongside him he stepped into the aisle and walked beside her to the chancel steps.

They had chosen Crimond for their first hymn. Hugh handed them a hymn book opened at the right page, then took one for himself and began to sing lustily. Richard turned to Anna.

'You look lovely,' he said.

She smiled at him, then remembering that the rector had advised them to sing the first hymn so that their voices were clear for repeating their vows, she turned back to the book. Richard must have remembered this too because when verse two began he joined in the singing. By the time his father invited him to repeat, 'I, Richard James take thee Anna Elizabeth,' his voice was firm and strong.

In his address to the newly married couple Tom Trevanion spoke of the need to build a relationship which would withstand the stresses of life and enjoy its blessings. It should be a life in which God played a vital role and Christian beliefs were the foundations. He reminded them of their vows to keep only unto each other as long as they both should live and wished them every happiness together.

After the signing of the register Mrs Pearse gave what she thought was one of her most accomplished performances of the Wedding March. Richard led Anna from the vestry, their faces wreathed in smiles. Mr Trevanion had removed his vestments and he walked down the aisle with Anna's great aunt on his arm. Matthew escorted the other aunt and Hugh came with his mother. Jane and Kate, yet again, brought up the rear.

It was too wet to pause at the church porch for any photographs to be taken and everyone rushed into the church hall where the Ladies Guild had laid on sherry and mince pies for everyone. Richard and Anna had not been told about this and they were delighted by the surprise. It gave them a chance to speak with friends from the village and with the few from the university who had travelled a long way to be there. The reception at the rectory was a buffet lunch for the family and closest relatives, although determining the measure of closeness had been left to the relatives' discretion, and in this they were generous. Hugh made a witty best man's speech and took several photographs. Richard's response was equal to it, but then these two had been having verbal sparring matches all their life. This was the sort of gregarious family occasion to which they were well accustomed and at which they were perfectly at ease. Anna found it much more of a strain. She felt uncomfortable in mass gatherings and she looked forward to getting away from this one.

They were going to spend two days on the north Cornwall coast before they went back to the flat in London. Mr Trevanion was lending them the family car so they were free to leave at any time. Anna was longing to go but Richard was enjoying the party and did not seem to notice. It was his mother who finally suggested to him that perhaps they should drive some of the way in daylight; she also suspected that there would be some tin cans and confetti to be shed from the car somewhere along the route.

That night Mrs Trevanion lay in bed thinking. Usually she slept easily but she needed to reflect quietly upon the events of the day.

'I hope it will work out well for them both; they seem so

very young.'

'Not much younger than we were when we married,' Tom replied.

'They seem younger, at least Richard does. I suppose he did want to get married before he finished at college. . . he doesn't seem old enough somehow. . .'

'Well there is nothing that you can do about it now,' said Tom with a laugh, 'so you might as well go to sleep.'

In a hotel room listening to the sea pounding on the rocks below, Anna lay in bed waiting for her husband. It had been a happy day yet, not for the first time, she was troubled by ambivalent feelings which she was experiencing. She wondered if, after all, it had been wise to marry at this stage in her life.

3

On Friday they returned to London, Richard with some reluctance because he much preferred being in the country, Anna with pleasure because she was going home. Having taken two weeks holiday which, apart from when her mother died, was the longest break from academic work which she had ever allowed herself, she was at the end of it restless and keen to be back in her research laboratory.

Richard had another week of his vacation, some of which he spent preparing lessons for his teaching practice and much more of it getting fit for the second half of the rugby season. He had had two weeks break in his training programme and he soon realised how out of condition he had allowed himself to become. In less than two weeks was an important match for which he now, rigorously, had to prepare himself.

The flat felt strange to him, particularly when Anna was not there. It was home to Anna and it still belonged to her. She had suggested transferring it to joint ownership but Richard's pride had not allowed this to happen.

'We'll have that when we buy a house,' he said and there the matter ended.

They had moved his few personal belongings over before they had gone down to Cornwall. The only change they made was to convert the dining room into their bedroom, so that Anna could retain her old bedroom as her study and keep it furnished as it had been. In buying their double bed Richard, most uncharacteristically, had insisted upon extravagance.

'A man should always buy the best in beds and boots,' he was told by the salesman in the furniture department 'for it is in these two that he spends the greater part of his life.' At the time Anna had felt quite embarrassed.

The household tasks they shared. Anna did most of the cleaning; Richard took the washing to the launderette. Whoever got in first at night started preparing the evening meal. Richard was quite happy to do the shopping which Anna found tedious but she always did the ironing which was a job which he hated. It was the routine of their marriage for several years although as time passed one of the partners was to find the balancing of household tasks to be even no longer.

Adjusting to living together was less easy than each had separately anticipated. As well as being a relaxed, easy going and good natured person, Richard was slightly haphazard, rather untidy and inclined to leave things until the last minute. Anna could be regarded as the perfect antidote in that she was almost obsessionally tidy and her meticulous organisation was a trait which enabled her to get the most out of every minute of each day. Sometimes she looked at the flat and it was as if a whirlwind had been through it. On rare occasions Richard felt the presence of Anna's mother watching him as he tried to be a little more systematic in what he was doing.

They had their first row about something very trivial. Mrs Trevanion wrote regularly each week to those of her children who were away from home. Richard enjoyed having these letters but in his bachelor days he rarely got round to replying and it was only when his conscience really pricked him that he would telephone, sometimes needing to reverse the charges, and let his parents know that all was well. Anna had not been away from home so the weekly letter was a new experience and now that she was included she felt duty bound to respond with the same regularity. Richard happily let her do so until Anna began to think that it was a little unfair and told him so. The whole incident was out of proportion. He had had to stay late at school and had forgotten to buy the sausages planned for supper. Anna got in from the university before him, feeling tired and had had to make a start on preparing the meal. While she waited for Richard and the sausages she began a letter to his parents.

When he came through the door and saw that she was writing he said quite casually, 'Tell Mum that I saw John Martin at the rugby match. . .'

'Why don't you write and tell her yourself; I'm not here to act as your unpaid secretary.'

'You don't have to write each week; Mum knows that we are busy and she never expects it.'

'She may not expect it but she likes to have a letter. She has done a lot for you – and for me since I got to know your family – and it's only right that she should hear our news. Have you got the sausages?'

'Oh dear, no I forgot to go.'

'Richard, how can you be so unreliable and so vague. . .?' They had omelettes instead and ate them in silence. Ann went to her room to work; Richard had a rugby club meeting. He stayed later than usual having a drink with his friends. When he got home Anna was in bed. He was not certain that she was asleep but she gave every indication of being so. Next morning it was all over, but it had been a salutary experience for them both.

That evening Anna, having bought some meat herself on the way home, had the meal ready when Richard got back. He had bought her a bunch of snowdrops and a pound of sausages.

Although Richard had a county trial he was only named as a reserve in the early part of the season and played one full representative match towards the end. However, at club level, he played well and with much enjoyment and he was nominated to be team captain for the following year. Initially, he thought that he could not accept the responsibility because he was not sure where he might obtain his first teaching post. Until he had married he had been free to apply for any job to which he felt attracted. Now he had to look for one within daily travelling distance of where they were living. None seemed to be advertised and by Easter he was feeling a little apprehensive. At the beginning of the summer term he was called to the headmaster's room and told that they had been successful in getting approval for an additional member of staff in the geography department. Although the post would have to be advertised both he and the head of geography would like Richard to apply and they hoped that he would be appointed. It was completely against their usual procedure to appoint someone who had done their teaching practice in the school but they considered that his contribution had been outstanding and they really would like him to become a permanent member of the teaching staff.

Richard duly applied and was appointed. Anna was genuinely charmed by his success, but also much relieved that any move of home was, at least temporarily, not necessary. By the autumn of that year Anna had completed more than half of her research programme for her doctorate; Richard had gained his qualification with a distinction in his teaching practice, was in his first post and had received a monthly pay cheque. He had also been able to accept the captaincy of the rugby team and was leading them in what was developing into a very successful season. They went to Cornwall for Christmas and to celebrate their first wedding anniversary.

At the end of one year of marriage they both could acknowledge to a living together which was somewhat independent. Each worked in quite separate disciplines with differing roles, he the qualified practitioner; she the research student, he the sportsman; she the scientist. Every Saturday Richard would referee school matches in the morning and play club rugby in the afternoon. Anna never went as a spectator and on most Saturdays she went into the laboratory because it was quieter at the weekend and she found that she could get much more work done. The danger signals of divergent paths were neither noticed nor anticipated. She did go with Richard to the school staff dinner and he joined the research students for a theatre outing. On some Sundays they took cheap day returns into the countryside and spent the day rambling together. These were outings which in the years ahead they were to look back upon with much pleasure and considerable regret that they had come to an end.

The spring heralded the publication of Anna's first scientific paper which was received with acclaim and soon was appearing in the bibliography of other scientists' written work. She was producing data of such scientific significance from her research project that her professor encouraged her to get into print as quickly as possible. Long before she had begun to write up her doctoral thesis Anna Trevanion's name was to the fore in the scientific journals. It was this flurry of publishing activity which led to Anna and Richard spending their next Easter in different parts of the country. In the Easter holiday the geography department took the sixth form on a field trip. It was an opportunity for much of the theory of the classroom to be demonstrated in the landscape of a selected region, and it was also a time when staff and pupils really got to know each other and could feel comfortable with the demands that each was to make of the other as the A level examinations drew nearer. Since the choice of location was invariably an attractive one, it was customary for the staff to take their spouses along. Richard asked Anna if she would like to go to Scotland with them. She thought about it but then decided that rather than spend ten days paddling through peat bogs and admiring U-shaped glaciated valleys she could use the time more profitably in writing up two more papers. In some ways Richard was disappointed, but in others he was relieved because he could now really concentrate upon his input as a leader in this, his first school excursion. He knew Highland Scotland far less well than he did the South West of England so he would need to do quite a lot of preparation.

All three geography staff members would be going. Joe Blackmore, head of department was taking his wife for the first time in many years. Their children were old enough now to be left and, although it would hardly be a holiday, it would be a visit to a very pleasant part of the country. Mary Swaine was single and as Anna was not going there was a convenient weighting of the sexes to manage a mixed school party.

The original plan was that Richard and Joe would drive up three days in advance of the main party to check out several of the excursions which were planned, leaving Mary and Mrs Blackmore to travel up on the coach with some twenty members of the upper sixth form. At the last minute the Blackmores had a family bereavement and had to attend a funeral the day before the main party was due to leave. In consequence the plans had to be rearranged. Joe lent Richard his car and delegated his preparatory work to Mary. He and his wife would travel up on the coach. It was a logical solution but it left Richard feeling somewhat apprehensive. Although he had taught for a year in the same department as Mary Swaine he felt that personally he did not know her very well. He supposed that she must be in her mid twenties. She had graduated from a Scottish University, specialised in physical geography and was very well liked by the pupils. She had also been very helpful to him as he got established in his post. However, he felt that it was with something of a stranger that he set forth one April morning to drive north. At the end of the journey he knew that he had a friend.

They shared the driving and were able to do the whole journey in one day arriving at the hotel just before nine o'clock in the evening. As hotels went it was quite frugal for every economy had to be made to ensure that every child who wanted to could afford to go. For Richard, whose rectory upbringing had never been able to stretch to holidays, let alone holidays in hotels, staying in even a cheap one was a treat. He relished the joy of a meal being served to him and not having to wash up at the end of it.

Next morning he and Mary made a relatively early start. There was still snow on the mountain peaks but on the lower slopes the grass was beginning to grow and young lambs were much in evidence. Everything was perhaps as much as four weeks later than in Cornwall where invariably lambs were born in the wettest weeks of February. They took packed lunches with them and spent the day checking the glacial features of several areas before finally deciding which one would demonstrate the most. They made notes on land use and rural economy and in the following days studied the very limited industrial development and tourism. By the time the main party arrived they were familiar with the location and confident in the learning opportunities.

The hotel had opened for its summer season two weeks earlier than usual to accommodate the school party so they were the only guests. Joe Blackmore knew the owner and as a result gained beneficial terms and the acceptance of a school booking which may not be every hotelier's choice of

guests. Joe's philosophy was to give youngsters self responsibility and they would behave accordingly. A time for
lights out was not mentioned but so rigorous was the day's
schedule that after the first night nobody could keep awake
long enough to burn the midnight oil. He turned a blind
eye to the youthful relationships which developed, relying
upon the restraint of group overcrowding to enforce some
parentally expected degree of morality. As a result it was a
very happy party which tramped through the glens
studying the geography and admiring the grandeur of the
scenery. For one young school master it was the most
pleasurable week's work he had so far undertaken. After
the quietness of his marriage he relished the noisiness
reminiscent of his childhood days. He enjoyed the buf-
foonery that went on amongst the youngsters and he liked
the relaxation of school discipline which could happen on
this sort of activity.

On the last evening Joe took his wife, Mary and Richard
out for dinner at an old pub which he knew well. They left a
prefect nominally in charge and gave him a telephone
number for emergencies. The food was excellent, much
better than they had been having at their hotel where the
priority had been on filling hungry young peoples'
stomachs rather than tempting the appetite. They also
allowed themselves to have wine with this meal. They
talked and laughed together for four hours. Joe and Mae
Blackmore had a very easy rapport with everyone and with
each other in particular. It was a skill to which Richard
readily responded and despite the generation gap the four
of them had a memorable evening.

It dawned upon Richard as they drove back to the hotel
that this was something very lacking in his life. Anna and he
did virtually no entertaining and seldom went out to visit
friends. He also began to realise that they did not talk to
each other as much as perhaps they should. It was a matter
that they would have to do something about. Then he
remembered that he had not written to Anna.

☆ ☆ ☆

Every research project has a bad patch; most researchers

experience a phase of being tempted to abandon what seems to be the very little so far achieved and to try to begin elsewhere or even to vow never to start again. The doldrums of Anna's research life were suddenly encountered in the early summer following Richard's trip to Scotland. Numerous experiments gave contradictory results; none of the latest calculations was of any significance and the harder that Anna worked to try to clarify the meaning of her data the greater seemed to be the confusion. She spent longer in the laboratory and arrived home late every night. In his supervision her professor was encouraging; at home her husband was supportive, yet Anna began to feel despair. As her research project seemed doomed at worse to failure and at best to incompletion, her emotional response was to jettison more of her marital responsibilities, although intellectually she knew that her marriage was in no way and never would be a brake upon her academic career. To each aspect of her life she felt ambivalent.

It was Richard who rescued her. None of the pressures in life which Anna created for herself ever carried over to Richard. He worked hard at his job and for the most part enjoyed it, but he also had a life outside which revolved principally around his sport. From this he had a wide network of friends and colleagues and in the background all the security of his Cornish childhood. His personal recognition of the significance of roots led him to suggest casually a week before half term that they should spend a long weekend in Yorkshire. Anna had not been back to Garside since she was a child and Richard had never been there. The suggestion was a straw in the wind which he did not expect Anna to grasp and he was to be very surprised by the enthusiasm which she showed for the idea.

They spent three days in the Dales, three warm summer days when nothing was planned in advance and they did on the spur of the moment just whatever they felt like doing. It was alien to Anna to live like this but, for once, she let Richard take complete charge and found that it could be a pleasant experience. They stayed in the local pub and in the evening sat on the wall outside with a pint of shandy talking to the locals who remembered Anna from years before. She showed Richard the little terrace house where she had lived and also the cottage where her beloved Mrs Hoggs had lived until she had died two years before.

Whenever Richard was away in rural areas he was always aware of sheep. There had been many times when he had thought about doing agriculture for a career and if he had he would have been a sheep farmer. The fells above Garside resounded with the cries of young lambs seeking their mothers and the call of ewes to their offspring. They heard the cuckoo and saw swallows darting for insects in the evening sky. As they walked in the high Pennines they talked about the things that they believed mattered in life. They both knew, although neither said anything, that they had neglected their marriage and that there was a need to reaffirm their commitment to it and their love for each other if their future was to withstand life's pressure. When Anna reflected back upon this weekend she was to realise that she had felt closer to Richard than she had done at any other time in their relationship. Fleetingly she contemplated whether or not this relaxed, seemingly carefree life was preferable to the academic world. But, for her, it could never be a realistic choice. All her life, from the earliest years, had been programmed towards an academic career. There was no going back upon this and she knew that, despite the difficulties, she did not want to.

Anna returned to the university with renewed enthusiasm and, inexplicably, the breakthrough came. Results began to confirm revised hypotheses, calculations gave the empirical evidence and the time to think about beginning to write up the thesis was fast approaching. Anna was buoyant and radiated her happiness at home and at work. She seemed to have endless energy and the laboratory was a joyous place in which to be.

But life rarely runs so smoothly for long and Anna's appeared destined to swing from peaks to troughs. There did not ever seem to be long spells when things just quietly ran their course. Suddenly all her supplies of energy seemed to have been dissipated. She felt tired, she felt sick, she missed a period and she realised that she might be pregnant. It had not been planned to happen for several years and her initial reaction was anger at their incompetence in starting a pregnancy at such a completely inconvenient stage in her career. How could she complete her doctorate and become a mother at the same time? What made it worse was that she knew as soon as she told Richard he would be delighted, would be more caring, take on more household responsibilities, make more personal sacrifices and compound all her feelings of guilt. It was not that she did not want a baby, it was that she did not want one then.

It did not help that Richard responded in exactly the way that she knew he would. He was overwhelmingly enthusiastic and accommodating to the extreme. It was not many years since Kate and Jane had been babies and he felt confident at being able to cope with this one. But Anna had not had this experience; she had never known any young children and was not sure that she even liked babies. She certainly did not enjoy being pregnant and continued to feel wretched for several weeks. She also missed her mother far more than she was prepared to admit, and being pregnant intensified her feelings of loss and bereavement. And what of the future? Her research so far promised a university career with high academic honours. Where did motherhood fit into the scheme of things? Would it be possible to continue the two roles or would both be compromised? Anna wept. It was so unfair. She had worked so hard and determined with great single-mindedness to reach the top of the academic world which was what she wanted from life. Why did her male colleagues have it so easy? Why did Richard not have to face the dilemma that their baby was causing for her? All these thoughts she kept to herself but it was a very subdued Anna who went about her daily tasks.

It was not until the feelings of nausea ceased that Anna began to think slightly more positvely about her pregnancy. Richard played less cricket during the remainder of the season so that he could be at home more. He did all the cleaning and took the washing to the launderette. Although he had always tried to avoid doing the ironing this was another task which he found that he had to take on. Anna began to write her thesis and although she went into college often, much of the drafting was done at home.

In August they went to Cornwall for a few days and

basked in the rectory excitement of the first grandchild being on the way. Mrs Trevanion had feared that there might be no children in this marriage, was surprised that there was to be one so soon and not a little anxious about the continuing academic career combining with family life. For her there had been no choice. Her role as homemaker was clearly defined from the day that she had married Tom Trevanion and any opportunities she may have had for working outside the home were sacrificed the day she became a parson's wife, and that was the way that she wanted things to be.

It was the hallmark of her organising ability that Anna could complete one important part of her life before embarking upon another. For her it was vital to complete her thesis before the baby arrived and, if possible, to have been examined also. She would need to have the copies bound and to the examiners as early in January as was possible. She knew that she was a strong candidate for a university lectureship in the next academic year, by which time the baby would be six months old. Richard had suggested that they should think about having an au pair living in to look after the baby while they were both at work. At some stage they would need to look for a house larger than the flat in which they now lived.

4

One day in November Anna had a small bleed and after mentioning this to Richard was persuaded to telephone their general practitioner. Dr Norris listened to what Anna described and said that she ought to go to hospital as soon as possible.

'But it has only been a very small loss of blood,' said Anna.

'It may be of no consequence whatsoever but, nevertheless, we want to be sure that everything is all right. I'll telephone the clinic and arrange for you to be seen today. And another thing, don't travel on public transport.'

'Why ever not? I feel really fit and well and we don't have a car of our own.'

'Is your husband with you?'

'No he has gone to school.'

'Then you must go by taxi.'

'Doctor Norris, is this serious? Am I in labour?'

'It is probably nothing to worry about whatsoever, but it would be foolish to take any unnecessary risks, particularly if it meant that you might lose the baby. I'll ring you back and let you know at what time they can give you an appointment.'

Ten minutes later the telephone rang. It was Richard ringing between lessons.

'Anna, love, what did Dr Norris say?'

She told him, reassuring him that it was absolutely nothing to worry about. She just had to go into the antenatal clinic for a routine check-up and she would be home again before he came in from school.

But it was not to be. At the clinic Anna was scanned and

the registrar told her that she had a placenta praevia and she would need to be admitted to the ward immediately and, in all probability, have to remain there until the baby was born. Anna was dumbfounded.

'Surely not? I can rest at home. I am working at home at the moment and spend most of my time just sitting at my desk. If necessary I could work in bed, but I must be at home to have access to all the material I have gathered. I am in the middle of writing a thesis and I've got a deadline by which time I must have it ready to go to the typist. I promise you that I would not do any housework or anything that was the slightest bit strenuous, but my work is very important. Well it is to me.'

The registrar was patient with her but he was also very honest. He explained that the gravest risk with her condition was that she could have a serious haemorrhage and lose not only the baby but put her own life at risk. With rest and close monitoring they would hope to maintain the pregnancy until the baby was as viable as possible, but they would plan to deliver the baby early and it would have to be by caesarean section. If she started to haemorrhage unexpectedly it would necessitate an immediate emergency caesarean section and she must be where an operating theatre was on hand. In his view to remain at home would be irresponsible in the extreme but, of course, no patient could forcibly be held against her wishes.

Anna was shattered. Everything had seemed to be falling into place with her planning but now this had wrecked all the arrangements she had been making. In the face of such strong medical reasoning she could do none other than concur with a hospital admission. She knew that she would not be able to work on a public ward; she dreaded having to share a room with other patients, having never shared a bedroom with anyone other than Richard. When the registrar left her Anna felt tears welling up in her eyes and she struggled to control them. A staff nurse came in to arrange for her to be transferred to the ward.

'Are you on your own Mrs Trevanion?'

'Yes, I didn't think for a minute that this was anything

other than a routine check-up. I haven't brought anything with me – nightdresses I mean."

'Can you telephone your husband? We'll let you use the phone in sister's office.' She put her arm round Anna's shoulder.

'Keep your pecker up, lass; you're in the best place now. Have a word with your husband and I'll get you a cup of tea.'

Anna telephoned the school secretary who promised to get a message to Richard as soon as possible and to ask him to ring back. Staff nurse brought in a cup of tea and said that it was all right for her to sit there until her husband called back. She did not have long to wait. The school secretary had stayed with Richard's class of first formers while he had gone to the telephone. Anna explained what had happened. He said that he would go home as soon as he had finished teaching and collect all the things which she needed and then he would come straight in to see her.

She was taken to the ward in a wheel chair. It seemed so incongruous because she felt so well and she was not bleeding. The ward clerk took the admission details. Full name, date of birth, address, next of kin, occupation. . .

'I'm a student – well a sort of student.'

'What are you a student of?'

'I'm doing some research – well I've finished it really – I'm writing up the results. I had hoped to get it finished before the baby was born had things gone as they were expected.'

'You won't have much time for studying when you become a mother,' said the clerk with a laugh. 'I had to wait until my youngest started school before I could go back to work and then I'm only working part time.'

'Oh no,' thought Anna, 'how can this happen to me? I'm so nearly there and now this.'

She sat on her bed in the ward. There were three other beds in the room and none was occupied. One of the nurses brought her in a hospital night gown and told her to get undressed and into bed so that the houseman could examine her.

It all seemed so repetitive. The ward clerk had taken details, most of which must have been in the medical notes already. The houseman was coming to do her admission examination although she had just been seen in the clinic and examined there. Anna remained silent, drew the curtain round her bed and got undressed. She put her clothes and handbag in the locker and climbed into the bed. It felt incredibly hard and she felt the plastic undersheet which seemed to be so ominous. The top of the locker was bare except for a jug of water and a glass. She had nothing with her to read and she did not like to ask if there was a newspaper or anything which she could look at. She glanced at her watch yet again. Richard would be leaving school about now; he should be in soon.

Richard went everywhere on his bicycle. It kept him fit, in London was quicker than going by bus and it was cheaper than running a car. He was almost the first person through the school gate that day and he pedalled home quickly to gather the things which he thought Anna would need. He packed these into his small rucksack and rushed out. It was raining slightly as he set off but he did not stop to put on his waterproof trousers. Anna had sounded very upset on the telephone and he was not sure that he understood why she had been admitted, other than she might lose the baby. As he approached the main hospital entrance he noticed a flower stall on the side of the road so he stopped to buy some flowers. He had ideas of a delicate spray of freesias or some red roses but he had not much money in his pocket and there was no choice other than different coloured chrysanthemums. As he balanced them on the handle bars he thought of the beautiful flowers which came from the greenhouses in the valley at home and considered that the rust coloured flowers that he had just purchased were quite ugly and even morbid.

He padlocked the bicycle outside the maternity block and went inside to find the ward. He stopped at sister's office and asked if he could visit Mrs Trevanion.

'Are you her husband?'

'Yes, I couldn't get here sooner because I was at work.'

'She is in room three, Mr Trevanion, and Mr Parget, the registrar, would like to speak with you. Go down and wait with your wife and I will give him a bleep. I will let you

47

know when he can see you.'

Richard had never seen Anna looking so forlorn as she did when he walked into the ward that afternoon. He could see that she had been crying and she was just sitting in the bed in the partially lighted ward doing nothing. He bent down to kiss her.

'You're wet,' said Anna, 'is it raining outside? I haven't looked outside since I was admitted so I hadn't noticed.'

Richard put the flowers on the locker and unloaded the clothes, her toilet bag and some books on to the bed.

'The doctor wants to speak with us,' he said. 'What exactly have they told you?'

Anna explained what she had understood from the earlier session with Mr Parget. As she spoke she began to cry again. Richard sat on the edge of the bed and put his arms around her.

'You are not supposed to sit on the bed – oh there are so many rules and regulations; it's awful. Richard, what am I going to do? I may be stuck in this ward until February and, if I am, I think that I shall go mad. I can't work here and I'm not going to be able to get my thesis done in time for the January submission and I could lose the baby at any time.'

It was the first time that Richard had known Anna to be so emotional and it was very much at the expense of her normal, highly logical, analytical approach to problems.

When the registrar joined them he repeated what he had told Anna earlier, stressing the dangers of haemorrhage being minimised by her being on the ward. He was reassuring about the chances of the baby being all right, provided that the caesarean section was performed as soon as there was any cause for concern. He was puzzled by Anna's considerable distress, reassuring her that there was very little to worry about now that she was in hospital. Richard explained that it was not just the complication of the pregnancy but that Anna was at a crucial stage in her career and that she was facing two possible losses. She had a thesis to complete and had hoped to have it done in the next six weeks. Mr Parget thought for a minute.

'Supposing that we could move Mrs Trevanion into one of the side cubicles – we are not particularly busy at the moment – it would be relatively quiet and perhaps she could carry on with her work. Of course, if a patient came in with a greater medical need for a side ward we would have to respect that and move her back into the main ward. I'll go and have a word with sister.'

Anna later sensed that sister was not too pleased by this request, no doubt questioning why this patient should have what appeared to be preferential treatment. She was later to learn that Mr Parget had only recently passed the second part of his FRCS examination and understood only too well her need for peace and space to study. He also recognised that a happier patient would make the management of her obstetric problems easier.

That evening Richard, equipped with a long list, sorted out in Anna's study the things that she had said she was going to need. He packed everything into a large suitcase and this time wore a raincoat and travelled by bus.

'Is that the case for taking your wife's clothes home?' enquired sister when he returned to the ward.

'Er – well – er no; it's some books and papers which she is going to need for her work.'

Sister sniffed and gave a sort of snort. 'Mrs Trevanion has been admitted to my ward for complete bed rest and we are here to ensure that she does just that. For the sake of the baby I cannot see why all this book work cannot wait. We are only talking about a few weeks. . .'

Richard gave her one of his most disarming smiles assuring her that both he and his wife understood the situation and that all that she would be doing was a little writing when she was not having any treatment or being needed for anything else. By the time he reached the side ward into which Anna had been moved it was nearly the end of visiting time. They unpacked the case putting as much of the precious data as possible into the locker where it was both safe and not an overt aggravation to sister. They both felt in such awe of sister that the minute the bell rang signalling the end of visiting Richard sprang up, kissed Anna quickly and shot out of the room. He thought that Anna seemed a little happier and more accepting of the need for her to be in hospital.

He went back to the flat and cooked an omelette for

supper. He had been doing all the housework for several weeks now so that would not change. Somehow he would have to find an extra two hours each day for hospital visiting and, with out-of-school activities increasing in the run up to Christmas, it was going to need meticulous organisation. Then he thought about Christmas; they had been planning to go to Cornwall as usual and that would not now be possible. He would have to ring his parents during the week. It was nearly ten o'clock when he started to prepare his lessons for the following day, and almost midnight when he fell exhausted into bed.

Anna could not sleep that night. There was noise in the corridors and some commotion in the grounds outside the windows. She could hear babies crying on the other side of the courtyard and she found it irritating. She did not like to switch the light on to read because she feared that she might be pressed into taking a sleeping tablet which she did not want to do. She thought back over the day's events. Although she struggled hard to be logical she felt angry. If she had not mentioned the show to anyone she would not have been in hospital. There had been no more bleeding and she felt well. She could have carried on working at home and probably there would have been no problems for a month at least, by which time she would have got the thesis finished. She tried to counter these feelings by acknowledging that the scan had shown the placenta to be in a dangerous position and the registrar had been quite emphatic that she was living with the risk of starting a haemorrhage. But it did not stop her feeling that it was all so unfair. She had not wanted to be pregnant in the first place, not just now when she had so much to deal with in getting her doctorate completed. Fleetingly she allowed herself to wish that she did miscarry the pregnancy and then she could get on with her work. Immediately she felt guilty because she did not wish death to any baby and particularly not her own. In the semi-darkness she began to weep again. She anticipated that she would be in-competent as a mother and yet it was this state that was being thrust upon her at the expense of what she knew could only be a very successful academic career. It seemed that every obstacle was being placed in her way. She so desperately wanted to get her Ph.D. and so much coveted the university lectureship. She even felt herself to be at odds with Richard. He was so accommodating and insisted that every problem could have a solution of sorts if only given time. Mostly, in their lives, it was by him making the sacrifices. How much was he sublimating his career to hers? How much was she prepared to let him take over the domestic responsibilities to facilitate her forward progression? Why did he never dig his heels in and make a stand for his rights? Were all parsons' sons so selfless or was this one quite exceptional? Finally Anna slept.

The next week saw the emergence of yet another improvised routine in Anna and Richard's life. For Richard who had had to learn to be more organised when he had married Anna, planning ahead was still far less well accomplished by him than it was by his wife. By now Anna did not have a lot of opportunity to programme her day. She had to fit into the ward routine of being wakened early and always at the same time, of meals arriving at regular intervals, of numerous interruptions for ward rounds and tests to be done and, of course, visiting time which spread over several hours of the day. However, between the interruptions she disciplined herself to keep on writing. It was much more difficult to concentrate here compared with being in her quiet study at home, but her determination was so great that she found she could block out the background activity and noise.

If he was not involved in after school sports or clubs Richard stayed in school doing marking and preparation until it was time to go to the hospital to visit Anna, and after that he went home. It tended to be the shopping that got left out of his schedule and when he got home he would remember that he had needed to get some more supplies and would end up having yet another omelette. It became something of a staff room joke that the expectant father was living on a diet of eggs. On the Tuesday afternoon Richard was sitting alone in the corner of the staff room doing some marking when Mary Swaine came in.

'Have you got a lot of work to do tonight, Richard?'

'I've nearly finished these fourth form books and then

I've got a bit of preparation to do for tomorrow, but most of Wednesday's teaching for me is on the rugby pitch, thank goodness. I'm trying to get it all done before I go to see Anna.'

'Would you like to come to my place after you have been to the hospital and have some supper? It will save you cooking and I promise you that it won't be omelettes!'

'That would be really great, Mary. Visiting finishes at 8 pm. Will that make it a bit late for you?'

'No that is fine. I'll see you later then.'

Although he did most of the cooking, Richard always preferred to have his meals prepared for him. Basically, and in jest, he would claim that he considered himself to be a male chauvinist who needed to have a woman to wait on him and it had been his misfortune that he had not organised this part of his life better. Whenever he told Anna this she always laughed and said that he was too fond of his food ever to wait long for her culinary achievements which she acknowledged were more rudimentary than his.

Anna had had a productive day and had written more than on any other day since she had been admitted. She smiled when he told her that he was going to Mary's house for supper and said that it would be an opportunity for him to practise his male chauvinism. She liked Mary whom they had got to know a little since the field trip to Scotland. Mary had called at the hospital over the weekend with some flowers for her.

Richard was not quite sure where Mary lived. She had given him directions and it was not very far from school. It was cold cycling that night and he was glad to find the road easily. Mary lived in a little terrace house. He rang the door bell and then put his hands in his trouser pockets to try and warm them.

'You look nithered,' said Mary when she opened the door.

'That's a real north country phrase; I didn't realise that you came from that part of the world.'

'I don't but my father is a Yorkshire man and he always says nithered.'

Mary had a coal fire blazing in the living room. When

Richard admired it she explained that it always seemed worth the extra work to have an open fire to sit by and most winter nights when she was at home she lit the fire. She gave Richard a drink and a newspaper to read while she set two places at the table. Delicious smells of food cooking made him realise just how hungry he was. When the meal was served it was chicken casserole which was always one of his favourite dinners. She had also made an apple pie to follow.

'How did you manage to do all this since you came in?'

'I made the pie this morning to bring it into school for you; then I decided that it might be more helpful if I cooked a whole meal for you so that you would not have to bother with anything. I expect you have been making do more than usual.'

She did let him help her wash up and then they made a big jug of coffee and sat by the fire.

'How long have you lived here?'

'Nearly four years. It's a long story, Richard, but this little house has special memories for me and it's not just a house but a link with a part of my life which was very happy.'

'Is the house the reason why you have stayed at our school and not widened your experience by seeking another job? You must soon be thinking about a head of department post.'

'It's partly that but as yet I'm not ready to think about what next.'

Richard sat quietly gazing into the fire. He was suddenly aware that although he had thought that he had got to know Mary well in Scotland there was much about her life which she had not revealed, perhaps because it was painful. He asked about her family and they began to laugh together about their respective childhood experiences. Mary had two younger brothers and her parents ran a small farm in Wales. Her younger brother still farmed with them but she and her other brother had both moved to London. She loved to go back to the farm and had things been different would probably not have remained in London but moved into the country again. Richard looked at Mary. She hesitated and then began to

53

tell him.

'I moved into this house with Bill. He was in the merchant navy and I had met him when we were both youth hostelling in the Lake District. He did not particularly enjoy being at sea but in his late adolescence had believed that this was the way to see the world. He had another eighteen months to do and then hoped to go to theological college here in London. We were engaged to be married. I was going to carry on teaching to help support us while he trained for the ministry. Then we were going to leave London for somewhere more rural. We bought this house cheaply because it was so dilapidated and when he was on leave Bill did the renovations. He build this fireplace during his last leave – that was three years ago. You see there was an accident at sea. It was in a force nine gale and some of the equipment on the deck came loose. Somebody had to go on deck and tie it down. Bill knew the danger and would not ask anyone else to do it. The first officer was on the bridge; we know now that he should have turned the ship into the gale – Bill was caught by a tremendous wave which crushed him against the side of the deck. They said that he must have been killed instantly. They buried him at sea. There was an Inquiry – I went to it. They handed over some of his personal effects but it was a long time before I accepted that he would not be coming back.'

She got up and put another log on the fire.

'Mary, I know this sounds almost trite, but I am sorry – I had no idea – I wouldn't have asked.'

'It's all right Richard. I loved Bill very dearly and there will never be anyone to take his place. I stay here because it was our home and so many memories of him are with me here. It's not a shrine; it's not a sad place. It feels warm and full of the love we had together. But there will come a time when I shall be ready to move on, to leave London and to move back into the countryside. I suppose that I will stay in teaching but I've got well over thirty years before I am due to retire so who knows what else may turn up!'

Richard was silent. He understood now why Mary, although friendly and popular in the staff room, was also a very private person. He had got to know part of her in Scotland but maybe nobody was going to be allowed to get to know her well.

'I feel almost privileged to have been invited to come here tonight and thank you for telling me about Bill.'

'In a way it might make things easier between us now that you know. We are good friends who work together and you don't need to worry about my intentions in offering a poor, self-neglecting fellow teacher a meal! I did tell Anna that I would give you a meal sometime.'

'That is why she did not seem to be surprised when I told her that I was coming here tonight; she did not let on that she was party to the "look after Richard" campaign.'

'I'm not going to do your washing. . .'

'How about the ironing?'

'No, definitely not. But I will always babysit for you. . .'

Richard looked away.

'I'm sorry, Richard, that was a stupid thing to say at the moment. You must be worried about both of them.'

'The registrar is optimistic that the baby will be all right, but obviously the longer the pregnancy the better the chances.'

'If ever you want to come over and talk about it all I'm nearly always here. Often things don't seem so grim if you are able to share it with somebody else.'

Richard got up to go.

'It's been a splendid evening, Mary. You have a lovely home and I am envious of that open fire.'

Mary laughed.

'When you are both at work it is much quicker and far more economical to have an electric fire and central heating. It is much more sensible than carrying coal buckets and chopping up wood.'

Richard remembered what Mary had said about being sensible when he went into the flat. The central heating had switched off because it was past their usual bedtime and the place felt cold and not much like home.

Was their flat home, he thought, or was it just the place where they lived and from where they went to work each day? Anyway, it would be different when the baby arrived and by next summer they would have had to move to somewhere more suitable for a child. Perhaps they should look for a terrace house like Mary's; there was a small garden for a pram.

But in his heart Richard knew that the difference between houses and homes was to do with people, with attitudes and with relationships. He knew that Mary seemingly having lost everything had something still from her loving relationship which he did not possess and perhaps coveted. He and Anna had not reproduced the home life which he had experienced as a child and which he naïvely assumed would be automatic. He was beginning to know something about the penalties of careers.

The following evening when Richard visited Anna she was in good spirits and he thought that she looked well. She had completed another chapter since her admission and asked him to take it for typing. There were only two more chapters to complete and then what would perhaps be the most difficult one which was the concluding chapter in which she would summarise all the arguments which she had developed through the text. All her references and the bibliography had been card-indexed as she had gone along so she really felt that she was beginning to see the light at the end of the tunnel. If she could write a chapter a week the draft would be completed on schedule as she had planned. There had been some very slight bleeding since her admission but no other cause for concern. She was now twenty-eight weeks pregnant and had been told that the baby could now be viable – but only just. She was interested to hear about Mary's house and the meal she had prepared. For reasons for which Richard did not have an explanation he did not tell Anna about Mary's fiancé being killed. Perhaps it had been told to him in confidence. He thought that Mary would tell Anna herself sometime.

Richard was wakened by the telephone. He must have been in a deep sleep and he had no idea as to how long it had been ringing. He switched on the bedside lamp; the clock said 2.10 am. He ran downstairs. It must be the hospital.

'Hello,' he said, 'Richard Trevanion speaking.'

'Oh Mr Trevanion, it is the night sister from the maternity unit here. We thought that we ought to let you know that Mrs Trevanion has started to lose quite heavily. The registrar is examining her now but it is likely that she might have to go down to theatre.'

'I'll come in straight away. Thank you for telephoning me.'

Richard dressed quickly and set off to the hospital on his bicycle. The roads were clear and he did not seem to notice the frost. When he got to the ward the sister came from Anna's room to meet him.

'The doctors are with your wife at the moment; just wait in the side room for a minute or two and then they will let you know what is happening. The consultant obstetrician has been called in.'

'How is my wife?'

'She is fine. It may be a false alarm but she is bleeding quite heavily.'

Richard could not sit down. He walked round the room and then out into the corridor. He wished that they would let him see Anna. The door opened. Mr Parget came out accompanied by a grey-haired lady who introduced herself as Miss Craig, the consultant.

'I'm sorry Mr Trevanion but we shall have to take your wife down to theatre and do a caesarean section. She has started to haemorrhage and we shall need to get the baby out as quickly as possible. You can pop in to see her but she has had her pre-med and she is getting drowsy.'

He went into the room. The nurses were quietly, efficiently and very speedily getting Anna ready.

'Darling are you all right?'

He leaned over and kissed his wife. She opened her eyes and looked up at him.

'I'm sorry Richard; I must have done something to start the bleeding.'

'Don't be silly, you couldn't have done anything. Just relax now. I'll be waiting here when you come round.'

He walked down to the operating theatre beside the trolley and held Anna's hand. He was sure that her pulse rate was falling but he knew that he was feeling very panicky.

'There is a sitting room where you can wait, Mr Trevanion. We'll let you know as soon as there is any news about the baby.'

He sat in a chair. A nurse brought him a cup of tea. 'Do babies have any chance of living when they are so small?' he asked her.

'Oh yes,' she replied with great confidence. 'The Special Care Baby Unit is a wonderful place. We have had twenty-seven weekers survive. The baby will have to go into an incubator of course. . .'

Richard waited. It seemed an incredibly long time. He kept looking at his watch. Perhaps it had stopped. There was a clock on the wall. It was the same time. He heard some movement in the corridor and went to the door to look. He saw some staff dressed in green theatre gowns pushing an incubator towards the theatre. It was not yet 3 am. A few minutes later Mr Parget came down the corridor. He was dressed in his green gown and trousers and his white wellington boots. He had dropped his mask round his neck. He smiled at Richard.

'You have a daughter. Congratulations! She is, as we warned you, only very small, less than three pounds I'd say, but we think she is twenty-nine to thirty weeks. She should have a better than evens chance. The paediatricians are working on her now and will be able to give you an accurate estimate of gestation weeks; she is in an incubator and has gone to SCBU. We'll let you see her as soon as they have got her sorted out. Your wife is fine. My colleagues are stitching her up. There shouldn't be any problems.'

Richard had never been into a baby ward and when he entered the Special Care Baby Unit he noticed how warm it was. When he went into the intensive care room he felt quite overwhelmed by the amount of technology. He peeped into the incubator at his baby. Her skin looked almost opaque and he could see blood vessels showing through it. She was on a ventilator and had several wires attached to her body and a tube into her nostril. She looked minute and she looked beautiful. The staff nurse and the sister were working swiftly together and explained to him what they were doing.

'She is going to be a fighter this little one,' said sister.

'Will she make it?'

'Why ever not? She is doing very well – only twenty-five percent oxygen now; that's good.'

He gazed at the little figure and all the machinery which was supporting her.

'Come on little one, fight hard, it's not such a bad old world waiting for you.'

Anna was in the recovery room. She was still very sleepy. Richard held her hand.

'Anna, I've seen our little girl; she is lovely and she is doing well.'

'I'm glad,' said Anna and went back to sleep.

'We are taking Mrs Trevanion back to the ward now,' said one of the nurses.

'May I stay with her?'

'Yes, of course. There is a big chair in her room. You might even be able to have a little snooze yourself, although we shall be coming in and out to do our routine observations. Have you got to go to work today?'

'I should do.'

'Well you had better try to get a couple of hours sleep otherwise you won't be up to much.'

But Richard was too excited to sleep and there was too much activity going on around. At 6 am he went down to the Special Care Baby Unit.

'Come as often as you can,' said the sister. 'If we are not doing any complicated procedures you can come and sit by the cot side whenever you like. It's good for the baby to have her parents there. We shall all get to know each other very well in the next two months.'

Richard telephoned his parents at 7.30 am and the headmaster an hour later. He was persuaded not to go into school that day.

'Stay with your wife and baby,' said the head. 'Come in tomorrow if everything is progressing satisfactorily.'

'Shall we come up to London?' asked his parents.

'Wait a day or two and see how things go. The baby has an evens chance of surviving at the moment. If there is any change in that situation I'll let you know.'

Anna was sleepy for much of the day. In the late afternoon the paediatricians thought that the baby had some respiratory distress and asked if her mother felt like coming down to see her. Anna was put into a wheel chair and Richard and a nurse pushed her down to the Special Care Baby Unit. Richard had tried to describe to Anna what it was like in the unit but she had been too drowsy to take in what he had been saying. When they got to the door of the intensive care room one of the doctors was taking a sample of blood from the baby's heel and they were asked to wait for a few minutes.

Richard could sense Anna's apprehension. He had already become familiar with the equipment and the washing of hands procedure before they went in. Anna, herself, was not feeling well; she knew that the baby was poorly and she was troubled by being asked to wait to see a baby upon which she had yet to set her eyes. When they were allowed to go to the incubator side her initial reaction was one of profound shock.

'She doesn't look like a baby.'

'But she is beautiful isn't she?' said Richard.

'How can you say that?' said Anna beginning to weep. 'She is so small and not properly formed because you can see through her skin.'

'Would you like to put your hand in the incubator and touch her hand?' asked the staff nurse.

'No, I couldn't do that.'

'Try, it will make all the difference to how you feel about her if you just touch her arm. Wash your hands in the sink over there and rub on some of the cream in the container.'

Anna did as she was directed with the tears streaming down her face. She was absolutely dreading what she was being urged to do.

'That's right, now put your hand through this little window and feel the baby's arm.'

As Richard watched he could feel tears pricking at the back of his eyes. He was worried by Anna's reaction to the baby. When it was his turn to put his hand into the incubator and let his finger gently caress the tiny arm he felt an immediate and intense affection for this tiny creature.

'What are you going to call the baby?' asked the nurse.

'We haven't decided yet.'

Anna looked at the identity card attached to the incubator. It said Baby Trevanion.

'It's nicer when they have a name,' the nurse continued, 'we know them all by their Christian names – they become part of our family here.'

'We will decide soon,' said Richard. 'We have got some ideas but as she has arrived much sooner than we expected we haven't made a final decision.'

He took Anna back to the ward.

'What name do you like?'

'I had thought about Jessica but she does not look like a Jessica – she doesn't look at all like what I thought my baby, our baby, would look like. . .'

Anna began to sob helplessly.

'Don't cry Anna. It is only because she is so premature. She will look so much better when she puts on some weight and when they are able to detach all those tubes. Did you notice any of the babies in the end room? Apparently several of those started their life in the intensive care room and they are now looking fine and are nearly ready to go home.'

'I don't think that I am ever going to feel that she is mine – I just don't feel anything.'

Richard sat with his arm around Anna. It was no use trying to use logic or trying to convince her that she would get attached to her baby given time. He stroked her hair and said nothing. But he could not help thinking that if this baby was going to survive she was going to need all their love and attention to help her pull through the crisis, and having just his was not enough.

The sister persuaded him to go home that night.

'You didn't get much sleep last night and it is important to pace yourself and to take care of yourself so that you can deal with the situation better. We've got your telephone number at home and at work and we will always ring you if there is any change in the condition of your baby or your wife. You know that the baby is likely to get worse before she gets better because that is what usually happens and we are prepared for that, but she will get better, you mark my words.'

The last comment was made with a twinkle in her eye and a finger waved authoritatively in the air.

Richard made a final visit to the incubator and was reassured by the close observation she was under. He quite liked the name Jessica but thought it was a mouthful with a name like Trevanion. He liked a shorter name and they had talked about Emma or Claire as possible choices. He thought it was going to be very important that Anna had the final say and then she might feel more strongly that the baby was hers. But there was no rush to make a final choice; Baby Trevanion would suffice for a few more days.

'Good night darling,' he whispered at the incubator side. 'God bless you.'

When he left the hospital Richard did not turn towards home. He felt that he needed some exercise and some fresh air after a very long day in hospital. He began to cycle in the opposite direction and soon realised that, either consciously or subconsciously, he was heading for Mary's house. She had said that if ever he wanted to come over for a chat about anything she was usually in. As he went up the road he hoped desperately that she would be in. He did not feel that he could just yet face the solitude of the flat. He needed somebody with whom he could share the anguish of the day and there was really only one person near at hand with whom he could do that.

Mary was sitting by her fire reading and listening to her record player. Richard squatted in front of the fire and warmed his hands. Mary went to turn off the record player.

'Please don't; it's lovely. I'm not very musical so tell me what it is.'

'It's Schumann's Kinderszenen.'

She left him listening to it while she made him some coffee and a sandwich. She came back into the room and put these on the side table beside him.

'Have you heard?'

'We all know why you were not in school today. The

head came into the staff room before assembly and told us what had happened. I'm so very glad that you have a daughter but we are all sorry that she is premature.'

'She is holding her own at the moment.'

'How is Anna?'

'They say that she is making a good recovery from the operation but she feels rather sore.'

He sipped the coffee but did not touch the sandwiches. Mary sat quietly and did not pester him with questions. The record moved on to playing the familiar section Trauerei. Suddenly the tears began to flow down Richard's cheeks. Mary got up from her chair and took the half empty coffee cup from his hand and then sat on the settee beside him. She put her arm around his shoulder and he turned towards her and as both her arms encircled him he put his head upon her shoulder and sobbed. He felt her hand gently stroking the back of his neck and he was aware of the closeness of her breast. He thought that at one point her lips had momentarily brushed against his forehead.

'You have had an awful day. I've thought about you and Anna and the baby so much today and prayed for you all. We knew that the baby was not well. . .'

They sat together for a long time until his tears had ceased and then Richard sat up and took Mary's hand in his. He did not feel embarrassed about showing so much emotion but he felt compelled to say something about it.

'I'm sorry; I can't remember when last I behaved in such a child-like way.'

'You wouldn't be much of a father or husband if you didn't act in a caring and concerned way. And you made me feel part of it too and it is always good for anyone to feel needed. I know, how about having something stronger than coffee to drink? I've got some brandy in the cupboard, goodness knows why because I never drink it, but let's have a drink and if we believe that it is for medicinal purposes we'll be convinced that it is doing us good.'

Richard then relived all the events of the day. He hesitated about describing how Anna had been when she had first seen the baby because he did not want to be disloyal to her and he was sure that it was only temporary, yet he was troubled.

'She really does not seem to like her even.'

'Well that often happens. Some mothers bond to their babies immediately, others take a while and, a very few, do not ever feel any real attachment. It is something of a fallacy that all mothers experience maternal instincts; some have to work very hard at this. And it is not a one-sided business either; some babies are not very lovable because they behave in ways which do not evoke affection spontaneously. Anna has been through a lot recently and she did have an operation today under a general anaesthetic which is bound to leave her feeling low. She may have had a vision that all babies are like those painted by Rubens and certainly I would imagine that a twenty-nine week premature baby weighing less than three pounds is not going to look like that. Give her time and don't make her feel guilty by expecting her to be experiencing strong maternal instincts.' She laughed. 'I must sound like your father in the pulpit.'

'How do you know so much when I, a married man and now a father, seem to be completely ignorant on these matters?'

'I've been around a bit longer than you.'

'Only a little longer.'

'Three years to be precise. I do read a lot and I have much more spare time for doing this than do many.'

Another cup of coffee countered the alcoholic effects of the brandy and eating the sandwiches made Richard feel much better. As he left the house he put his hand on Mary's shoulder.

'Thank you for being a really good friend.'

He bent forward and kissed her lightly on her cheek.

'Just a friendly gesture,' he quipped, but as he looked into her gentle brown eyes he felt a strong urge to kiss her more warmly than that and he knew that she realised this. He turned quickly to go. He knew that anything beyond what he had done would be deemed a betrayal to Bill, as he would consider it to be to Anna. Perhaps it was the effect of the Schumann and the brandy, he thought, but he knew that this was a rationalisation.

64

Richard called into the hospital on the way to school. After the strict visiting times on the gynaecology ward it was a joy to have unlimited visiting to the children's ward. Baby Trevanion was holding her own he was told. He thought he could see some improvement but then he, himself, was feeling better after a good night's sleep. Anna was experiencing some pain but she had been given pain killers and had slept.

'I've thought about names. I don't think I like Jessica quite so much now. I think I would prefer Claire and I know you like that name.'

'Claire Trevanion; yes that is lovely. Right, if you are sure, I'll write it on the card next time I am in SCBU.'

Once he got to school Richard had many enquiries, and not just from the staff, about how the baby was and not quite so many about how Anna was. Mary was in the staff room when he went in and, along with the group of teachers who were there, heard the latest report from the hospital. After that it seemed as if they were almost avoiding each other. In the cold light of the following day his grief displayed with her the previous evening now to Richard seemed excessive and he felt the embarrassment which he had not encountered then. They had nodded to each other later in the day but she had not come over and he did not seek her out or speak to her further. It was not until after school when he was boiling a kettle in the staff kitchen that she came near to him. He felt uncomfortable. She paused and looked at him.

'What is it? You are not having a delayed reaction to last night are you? I was glad that you came to my house; in fact if it doesn't sound too pompous I felt very privileged that it was me that you came to talk to.'

'You were great last night. I'm sorry that I made an ass of myself.'

'By crying do you mean?'

'Well, partly that. I don't usually behave in such a sentimental way. . .'

'What else then?'

He was silent.

'Ricky, shall I say what I think it is? Last night I found it very easy to put my arms around you and to feel you close

65

to me, and maybe I have felt like doing that before. I also sensed when you left the house that we would both have liked to have kissed each other good-night. No, it wasn't just you that experienced that feeling. I thought about this for a long time in bed last night. We are both, I suspect, or I like to think, fairly warm, sensitive people and the fact that we experienced what we did is not exactly criminal. You are in love with Anna and I am still in love with Bill and we are just good friends who have shared some deep and personal experiences with each other. That seems pretty reasonable to me, or am I being incredibly naïve?'

He smiled at her.

'It's a wise head on those old shoulders.'

'How about making me a cup of tea young man and then I'll be getting along home. And if, when you have been to the hospital, you feel a need for my shoulder and my coffee you know that you are more than welcome.'

But they both knew that this would not happen on that evening.

5

Claire's first week was not without its problems and although Anna and Richard were constantly being re-assured that this was to be expected they were both extremely anxious. Richard's parents kept in touch by telephone but on the fourth day when Claire had a set-back, they came up to London on the coach and stayed at the flat. Although, in the early days, grandparents were usually only allowed to view from the window, as Mr and Mrs Trevanion had travelled so far and because the baby was poorly, sister permitted them to go into the intensive care room. When she saw Mr Trevanion's clerical collar she took Richard to one side and asked him if they were considering baptising Claire while she was in the unit.

'It's not that we think anything untoward is going to happen but sometimes when babies are so small and not very well it does seem to be a wise precaution. Of course, not all parents believe in baptism but I see your father is a clergyman so I assumed that you would. It may be that you would like your father to perform the ceremony.'

'I'll talk to my wife. My father has never been a hospital chaplain; I doubt if he has ever baptised a baby in an incubator.'

Later, when he mentioned it to her Richard was sur-prised at how calmly Anna took the suggestion. She believed that it was the right thing to do. Although she had been brought up as a Baptist she was, in many ways, much more ecumenical than Richard who really only felt com-fortable with the Anglican ritual. In their married life they embraced both denominations but the agreement had been that any children they might have would be brought up as

67

Anglicans rather than being left to drift between the two. At a later stage the children could choose for themselves which, if any, religious persuasion they wished to follow.

The following morning Mr Trevanion borrowed the little portable font from the unit and placed it carefully on the top of the incubator. In the presence of Anna, Richard, Mrs Trevanion and the two staff nurses most involved with the baby's care, he put his hand through the side window of the incubator and baptised his first grandchild with the sign of the cross. It was a very moving moment and Mrs Trevanion was close to tears.

'We shall still welcome her into the church when she comes home from hospital,' he said and that made them all feel better. Mrs and Mrs Trevanion had to go back to Cornwall the following day but before they left they were told that there was a slight improvement in Claire's condition.

Anna made a good recovery from her operation but the aspect of motherhood which she found most difficult was having to express breast milk to be stored in the milk bank for Claire. She found the whole process of using a breast pump distasteful and dreaded having to do it. However, she was persuaded that it was in Claire's best interest that this milk should be available for her as soon as she was able to take a little by tube each hour. But it was an ordeal to visit the mother's room to do this and her apprehension about the task affected her attitude to visiting the incubator and seeing the baby. Although nothing was ever said she still felt a covert pressure that as a mother she was expected to be with her child. She found it easier to visit when Richard was with her, partly because he had a much more relaxed manner with people and therefore she felt more at ease. She tended to postpone visiting until he came in.

After ten days Anna was ready for discharge from hospital. She knew that Claire would have to remain in SCBU until she reached what would have been her expected date of delivery and that would probably be for at least another two months, assuming that everything went well.

'We hope that you will come in as often as you can and do as much as possible for Claire,' said sister, 'we only look after her on your behalf.'

Anna believed that it was obvious that she was already labelled an indifferent mother.

'I know she is my baby but she doesn't feel like it,' she thought.

Always at the back of her mind was her thesis. She still had two more chapters to write and it was December already. But she knew once she was on her own at home she would be able to work without interruption and ought to be able to complete the task easily. She would express the milk at home and put it into the refrigerator until she and Richard visited in the evening. She allowed herself to think that what had happened might be considered an academic blessing in disguise, but then felt guilty because she would not have wished for Claire to be born so early and to have such an uphill struggle in the beginning of her life.

When Richard broke up for the Christmas holidays he suddenly found himself feeling tired and quite depressed. The last few weeks had been hectic and the anxiety about Claire in the early days had been considerable. Although he really enjoyed going to visit her and would never miss a day, he was sad that they would not now be going to Cornwall for Christmas as had originally been planned. There was always something very special about Christmas at the rectory and despite it being busy it was always a joyous occasion.

He had warned Anna that she would feel tired when she first came home, and she did, but would not admit to it. She drove herself to the point of exhaustion to get the thesis finished by December 15th, this being the deadline which she had set herself to get her material to the typist. Richard began to feel utterly sick of the thesis. It seemed to dominate their life and appeared to be Anna's primary concern. On one level he could understand the necessity to get it finished but it did not prevent him feeling angry about the amount of Anna's time it occupied and which he was beginning to think was more and more at Claire's and his expense.

'As we cannot go away for Christmas I shall be able to check everything over the holiday and have it ready for the binders at the beginning of January. Once the thesis is bound and submitted to the university I shall be able to give more time to Claire. . . and you,' she added almost as an afterthought.

'And not before time,' snapped Richard. 'I'm fed up to the back teeth of being married to a career. All you think about is getting your Ph.D. We haven't bought anything for the baby yet, we have not decorated her room. And who is going to do these things? It's always me that has to do everything.'

Anna was amazed. She had never heard Richard speak like this before and it made her angry too.

'You encouraged me to carry on with my research. It was you who said that we could make marriage and a career work. Do you want me to give it all up? Do you want a wife at home all day waiting with your meals ready whenever you choose to return from playing rugby or cricket, or from leading another geographical excursion? What a waste of everything that I have worked for if all you want is a housekeeper.'

'What I want is a home with a contented wife who enjoys her family and I want my daughter to have a mother who is around.'

It was alien to them to be so vicious in argument. They were both angry and yet they were both soon regretting bitterly what was happening and what had been said. Anna was trying not to let the tears which were near the surface show. She would not be a weak little woman; if she was going to have to fight with even her husband to have the opportunity of a career then she was going to have to be tough. And Richard was equally determined that he was not going to be the first to apologise; what had been said needed to have been said.

It did not last long. The anger abated as quickly as it had come. As he turned to storm out of the room Richard caught his foot on the armchair and tripped. Anna tried not to laugh at his endeavours to make a dramatic exit ending up being so undignified. Even he had to see the funny side and as soon as that happened for both of them they were hugging each other and saying that they were sorry. But at later times when they reflected back upon this angry interchange each knew that the hurtful comments

70

had a basis in fact and that making a marriage work required more effort than they were really putting into it. They were both very conscious of their additional role of being a parent and that was something which now needed their special attention.

Following the argument and the completion of the draft of the thesis, Anna found that her enjoyment of hospital visits was much increased, particularly when she went in with Richard. It had been a momentous event when Claire had first been lifted out of the incubator, with all the tubes and wires attached, wrapped in a blanket and given to her mother to hold. As Anna gazed down at the tiny creature she felt a flood of warmth and love which she had never experienced before. Richard sat close beside her and when the staff nurse handed him the baby for a cuddle it was one of the most moving moments of his life.

Whenever he had been on holiday, or at the weekend, Richard would call into SCBU to see Claire.

'Is Mrs Trevanion coming in?' he would be asked.

'Yes, she'll be in this evening; I'm on holiday but she is working,' he would add, trying to justify why he seemed to be the only father around in the day time and she the only mother who was missing. 'If only they would let Anna develop her relationship with Claire at her own pace and not appear to hound her,' he would think and do all he could to protect Anna from these pressures.

As this was the first Christmas that they had stayed at the flat they went out together and bought some decorations and a little fir tree. Richard decided that they must have some balloons and as he blew them up he recounted how he and his brothers used to make yards and yards of paper chains, which despite using lots of spit and much hand hammering, still seemed to come unstuck as soon as they tried to hang them up. He remembered thinking that his mother had been unfair in not letting them hang paper chains in the sitting room, although she had let them put up paper chains anywhere they liked upstairs.

Hugh came to visit them on his way to Cornwall and was taken into the hospital to peep through the window at his niece. He had just got engaged to Sarah and appeared to have much more interest in children than had ever been

71

acknowledged before. He brought presents from everyone and took theirs for the family in Cornwall. After he had left Anna and Richard did the food shopping for the Christmas holiday together and they shared all the cooking and other preparations.

'Perhaps now the thesis is written,' thought Richard 'it is all going to be much easier.' He began to whistle as he was doing jobs; he felt and was a happier man. On Christmas Eve when they went into the ward Claire was no longer in the incubator but had been transferred into a little cot, still with her monitoring system attached. At the end of every baby's cot was a tiny stocking put there by the nurses ready for Father Christmas. A group of doctors and nurses was going round the wards singing carols and they stopped in the corridor near SCBU to sing 'Away in a Manger.' Although there was never any relaxation in the medical routines there was a very happy atmosphere on the ward over Christmas. The nurses had decorated the ward a long time before but on Christmas Day itself they decked their hats with pieces of mistletoe, a baby doll was put in the manger in the nativity scene and all the little stockings were filled with presents. There seemed to be an endless supply of mince pies and Christmas cake and the occasional drink, although alcohol was not supposed to be consumed on the hospital premises. Brothers and sisters came in with their parents to visit small babies and lots of new toys were in evidence, mostly strewn around the ward floor and over which doctors and nurses picked their way to carry out their medical duties. The consultants brought their own children in to visit the hospital wards and all the junior staff derived much pleasure from observing any so-called deviant behaviour! Anna and Richard spent most of the day with Claire and for the first time Anna did a tube feed. It was a happy and relaxed couple who left the hospital hand in hand to return home to cook their own Christmas dinner and to telephone the rest of their family.

January saw the return of Richard to school for the spring term, the submission of the thesis to the university and the rapid progress of Claire. Anna became more competent at handling the baby and more confident as a mother. She learned how to bath her and as Claire became stronger she was able to put her to the breast to feed. In early February Anna was examined and awarded her doctorate; by mid February Claire had reached 5lbs in weight and was deemed well enough to go home. Anna stayed on the ward for two days and nights and took over completely the care of Claire. She breast fed her three hourly day and night, although the nurses gave Claire one of the feeds in the night so that her mother could have a little extra sleep.

At home Richard set the central heating thermostat higher and got the flat really warm. He had decorated the nursery and they had collected the cot and the pram from the shop. Claire had had lots of presents from her relatives and her parents' colleagues and the little cupboard in her room was filled with clothes. It was both a proud and anxious moment when the taxi drew up outside the flat and Mr and Dr Trevanion first brought their baby daughter home.

It was, however, not long before they realised that two days had not been sufficient time to get to know how to handle Claire and Anna's self confidence quickly ebbed, a fact which Claire equally quickly perceived. A tension began to develop between mother and baby. Claire kept crying; Anna could not settle her. Anna's milk began to dry up; Claire got hungry. The health visitor came in regularly and Anna found that she was getting more and more dependent upon her support and friendly, down-to-earth advice. They began by topping up Claire with a bottle but in the end the health visitor with reluctance, and Anna with relief, agreed that Claire would have to go onto the bottle completely. This meant that Anna was not so tied to the baby and that Richard could now give Claire the occasional bottle in the night so that Anna could get some more sleep. But even by doing this Richard knew that Anna was far less happy being at home looking after a baby than she had been when she had had days on end in her study writing her dissertation.

One day the telephone in the staff room rang during the dinner break.

'It's for you,' called the history teacher across the room to Richard. Above the noise of talking in the room he tried to

73

hear what Anna was saying.

'I can't go on,' she sobbed down the telephone, 'Claire won't stop crying unless I pick her up. The health visitor has been in and she says there is nothing wrong with Claire and I have just got to be firm. But the crying is getting on my nerves. I've wrapped her up firmly and tucked her in her cot; I've shut the bedroom door and gone into the kitchen as was suggested, but then I feel worried and go back to listen outside the door and she starts to cry again.'

'Look, I'll be home soon after four and I will take over.'

'Can't you come before then?'

'No, you know I can't. I'm teaching all afternoon. If Claire has had her feed do what the health visitor says, close the door and leave her in the room.'

When he put the phone down his face must have revealed much.

'What is it Ricky?' asked Mary.

'Anna can't get the baby to settle and it's not just today, it seems to be every day and she is getting to the end of her tether.'

'Look come to the geography room with me and tell me about it – it's too noisy to have a sensible conversation in here.'

They perched on two stools in the deserted geography room and drank the two mugs of coffee which Mary made. Richard told her about life at home with Claire. She was doing very well, putting on weight and taking her feeds from the bottle without any problems. She was sleeping well at night and was usually good in the evening when he was home.

'Every baby I have known. . .' he continued

'. . .and how many is that?' interjected Mary with a smile.

'Well, about two,' he confessed, 'but they would have their restless time in the evening. Claire has hers during the day when Anna is there on her own and Anna is beginning to say that she cannot cope.'

'It is very understandable isn't it? Anna loves her academic life and she really had to battle against the odds to get her thesis finished and her doctorate awarded. She did not have an easy pregnancy and that's the understatement of the year. She had an awful time and she is bound to feel a bit resentful.'

'We are very lucky to have Claire at all; she nearly died at one stage. Anna ought to remember that and be very grateful that she has a baby at all.'

'She does remember and she is grateful and that is making things worse because she must feel guilty when she finds that things are getting on top of her.'

'It's all very well understanding the reasons why there is a problem; I don't know what can be done about it.'

'When is the university lectureship going to be advertised?'

'Probably in May or early June.'

'Is there any chance that Anna could do some temporary work in the university before then so that she was using her brain more than she is doing now?'

'She is trying to write some papers using material from her research.'

'Well that is fine but surely what she needs is to get out of the flat into the academic hurly-burly if only for a few hours each week.'

'We are planning to get an au pair girl after August when we have moved into a bigger house, but we can only start looking for a house when we know that Anna has a job. If she gets this lectureship then we shall have two incomes to pay the mortgage and the baby caring fees. It all sounds so full of ifs. If only Anna enjoyed being a mother more than she does, she loves Claire of course – there is absolutely no doubt about that – but she is not quite like I remember my mother being with my sisters.'

'I seem to remember reading that men always choose wives who were replicas of their mothers. . .'

He had to laugh. 'I know it will work out but we always seem to be contending with so many variables.'

'As a short term solution, how about me coming round tonight and baby sitting. I can change nappies and give a bottle, and if she cries I can carry her on my shoulder all evening. I should love to do that. Take Anna to the pictures tonight.'

'She does not like going unless there is something really good on. We've only been once or maybe twice since we got married.'

'Well tonight is different. I guarantee that Anna might even contemplate going to see a western, if only to have an evening out of the house with her husband. It might do you good too. You look far more worn and haggard with all your domestic responsibilities than you did when, as a fanatical sportsman and outdoor man, you first arrived at this school. You two miss out by not having any of your family near at hand to help so when it comes to baby sitting you will have to regard me as the much needed aunt.'

Mary was right in everything which she had predicted. Anna enjoyed her evening out; Mary did quite well with the babysitting and when the parents returned it was Anna who readily changed and fed Claire. In bed that night Richard mentioned the possibility of Anna doing some temporary work until the lectureship was decided upon.

'You don't mind?'

'I would rather have a contented wife and mother than an unhappy housekeeper. Why not ring the prof and talk with him about it?'

It was more than fortuitous that the Easter field trip for the sixth formers was this year to be on Dartmoor with the last three days spent studying the coastal features of Dorset. Richard would have been worried about Anna being left on her own with Claire for the ten days that he was to be away but as the field trip was going to be fairly near to his parents he suggested that she stayed there and that he came back in the evenings when he did not have any commitments to the field work party.

Richard hired an estate car for two weeks and they loaded all the baby things into the back, together with their own more modest luggage. Mary drove down to Cornwall with them because on the Sunday morning Claire was going to have her baptism completed by her grandfather in his church and Mary was going to be a godmother. This had been Anna's suggestion. She had become very fond of Mary in the weeks since Claire had come out of hospital. Mary was always willing to come over and baby sit, or just to talk and her apparent understanding of the conflicts which

76

Anna experienced made her a much welcomed friend. As one who, had things in life worked out differently had been destined to be a vicar's wife she seemed a particularly appropriate choice of godmother.

Mary fitted into life in the rectory well. She loved the atmosphere created by Tom and Elizabeth Trevanion and she enjoyed the company of Jane and Kate. Mary was the sort of person who could see which jobs needed doing without having to ask what she could do to help. On the Sunday morning in the pale April sunshine she carried Claire across to the church accompanied by Hugh's fiancée Sarah and one of Richard's school friends who were to be the other godparents. Tom Trevanion explained to the congregation that this was to be a slightly different baptism service in that Claire, when she had been so poorly in hospital, had been baptised by him in her incubator. Now, partly as a thanksgiving for her recovery, and mostly because her godparents had not been there to make vows on her behalf, they were now going to complete the ceremony and welcome Claire into the family of the church. It was a very moving experience for everyone but the only person who cried was Claire and she howled lustily when her grandfather tipped cold water on her head. There were those who commented with good humour to the rector later that it was pleasant to have another child from the rectory who behaved very noisily in church.

On the Sunday evening Richard and Mary had to join the school party which had travelled down from London by coach. After supper Richard was doing the opening session on the geology of Dartmoor. He had prepared this well and had some good slides of the features they would be studying. He also felt happier than he had done in weeks and this came over in the enthusiasm with which he presented the material. It gave the field class the right start. Next morning the group set off early and had an energetic day walking between tors. After the evening meal and the day's debriefing Richard drove back to Laneast, leaving Joe Blackmore and Mary to cope with the evening's activities.

Anna had been out with her mother-in-law pushing the pram. They had only made very slow progress through the village because everyone had stopped to admire the baby and to have a chat. Had Anna not been on holiday she would have found this very time consuming but she realised how much a feature of village life this was and how important it was for the rector to have his wife gathering the village news. By the time they returned to the rectory Mrs Trevanion knew about two sick people whom her husband would need to visit and another whose elderly father in Lancashire had just died.

Claire was the inevitable centre of attention and thrived on the adoration. When she cried there was always somebody to rock the pram or attend to her needs. Mrs Trevanion looked after her completely one day so that Anna could join the school party. Although Anna felt quite apprehensive about doing this and wondered if she would be able to keep up with their energetic programme she found that there were several of the sixth form girls who walked at a leisurely pace and she tended to join with them. At the end of the day she knew quite a lot about the land use of a national park, but the next morning, despite having a long soak in a hot bath the previous evening her body ached and she was glad to do nothing more energetic than pottering round the rectory doing the baby's washing.

It was too far for Richard to travel back from Dorset so he stayed there for the three days. Joe Blackmore was an expert in the geomorphology of this area so he led the teaching and the other two staff relaxed without the responsibility. Although the sea was icy they all paddled and their were some hilarious photographs taken by the youngsters of staff members with their trousers rolled up being pushed into the water, although theoretically they were all supposed to be looking for fossils. It was the end of a hard working trip and nobody was going to be too strict about how intensive was the fossil hunting. Mary was always very careful not to let the friendship she had with the Trevanions out of school intrude in the work situation, knowing only too well how gossip can develop from the merest casual remark or gesture. If there had been any rumours around stemming from her and Richard arriving together at the beginning of the course, the apparent close friendship between Anna and Mary evidenced on the day when Anna joined them would have done much to dispel the inferences.

The rest of the Easter holiday was spent back at the flat. Anna had been offered some demonstrating work in the summer term and they had advertised for a baby minder to look after Claire for the few hours that Anna would be working away from home. They both studied information from estate agents about houses and viewed some so that they had some idea of prices and location.

When Anna was duly appointed to the university lectureship they put in an offer for a house that they both liked near to the university. The child minder was willing to extend the hours she came and it would be much less travelling for her when they moved to their new house because it was in the road next to hers. In that summer term Richard found time to play some cricket, but never regularly for the team as he used to do. Things did, at last, seem to be working out, but it had not been the easiest of years for either of them. Richard sometimes allowed himself to feel envious of the carefree life which some of the unmarried members of staff seemed to have. They were able to socialise a lot, appeared to have plenty of money to spend on exotic holidays, and although he never really hankered after these things he did miss playing all the sport he had done before he got married. He kept very fit training with the boys at school but he no longer felt able to commit himself to being a regular member of a sports team. He would a little ruefully reflect that although he might never have been an international sportsman he could well have achieved a reasonable county standard for a few years.

6

Having been brought up in what he affectionately referred to as his dad's tied cottage and then moving into his wife's inherited ancestral seat, the buying of their first jointly owned home was an event of great significance for Richard. Because they had not had a mortgage on the flat, when they sold it they had a sizeable deposit to put down on a property and with their two incomes they could afford to buy something which would meet all their needs for a long time. Richard particularly wanted a garden but realised that in London he would have to be contented with something very much smaller than the rectory garden which he had always enjoyed working. Anna wanted a study with a view over the garden. They knew the moment that they walked through the front door of number nineteen that this was the home for them. It was a three storied semi-detached Victorian house with four bedrooms and French doors from the living room opening on to a very overgrown and neglected walled garden. On the top floor was a large attic room which the previous owner had used as a studio because there was a lot of light which came through the big window overlooking the back garden.

They moved in at the end of August when Claire was nine months old. Together they converted and decorated Anna's study so that as soon as she took up her appointment at the university she had a place at home where she could work. Then they turned the smallest bedroom into Claire's room and shared doing the decorating.

After that was finished Richard declared that he was

utterly sick of painting and wallpapering and he now wanted to make a start on the garden so all the other rooms would have to wait. Anna was not sorry. The rest of the house was in a reasonable decorative order and, although the choice of decor would not have been theirs, it was livable with until the spirit moved them to take up their paint brushes again.

Decorating was to Richard a duty; gardening was an absolute pleasure. He cut down all the overgrown shrubs and spent hours digging out huge roots. In the evenings he had bonfires to burn rubbish, which did not immediately endear him to the neighbours. There were two apple trees which had been neglected for years and had only a few undersized apples that summer. After he had harvested the meagre crop in the autumn he pruned the trees drastically to encourage stronger growth and perhaps a heavier crop the following year. In his mind he carried a design for his garden which included a lawn for Claire to play on, a sandpit and a branch of the apple tree to which he could attach a swing. There was also to be a vegetable patch, herbaceous border and a rose bed. Roses never grow well in Cornwall where the air is too pure and enables black spot to flourish. In contrast, the more polluted atmosphere of the capital city kept many of the diseases which adversely affected roses at bay. Anna gently reminded him that they were quite grandiose schemes for a pocket sized garden but he would let nothing dampen his enthusiasm. The move to number nineteen they would come to look back upon as one of the happier times in their marriage.

There were those who would consider Anna and Richard's marriage to be unusual. It had always been characterised by elements of role reversal which to traditionalists might be eyebrow raising. Outwardly they appeared happy together but to those who knew them well it became more and more obvious that the greatest joy for Richard was his little daughter. Because her mother tended to be away from home more than other mothers would be, her father compensated for this by being with her as much as he could. He was usually back from school before Anna came home and he took over from Chris, the

81

child minder, giving Claire her tea and then playing with her until Anna returned. Anna usually bathed Claire and then one of them would read her a story while the other started getting supper ready. After their evening meal both parents had work to do. Anna would go upstairs to her attic study; Richard would spread the books he had to mark over the sitting room floor and have the television on low which he would keep half an eye on and turn up the sound if there was something that he thought he would be interested in. Chris did all the washing and ironing and much of the housework so he was relieved of the domestic tasks which he never liked doing but had felt obliged to undertake. Now he had more time to spend on the things which he most enjoyed doing at home, playing with Claire and gardening, and these two activities he could often combine. Before Claire became mobile she would sit in her pram in the garden watching him until she became bored or just fell asleep. She did not finally take her first steps until she was nearly fifteen months, but by that time the lawn was ready for her to begin being coached in ball game skills. From the very beginning it was clear that if Claire had any prowess on the games field her father would ensure that she succeeded in maximising the potential. As the spring days lengthened he took her to the park to ride on the swings and to feed the ducks. Sometimes Anna got home early enough to go with him. Mary would often come over at the weekends. She now owned a car and on sunny days they would all go for a picnic in the country or even down to the south coast.

Anna's university lectureship was initially for three years but there was no doubt that she would be confirmed in post before the end of her probationary period. She had produced an excellent doctoral thesis and had published a number of highly rated papers. Her research was continuing and although her lectures were not yet as stimulating as those of some of her colleagues, they were carefully prepared and full of sound information. Development of an interesting lecturing style was some-thing with which she was seeking help and as her personal confidence grew she relaxed more in the lecture theatre. Claire was just turned two when Anna received her first invitation to address an international conference which was being held in America in June. She was very excited and the ever supportive Richard could see no reason why she should not go. It was only for ten days, Chris would come in as usual to look after Claire and he would be home in the evenings and at the weekends. If he needed any further help there was always Mary to call upon.

When the time came for Anna to go Richard and Claire went to Heathrow to see her off. Claire was excited when she saw the aeroplanes and kept telling other travellers that 'Mummy going up a sky.' They went out on to the balcony to watch the aeroplane take off and then caught the underground train back home.

As Anna had gone through the checkpoint she had turned back to wave to them. Richard was holding Claire and she had her arms round his neck giving him a kiss. He had obviously told her that Mummy was waving and she had looked round and waved her teddy bear at Anna.

'I know they will be all right,' thought Anna, but suddenly going all the way to America did not seem as exciting as it had done. Occasionally she felt a little resentful of the close relationship which Claire and Richard enjoyed, but Mary had suggested that there was a time when little girls were all over their fathers and then a time when it would be mother's turn. Once she was settled in her window seat and the plane was taxiing down the runway her enthusiasm returned. She looked across to the spectators' balcony but it was too far away to be able to see if they were on it. The plane moved out on to the main runway, came to a standstill and then the engines were revved up before it began to race down the runway to lift off and ascend into the sky over west London. The cabin crew came round with newspapers and then drinks. Anna unfastened her safety belt and looked down at the patchwork of tiny fields as they crossed over Ireland. A meal was then served after which she got out her papers to do some more preparation for the conference. She was fortunate in that the aircraft was only half full so she had nobody in the seat next to her and was able to spread out her work.

At Washington airport she was met by a conference

organiser who escorted her to her hotel. It was early evening but for Anna it was past midnight and she was extremely tired, so she went to bed. Next morning she woke incredibly early, read for a while, then dozed before she received the call which she had requested the previous evening. The organiser who had met her arranged to see her after breakfast and to introduce her to some of the other delegates who were staying at the same hotel.

'When were you last in the States, Dr Trevanion?' he asked.

'It's my first visit.'

'Well I never did. I thought with all that you had published that you must have been over here many a time. Are you going to stay on and see something of the country while you are over here?'

'I've got to get back to my little girl; she is only two and this is the first time that I have been away from home for more than one night.'

'My, you must be a busy person.'

'I've got a very good husband.'

They travelled together to the conference centre.

Anna was not presenting her paper until the morning of the fourth day so she had plenty of time to become acquainted with the atmosphere of the conference and to familiarise herself with the other inputs. She found the American delegates, in particular, to be very friendly and there were several other scientists from other countries with whom she wanted to make contact because they were working in areas closely related to her own research. She had promised that she would telephone home and she timed this so that it would be just before Claire went to bed. The line was rather crackly and Claire could not be persuaded to say anything although Richard said that she had a big grin on her face when he said that it was Mummy. As he was bathing Claire she asked him, 'Mummy come now?'

'Not tonight, darling; Mummy has gone to America to speak to some scientists. She will come back next week.'

Chris had told him that Claire had kept mentioning that her Mummy had gone into the sky, but apart from the fact that Anna was not coming home in the evenings Claire's routine was little affected by her mother's trip and she seemed happy.

As well as having a full programme of lectures, the conference had also arranged outings for delegates. After the Saturday morning session finished at noon the rest of the weekend was free, either to go on one of the outings or for doing their own thing. Anna's presentation was the second on the Saturday morning. She did not sleep well the night before and did not feel able to face the other delegates at breakfast. Instead she asked for a breakfast tray to be sent up to her room, but when it came she only drank the coffee and did not eat anything.

'All right, it is your first international conference,' she told herself, 'but if you are going to be an academic it's no use getting so worked up about giving a lecture. It's part of the job and you have got to get used to doing it.'

She skimmed through her lecture material; she knew that the content was good but so much was going to depend upon how she presented it.

She did not go to the first lecture but chose instead to use the time to walk through the park to the conference centre. She thought that the exercise and fresh air would steady her nerves. When she arrived everyone was having mid morning coffee and there was about another half an hour before she was due to speak. She took her slides to the technician and then made her way into the foyer where coffee was being served. The chairman was watching for her and when he saw her hesitate at the door he came straight over.

'Have some coffee?'

'I don't think I will, thank you.'

He smiled at her.

'If you haven't got a horrible knotted feeling in the pit of your stomach you are a very rare person. No matter how many lectures I give I still feel quite sick until I get started and then it is all right. A cup of coffee is very good for dealing with the stomach butterflies.'

She allowed herself to be persuaded to have a drink.

'Once you have got your first slide on the screen and are into the matters you know most about you will be fine.'

Anna nodded gratefully but as she walked up on to the

platform with him her knees felt weak. She was glad to sit down while he introduced her. She looked out across a massive sea of faces and took a deep breath. She was only half hearing what the chairman was saying.

'. . . and we are delighted to welcome Dr Anna Trevanion from the University of London, England, who is now going to address the conference on. . .'

'This is it. I have got to stand up now and start.'

Polite applause followed the chairman's remarks. Anna rose to her feet. The chairman adjusted the microphone. The lights in the main auditorium were dimmed and Anna began to speak. As soon as she started her nervousness melted away. The first slide came up on the screen and she was able to give a half smile to the chairman to let him know that he had been right and she was now feeling on top of things again. She knew her material well and she was able to distance herself from her notes and speak spontaneously about the slides and the features she wished to emphasise. The audience was quiet – 'Are they bored?' she wondered. 'They are not shuffling papers, they must be listening to what I am saying; I'm doing all right.'

At the end of her lecture there was an enthusiastic outburst of applause and when the chairman invited questions there were many spontaneous and interested comments and enquiries about the research she was doing and the results that were being obtained. Anna was good at thinking on her feet, she had an excellent memory and she knew her subject well. The question time was perhaps the best part of the session and it over ran into the lunch break without anyone seeming to mind. The nervous creature who had stood up at 11 am was now a confident and charming lecturer. The chairman was the first to his feet to lead the applause which ended the morning's programme.

'Absolutely first class,' he said, 'well done!'

For the first time in her life Anna thought she knew what it meant to be walking on air as she gathered up her notes and walked off the platform. From being a non-entity at the conference up to then she had suddenly shot into the limelight and she found that it was to her liking.

Her adrenalin was still pumping hard in her system as she joined the rest of the delegates for lunch and by now she was really hungry. After lunch she had already signed up for a coach trip to the Blue Mountains.

'There is just time to telephone home and let Richard know how it has gone and perhaps Claire will speak to me this time,' she thought. 'If I ring now I should catch Claire before she has her bath.'

But there was no reply. She felt more than a little disappointed but then remembered that it was Saturday and they might have gone out somewhere. Allowing for the five hour time lag by the time she returned from her outing they would have been in bed for hours.

'Oh well, I'll try again tomorrow and if I don't get through it doesn't matter because they know when my plane is due in on Wednesday.'

On the coach that afternoon Anna sat next to a very pleasant young delegate from New Zealand who, like Anna, was attending her first international conference, but unlike Anna was not presenting a paper. For the first time since she had arrived in America she felt really relaxed, and as the coach sped through the beautiful scenery and she chatted to Margaret she could not help thinking that a life of such luxury was very enjoyable. If all this went with the academic role then her chosen career was very worthwhile.

Mary had suggested that unless it was pouring with rain on the Saturday she should come over in the car and take Richard and Claire down to the south coast. Claire loved playing in the sea even when it was cold, but that morning dawned sunny and warm. They got off to an early start and took a picnic. It was a low tide when they arrived and the rest of the morning was spent building sand castles, all with moats and channels in preparation for the incoming tide. After they had their picnic Claire had a sleep in her pushchair while Richard and Mary stretched out on the rug to sunbathe.

'How about a swim?'

'You are mad,' she replied, 'the sea in June is still icy cold. I'm perfectly happy just to paddle when Claire wakes up.'

He was not to be deterred and raced off down the beach to the water's edge. She saw him pause as his feet felt the temperature of the water but his pride would not let him give up now and he plunged into the waves. It was paralytically cold and after the briefest of swims he had to go for a long run up the beach to get his circulation going again.

Mary read her book and watched Claire. It never ceased to amaze her that such a tiny, premature baby, who for so many days had clung to life by a thread, could grow up into such a beautiful, healthy little girl. Perhaps because she was her godchild Claire felt special to her. Mary now had a nephew and a niece but she did not feel quite the same about them even though they were her own family. She did, of course, see much more of Claire and knew her very well, whereas the other children lived in Wales and she only saw them two or three times a year. When Claire woke up the tide had turned so she and Daddy extended the channel down to the water's edge.

'Aunty Mary, come and see,' she called.

They had found a tiny crab which they had put into a bucket of water for her to take to show Mary. They gathered some shells and put them in the bucket too, then a long pice of seaweed. Claire was avidly collecting treasures to take home. As the sea came in it filled the moat round the castle and then with incredible speed the waves broke down the sides of the castle.

'A very good example of coastal erosion!' commented Richard. 'Five waves and a fortress is demolished.'

They persuaded Claire that her baby crab would be happier with his Mummy and Daddy in the sea but said that she could take all her shells and her seaweed home. If things were explained clearly to Claire she was amenable to suggestion and most times went along with what was proposed. They made a little pool for the crab and then they all squatted down and watched him dig himself into the sand.

'Is his Mummy in the sand?' asked Claire.

'She will be looking for him somewhere along the beach.'

'Has his Mummy gone away?'

'No, Mummies come back to their children. Your Mummy is coming back in five days' time.' Mary held up her hand and together she and Claire counted her fingers – Saturday, Sunday, Monday, Tuesday, Wednesday. Wednesday was her little finger. 'That is the day when Mummy will come back on the aeroplane.'

They packed up all their things into the car and then walked along the sea front to buy some fish to take home for supper. On the journey back they sang nursery rhymes to keep Claire awake because they anticipated that if she had another sleep before they got home she would not be ready to go to bed for hours. Once back at number nineteen Mary bathed Claire and put on her pyjamas and dressing gown while Richard cooked the supper. Claire sat up to the table with them balancing on two cushions on the kitchen chair. She ate some of the fish but she was very tired and her eyes began to droop. Mary carried her up to bed and only needed to read two pages of the story before Claire had fallen asleep with her arm around Mr Ted. Mary gently kissed her forehead and whispered, 'God bless, darling,' then went downstairs to finish drying the dishes.

After they had unpacked the picnic things and shaken the sand out of everything Richard took Mary on his daily tour of inspection of the garden. In slightly less than two years he had created something beautiful out of a near wilderness and he was justifiably proud of it. The vegetable plot was weed free and, although the ball often got kicked on to the patch, Claire was careful about not treading on 'Daddy's plants'. The young rose bushes which he had planted the previous November were coming into the first flush of flowers. Richard bent down and picked a single scented deep red rose and gave it to Mary. Neither said anything. They went back into the kitchen to make some coffee and Mary filled a tiny vase with water, put the rose in it and stood it on the window sill. She remained with her hands resting on the side of the sink, gazing at it and across the back garden. She felt

Richard come up behind her, then put his arms around her and gently turn her to face him. He drew her close to him. His mouth came down hard upon hers and he felt her body press against his. Her mouth opened slightly; his tongue began to explore her lips and then the inside of her cheeks. Her tongue responded to his searching as his hand unbuttoned the front of her blouse and gently caressed her breast.

Suddenly Mary drew back.

'Ricky, we must not do this.'

'I know, I'm sorry, but I so desperately need you.'

She switched off the kettle which was billowing clouds of steam all over the kitchen and got out two mugs. She put a teaspoon of coffee in each, opened the fridge and took out a pint of milk and added it to the mugs. Richard never took his eyes off her.

'Come and sit down,' said Mary, 'we've got to talk about this and we've got to do it now.'

He closed the French windows because it was cooler and drew the settee near to them so that they could look across the garden. Mary was going to sit in the armchair but thought it rather churlish since he was making it very obvious that he wanted them to sit together.

They sipped their coffee.

Richard first broke the silence.

'I know that I should not have taken advantage of you after we had had such a happy day out with you. . .'

'Oh Rick, don't be so pompous and old fashioned. . .'

'I am old fashioned in lots of ways and I'm not ashamed of it. I'm so old fashioned that I deliberately picked a red rose and gave it to you with an old fashioned message. Perhaps you are not sufficiently old fashioned to know what that message was. . .'

'Ricky, don't let's quarrel about this. We have got to be very honest with ourselves and with each other, and we have not got to leave unsaid things which we know must be said.'

'I believe that I am falling in love with you.'

Mary was silent and when she turned towards him she had tears in her eyes. She looked at him but she had to wait until she thought her voice was going to be steady

90

enough to speak.

'For a long time I have realised that I am very fond of you but I have struggled hard to keep that affection under control and not let myself think of you other than as a dear man, the father of my godchild and husband of my close friend. You are a married man, you have a marriage to sustain and nurture.'

'It's not much of a marriage being married to a career.'

'Stop basking in self pity. You knew when you asked Anna to marry you that she was destined to achieve high academic honours. You do benefit in many ways from her success. She had a terrible pregnancy and still managed to complete her doctorate despite all she went through.'

'That pregnancy has put her off having any more babies. When I suggest that we ought to have other children before Claire gets too old she keeps saying that she first needs to get established in her career.'

Mary was quiet. She had suspected that Anna had been sleeping in her study and had wondered if all was well with the marriage.

'Anna does not want me to make love with her. Since Claire was born the number of times we have made love I could count on one hand and I am no monk you know.'

'I'm sorry, Rick, really I am. Have you talked together about it? Have you sought any help?'

'What sort of help?'

'Counselling. . .'

'I've spoken to our family doctor. He just says give it time, be patient.'

Mary took hold of Richard's hand.

'The easiest thing in the world now would be for us to go upstairs and get into bed together. Every part of my body aches for you. There is nothing that I want more now than for you to make love to me. I need you as much as you need me. Nobody would know. Anna is on the other side of the Atlantic; Claire is sound asleep in her room. But we cannot. Everything that we believe as Christians is that we have a duty to remain loyal – "keep ye only unto her so long as ye both shall live" – oh yes, Bill and I made love. We weren't married and he was planning to go into the ministry but our passion was too strong to be under the same roof and not living together. So I have a duty to his memory too. Think what we stand to lose if we don't curb our relationship. I would have to change schools immediately, possibly sell my home and move right away, not be able to come and see Anna and my godchild and we would never meet.'

'I am not sure that I am going to be able to control the strong physical desire for you that I have. I could not in the kitchen and I know that you felt the same. I believe it is more than is humanly possible for us to carry on as we have done for the last three or four years knowing that we feel about each other as we do.'

'We have no choice but to do this. You know as well as I do that Christ said to follow him would not be easy and it isn't, but we are not going to hurt Anna by our lust.'

'It's not just that and you know it isn't.'

'I'm trying to be brutal and to get everything in perspective. I know I am so near to being weak and if you don't help me to keep strong we are both going to do things that we shall regret.'

Richard then realised how selfish and childish he was being and how hard he was making it for Mary by putting all the responsibility for being restrained upon her.

'You are a very, very dear person, Mary. My family needs you and whatever I feel for you and you feel for me has to take second place to that. But perhaps our Lord would understand and let us comfort each other from time to time.'

'I know the wise thing is for me to go home now and that I am going to do. It has been a lovely day and nothing that has occurred has changed that, in fact what we have said to each other has added to those good memories.'

She stood up and put out both hands to him, drawing him to his feet and then to her.

'I want you to know always that I love you, find you a very attractive man and that makes everything so very much harder.'

She kissed him good night and left quickly.

That night in bed Mary wept and the following morning she did not get up for the communion service. Richard lay awake for most of the night and agonised about the situation. He had tried to keep up the facade of a happy marriage instead of trying to work out with Anna a way of solving at least some of the difficulties which existed between them. Perhaps it was that he had not tried to do this because he did not want their problems to be solved, yet he was fond of Anna and the last thing that he wanted to do was to hurt her.

The dawn was breaking when he finally dozed off but it was not long before a little figure scrambled into bed beside him full of the joys of living and eager to start another day.

☆ ☆ ☆

Anna shared a cab to Washington airport with her friend from New Zealand and two other delegates. She was still experiencing some of the elation which followed her very successful lecture and had enjoyed the kudos which went with it. They all felt somewhat akin to VIPs as their luggage was transferred by porter from the cab to their various check-in points. Their flights left before Anna's but there was still plenty of time for them to have coffee together before they went their separate ways.

The next international conference was in two years' time in Sweden and they all hoped to be there. Suddenly the world seemed to be Anna's oyster and she knew that she would no longer be contented with researching and lecturing in one university city. She needed the stimulation of international travel and the academic contact that went with it.

It was early evening when she boarded what was to be the overnight flight to London due in to Heathrow at 8 am local time. It would have been impossible for Richard to meet her at this time and be in school an hour later and they had agreed this before she left. As it was, the flight from Washington was delayed by mechanical trouble and by the time they got over Heathrow the plane had to stack for a while waiting a turn to land. Anna did not sleep very much on the journey and by the time they landed nearly two hours' late she felt extremely weary. She waited at the baggage conveyer with a trolley and then pushed it through the nothing-to-declare section of customs.

'Oh well, after the Lord Mayor's show comes the dustcart,' she thought, but it felt very different to the send-off she had experienced on the other side of the Atlantic.

'I'll have to get a taxi; I'm too tired to struggle with the underground, even if the rush hour is over. But everyone else had the same idea so there was a long queue and an equally long wait.

When the taxi drew up outside number nineteen Chris said to Claire: 'Mummy is here; come and meet her,' and they both went down to the front gate where Anna was paying the driver.

'Where is Daddy?' asked Claire.

'He is in school,' said Chris. 'Mummy has just come back from America.'

Anna bent down and picked Claire up and gave her a kiss and a hug.

'Hello darling. What have you been doing while I have been away?'

'The crab went to find his Mummy.'

'What crab was this?'

'The crab in my bucket.'

'Aunty Mary took Claire and Daddy to the sea-side last Saturday,' explained Chris. 'Claire brought you a piece of seaweed back as a present.'

Chris carried in the case and Anna carried Claire, then they all sat down and had a cup of tea together. After this Chris got on with the housework and Anna unpacked her luggage, helped by Claire.

'I've got you a present.'

'Show me my present.'

Anna had brought her a cuddly brown bear which she had bought on the trip to the Blue Mountains.

'You could take him to bed with Mr Ted.'

Anna went to bed and slept for two hours, only to be wakened by the telephone ringing.

'I'm sorry,' said Chris, 'I tried to get to it before it wakened you. It was Richard just checking that you had got home safely. He sends his love and said that as you

94

were here today he might be a little later than usual because he was going to stay on and do some cricket coaching tonight.'

When Richard came in at 6 pm Claire was bathed and ready for bed and a meal was prepared.

'What a treat,' he said, 'no chores for me tonight.'

'You poor hard-done-by man; your turn tomorrow.'

But it felt good to have a wife and mother at home when he got in from work.

In most respects it felt good to Anna to be home. She had really been looking forward to seeing them again, and especially Claire since this had been the longest time that she had left her. But things had not turned out quite like she had thought they would. Claire had her routine for the day and Mummy being there was not part of it. After lunch Chris usually took Claire for a walk or to do the shopping and they often ended up playing on the swings in the park. As Anna was home for the day Chris went early.

'Mummy is home today so she is going to take you out.'

'I want to go to the park with Chris,' wailed Claire.

'But you have Mummy today.'

'Don't want Mummy; I want Chris.'

It was all right when Chris had left. Claire went happily to the park with her mother, but it left Anna, not for the first time, feeling slightly envious of the relationship between Chris and Claire. On one level she understood it; on another she resented it. If Claire spent most of her time at home with Chris and then with Richard it was inevitable that she would get close to them. It was the price which a working mother had to pay, but at times it hurt.

95

7

It had been the Christian Union which had brought Anna and Richard together in the first place and, although they belonged to different denominations, their Christian beliefs could have been a unifying factor in their relationship. But as time went by it became somewhat divisive. There had always been an expectation in the Trevanion family rectory that one service on Sunday would be attended, but there was never any pressure extended to do so. When adolescence brought its normal temporary rejection of the parental Christian belief system it was understandingly tolerated, but no doubt actively prayed about. Richard had long past established a routine of taking communion at the early service on Sunday mornings and this he only rarely missed and then only with very good reason. Although he was fairly accommodating about most things he knew that for him the Church of England was right and that he could not share meaningfully with Anna's more fundamental evangelism. They had agreed that Claire should be baptised into and brought up as an Anglican because Anna knew that this was something which was very important for Richard and about which she felt far less strongly. She still went fairly regularly to the Baptist church which she had attended when her mother was alive but she did not take on any further responsibility because her time was limited. In the early months of their marriage Richard had accompanied Anna to the morning service but gradually this had lapsed and when Claire was a tiny baby this was a very good reason for discontinuing the practice permanently.

When Claire was staying in Cornwall she always went to

church. As her father had done a generation before she went first as a small baby in her pram and then, as she got older, she progressed to joining the family in the front pew. She liked to sit next to her grandmother but soon became restless and would stand up on the seat and turn round to face the congregation. On one occasion she had got excited when Tom Trevanion came in at the beginning of the service and called out, 'Grandad, hello Grandad'. He smiled at her as she jumped up and down in the pew and in no time she was walking up the chancel steps to see him. Richard had gone quickly after her fearing that she might protest noisily when he picked her up but, in fact, she came back quite happily to her place and to having a story read to her. Children were very much part of the services in Tom Trevanion's church. He never minded how much noise they made or how mobile they became in the service. This was the church's congregation of the future and he wanted it to feel at home from a very early age. But things were very different in the church which Richard attended in London.

He went to the one which was nearest to his home which tended to have an elderly and rather sparse congregation and children were but rarely seen. There was not a Sunday School or seemingly any attempt to bring the young people into the church. When Richard had discussed this with his father his response had been to ask his son what he could do about it.

'You are a teacher; why don't you start the Sunday School?'

But Richard felt that he had enough responsibilities or perhaps he did not share the same conviction as his father that God intended him to fill the breach. However, the matter of taking Claire to church more regularly than the times they were in Cornwall prompted her parents to have a long talk together one evening.

Since Anna had returned from the States there had been a certain amount of separateness between them. They had chatted about the conference and how Richard had managed looking after Claire but between them there was a

97

feeling of restraint. It had been a long time since they had had a meaningful discussion about important things. Mary had chastised Richard for moaning to her about difficulties in the marriage instead of discussing them with Anna, but he found it so much easier to talk with Mary. He still felt guilty about what might have happened between him and Mary had she not been so determined that nothing was going to happen. It was not something that he was ever going to be able to tell Anna about.

Anna knew that she found it difficult to show emotion and to share feelings. That was probably a reason why she was a scientist who dealt always with facts but it was a way that she coped with interpersonal stresses. She would immerse herself in her work. The times when she had been most stressed emotionally had often been her most productive scientifically. The weeks preceding Claire's birth followed by the great worries over whether or not the baby would survive produced from Anna a thesis of outstanding merits. She had recently retreated more and more into her attic study working on a very important paper when she knew that she and Richard must talk about her fear about having any further pregnancies.

'I wish we lived nearer to Dad's church,' said Richard out of the blue over supper one evening.

'Why do you suddenly say that?'

'I have been thinking that we don't take Claire to church except when we are down in Cornwall because the churches round here don't seem to encourage children's attendance.'

'You can put children off religion for life if you give them an overdose of it too early on. I don't think Claire would like to go to church round here because it is so starchy.'

'Well, do you think she should go to church at all?'

'Yes, when we are in Cornwall, but that's enough while she is so young. Children would rather be outside playing than being inside a dark old building.'

'Not all churches are as dreary as you imply.'

'A lot of Anglican ones are.'

Richard continued to eat his meal in silence for a while.

'I wish there were more children around us for Claire to play with.'

'You're doing a lot of wishing tonight,' said Anna with a smile.

'Well don't you think Claire ought to have more young company? She spends her time with Chris, you and me and the occasional outing to see Mary and we are all adults. I know this is probably why she is so forward with her speech and language development but it can't be good for her to spend so much time with adults. She needs to be able to go out to play with other children. When we go home its different because Mum has other little children to come round to play while she is staying and she loves it.'

'We could book her into a playgroup near here. . .'

'Or we could have another baby.'

Anna looked down at her plate. When this had been said previously she had always fobbed it off with a remark about it being too soon yet but she sensed that Richard was not going to accept this as a valid reason any longer.

'Don't you want another baby?' he asked.

'I'm not sure. . .'

'Only children miss out on so much'.

'I had a very happy childhood and I don't think I missed out all that much.'

'No, but you were living in a small community; there were lots of children living in Garside and from being young you were able to go out to play because it was so safe. It's not like that in London and anyway society is different. We would never dare let Claire go out to play like we used to do when we were kids. We are both out at work each day so we don't get to know our neighbours with children. She is going to be a very lonely child until she starts school and probably then as well. The only solution that I can see is to increase our family size preferably with twins since they do run in the family!'

It was typical of Richard to make a flippant remark when he thought there was a tension in the conversation and, whereas in the past Anna found this quite amusing, more recently she found it irritating.

'It is easy for you to talk about having another baby as if it was the easiest thing in the world to accomplish. Think back on my last pregnancy. I was sick for three months, felt better briefly then started to bleed and had to have weeks in hospital, a caesarean section, a premature baby who nearly died and who was needing much more additional attention when she did finally come home from hospital than any baby normally does. I know you always shared the responsibility but you don't have to be pregnant and I do.'

'The chances of it being as bad as that again are very remote.'

'I know that but the chances are always there. I'm at a fairly crucial stage in my career and I think I want to be more secure about that before I start taking maternity leave.'

'You know there is not the slightest doubt that you will be confirmed in your university lectureship at the end of the three years. Is there ever going to be a stage when it is going to be convenient to have more children?'

'That sounds a bit nasty.'

'Well I don't mean to be but I like children and I particularly like my own. I will always support you in your career and whatever you want to do but there surely must be a bit more give and take in our marriage. If I want a large family and you only want one child there must be a compromise number between that?'

'You are being flippant again. . .'

'I'm not; I'm deadly serious about this. I'm willing to live in London to further your career when, if I were truthful I would much rather live in the country, I'm willing to give up most of my hobbies and outside interests so that I can be at home to help run the place and give you extra time for your studies. I am very happy to do this because it gives us a family life which I certainly want and believe you do to. But I don't think that we have a complete family with only one child.'

'I'm not saying I won't have any more children. You make me feel as if I'm being very selfish. . .' Anna paused. She found it so very difficult to talk about their emotional relationship and even more difficult to talk about their sexual relationship. . . 'sometimes I feel that you don't really love me as a person and that when you make love to me it is only because you want children.'

He only just stopped himself saying breezily that marriage was ordained for the procreation of children. It

100

was not a moment to be jesting. Anna had given them an opening to discuss something which was crucial to their relationship and he knew that he must say nothing which would terminate the opportunity. But what should he say next? How could he tell Anna about his feelings about making love to her. Could he tell her that he felt very rejected when she went to her room to work at nights, and often slept on her divan up there, the excuse being given as not wanting to wake him up when she finished work late. Was it because she feared getting pregnant again that she avoided getting into their bed unless she was sure that he was too tired to be interested in any thing other than going to sleep? Was there any truth in what she had suggested that he only made love to her because he wanted children? Was it possible that he was in a forbidden love relationship with somebody else and that he was not able to love his wife as he had vowed he would do? He had on occasions reflected back upon the speed with which they got married and, in moments of being down, wished that they had delayed this until they had got their lives more sorted out. He knew that he was a very immature young man when he had proposed marriage. What he had not realised was just how hard a marriage relationship could be and just how much tender care it needed to keep it flourishing and intact.

'When we were first married, our physical relationship seemed to be all right,' he began tentatively.

Anna nodded.

'In fact, it was quite good.'

Anna nodded again.

'Was it having Claire that changed things?'

'I did feel very tired after I had had Claire and while I was breast feeding her and I had not much energy for doing anything. . .'

'. . . except writing your thesis.'

The minute he had said that Richard was sorry. He had not meant it in quite the vicious way that it had sounded and he knew that it had hurt Anna when she was feeling vulnerable.

'I'm sorry Anna; I really don't mean that. I am very proud of my scientist wife and I thought you were great to get your Ph.D. when the odds were really stacked against you. It's just that being that very distinguished person that you now are takes up a lot of your life. Oh I know I want the best of both worlds. I want a famous wife but I also want a housekeeper, a mother of a vast brood of offspring and a bed warmer whenever I need one.'

'Would you be much happier if we were to move out of London?'

'We can't do that. Your job is at London University.'

'There are other universities. . .'

'Not doing the research that you are engaged in.'

'Well that could be changed.'

'No, living in London is not really a problem, so long as I get regular doses of Cornish air and I'm lucky that my parents live in such a lovely part of the world and that I have long holidays, part of which I can spend down there. I'd like Claire to grow up there in some respects but in others she will have more advantages living in London.'

'Don't forget that I'm not a Londoner. I grew up in rural Yorkshire you know. I like being amongst the green fields too!'

It had got quite dark in the room and they were still at the table.

'Let's clear the table and have some coffee and cheese and biscuits sitting in the easy chairs. It's too late to do any work tonight.'

'Speak for yourself dear wife; I've got lessons to teach tomorrow that I haven't thought about yet!'

'Well you will have to plan them on the way to school tomorrow! You have more important things to deal with this evening.'

They sat on the settee together and ate their cheese and biscuits; they watched the news on television and they went to bed early. That night Richard was very gentle and loving with Anna and she did not turn her back to him or pretend to be asleep. But it was going to take more than an evening of talking together to retrieve the better sexual relationship that they had once enjoyed.

8

In the spring of the following year Mary Swaine was awarded a school teacher fellowship to spend the term at Cambridge University. A locum teacher had been appointed to the school while she was going to be away but, inevitably, it did mean that Richard would take on some extra work to ensure that the pupils who were coming up for major public examinations did not miss out in any way. He did not mind this in the slightest but as the spring term approached he realised how much he was going to miss having Mary around. Since their trip to the sea while Anna had been in America they had not spent any time on their own together and this was of Mary's choosing and not his. Anna had invited Mary over many times to the house and she had always come when she had been asked, but she had stopped just popping in unless she was absolutely sure that all of them were at home.

Mary realised that sooner, rather than later, she would have to change schools. She did not think she was ready yet to sell up her home and move back to Wales but she knew that the wise thing would be a job change. As a step towards that she had applied for the teacher fellowship, not believing for a minute that she stood any chance of being awarded one. When she heard that she had been successful she was very excited, but also took it as an indication that her planning to move away gradually was the right thing to be doing.

'It's only for a term,' she said to Richard 'and it would be lovely if you could come up with Anna and Claire one day and we could all explore Cambridge together.'

As it was things turned out better because Anna had a

scientific meeting organised in one of the other Cambridge colleges while Mary was up there and they might be able to see something of each other. It might even be possible for Richard to bring Claire up at the weekend but they would see how things worked out.

As had become customary Richard, Anna and Claire went to Cornwall for Christmas. Now that Claire was three she was very aware of all the preparations for the Festival and knew that she had to hang up her stocking on Christmas Eve because Father Christmas would be coming. But she was even more excited by the fact that she would have a baby cousin coming to Grandad's house that Christmas. Hugh and Sarah had had a son the previous October and this would be the first time that Claire had seen him.

'Is he my cousin?' she had asked. 'Will he sleep with me in my room?'

'I expect he will sleep with his Mummy because he is only small and will want a feed in the night.'

'Will he see Father Christmas when he has his feed in the night?'

When cousin James arrived Claire was fascinated by him.

'He's not very big, can he come out to play with me?'

She was allowed to help when he had his bath and was intrigued by his little penis.

'What has he got that thing for?' she asked Sarah.

'All little boys have one,' explained Sarah.

'Will I grow one?'

'No little girls do not have them.'

'Oh.'

Sarah had had an easy pregnancy and was relishing the joys of motherhood. She was very happy to be at home all the time and had no plans to pursue her career while her family was young. She and Hugh hoped to have several children. Richard was interested to note how much being a father seemed to have changed his brother. He was far less pernickety than he used to be and did not seem unduly upset when James wet all over him. Claire found this incident particularly funny and told everyone whom she met that day that James had done wee-wees on Uncle Hugh.

'Your daughter's education has been neglected,' remarked Hugh to his younger brother when they were washing up together. 'Isn't it time she had a brother so that she is familiar with all aspects of the male species?'

'I wish she did have a brother or a sister.'

'I'm sorry, Rick, I shouldn't have said anything.'

'It's OK.'

Hugh presumed that perhaps there were problems obstetrically for Anna, because otherwise everything seemed fine for them and they found it easy to organise Claire's life into their careers. Presumably it would be almost as easy to make arrangements for other children.

Matthew was still single and seemed to show no inclination to get married. Neither did the twins have any plans to 'settle down' as they termed it. They were going to see the world and enjoy themselves and they were not going to be tied by 'wailing brats'.

'That's a horrible way to speak about children,' said their mother.

'Well they are a tie,' said Katie.

'Not necessarily so,' said their father 'Anna manages to have a very successful career and bring up her daughter.'

'That's because Richard is good at changing nappies and doesn't want to be a headmaster.'

'I think we may be talking about things that are none of our business,' said Elizabeth Trevanion but there had been times when she had let herself think that perhaps Richard was making most of the sacrifices. She had been sorry that he had not carried on playing rugby for a few more years because it would have been good for him to excel at something and to know the glory that goes with it. But she had to reprimand herself for thinking along these lines and acknowledge that she had always worried in case he got a neck injury playing what she really thought was quite a barbaric game.

Once the New Year was over the rectory emptied of visitors and Richard and Anna returned to London with a somewhat disappointed Claire. She always loved the endless flurry of activity in the rectory and the freedom which she had when she was down there. But once she was back home and in her familiar routine again she was happy.

Richard had quite a lot of preparation to do for the new term which was to be without Mary.

She invited them all round for the last Sunday before she went up to Cambridge. It was pouring down with rain so they could not go out for a walk. Instead they played a game of hide and seek which Claire loved, except she could not keep quiet about where she was hiding and they had to pretend that they could not see her.

Richard felt quite bereft when he went into school on the first day of term. He missed having Mary around more than he could admit to anyone and although he found it almost intolerable at times not to touch her hand or put his arm around her shoulder he had at least seen her every day at school and had many things geographical to talk over with her.

Mary drove up to Cambridge on a bright crisp frosty morning and her first impression of the city when she saw the colleges in the pale winter sunshine was to fall in love with it.

'How can I bear to live in London when there are beautiful places like this?'

Her college rooms were far more spacious than anything she had ever had when she had been at university previously. Perhaps it was something to do with being at a Scottish university and they were more frugal in their provision of student accommodation. She unpacked her things and put her few books on the shelves. That evening she dined in the hall and met the other school teacher fellow who was from Northumberland. The following morning she met the don who was nominally to oversee her project and then went to the library to begin searching out references. What she was determined about was that she was going to get the very most out of her all too short time in Cambridge.

Anna came up during the third week in February. They were both free on the Wednesday afternoon so went for a long walk together along the backs. There were several oarsmen on the river that afternoon and they stopped to watch them practising.

'It really is an idyllic world.'

'Is it idyllic but also artificial?'

'In some respects it must be. The dons of the college seem to be immune to the pressures of the outside world. They live in the college with every creature comfort provided, their incomes assured by endowments of long ago, and they carry on researching into topics which are of immense interest to them.'

'It's that part of the academic culture which is so attractive, but there is another side.'

'I can't believe it but I'm sure there must be.'

'It can be a rat race you know. Too many bright young things chasing too few chairs. Too little sponsorship of research and the inevitable scrambling to get the finance. And there is always the pressure of suspecting that somebody else is already doing the work in the field that you think is exclusively yours and will publish results just before you.'

'Is that why you rarely give yourself a break?'

'I suppose so, although I really do enjoy my work. But the next few years are vital. I have got to establish a reputation for myself and then, hopefully, I will have some sort of academic security. My lectureship is only a three year contract which will be up this summer.'

'But surely you will be given another?'

'Yes, I think I will; I really do let myself believe that I am good enough to be kept on.'

'It must be quite an achievement to have been invited to give a paper at an international conference when you are so early into an academic career.'

'Just luck you know! I was doing the right piece of research at the right time and somebody who was responsible for conference programming was told about it.'

'The bit of me that is the geographer envies the part of your job that is to do with travelling the world; the rest of me is quite happy not to be in your shoes. I think I would not be able to cope with the intellectual demands of the academic world.'

'I may never get another invitation to go abroad, but I am hoping to go to the conference in Sweden next year, even if I have to pay the costs myself. It would be nice if Richard and Claire could come too but these conferences are always coming up in term time and he is not free to go. You must think me very selfish because I'm the only one that has had the trip abroad and Richard hasn't been anywhere other than having a holiday in Cornwall.'

Mary did not say anything immediately. She linked her arm into Anna's and continued walking and thinking.

'If I'm honest I must admit that sometimes I find it hard to understand the compulsion which seems to drive you when it comes to your career. You have a super man for a husband and a dear little daughter. . .'

'. . . and how can I bear to leave them and be away at work for so much of the day?'

'No I'm not really saying that. When I was engaged to Bill all I wanted to do was to settle down with him into the vicarage and have a large family. Things did not work out like that and here I am pursuing a teaching career with nothing like the dedication which you have for yours, yet for me it really is the only life I've got.' Mary laughed. 'That really sounds as if I'm miserable with my lot and covet what you have and it's not like that at all.'

'You are very fond of Richard.'

'Yes, I'm fond of Richard, and Claire, and I'm very fond of you and because of all that affection I don't want anything to happen to spoil things between us all.'

'Could it?'

'Not if I have my way, but that isn't always the way things work out.'

'Richard very much wants to have a large family, I suppose because he was one of five children, and he is keen for us to start another baby. After the experience of my first pregnancy I'm quite apprehensive about starting another but I suppose I shall have to give way.'

'That's not the most positive way to approach motherhood.'

'I do love Claire but I'm not sure that being a parent is my most natural inclination. She is at a lovely stage at the moment and all the business of nappies and bottle feeds is well behind us. I'm not sure that I want to face it again but I know that Richard does and I don't want him to feel resentful of me for not being as enthusiastic as he is.'

They carried on walking together for a long way in silence but it was an amicable and comfortable silence.

There was nothing further for them to discuss; it was a matter between Anna and Richard in which Mary did not wish to be involved.

Anna had an evening session that she was going to attend but before that they went back to Mary's rooms and had tea.

'I must say the accommodation which you have in Cambridge is infinitely superior to mine in London. Perhaps I did go to the wrong university.'

'Well there is always the possibility of a post here in the future isn't there?'

'We can all dream dreams, but there are advantages to being based in London in my line of research. Now I must fly; thank you for being such a good friend to us.'

Anna gave Mary a hug and then went racing across the quadrangle. Mary watched her go feeling very mixed emotions and realising that she was being caught as a sounding board between this couple and that was something with which she did not think that she could cope. It confirmed for her the need to start actively looking for alternative posts and to distance herself from the Trevanions, at least in the immediate future.

☆ ☆ ☆

Claire was very excited because in the same term that Mary went to Cambridge she began to go to playgroup for two mornings a week. Sometimes Anna would be able to drop her off as she went to the university but usually it was Chris who took her over and collected her at the end of the session. Chris was wondering what she would do when Claire started school in less than two years' time because it was unlikely that she would be needed by the Trevanions in the way that she had been up till then. The beginning of the playgroup days was a testing out of the need for her as a full time child minder. She loved looking after Claire and found her parents really splendid, relaxed and appreciative people and she was sorry that the end of her employment could be in sight, although nothing had ever been said along these lines to her.

She was therefore rather apprehensive one morning in March when Anna was having a day working at home and as they sat down together for their coffee break she had said, 'Chris, I'd like to have a word with you about the future.'

'You would like to talk about me leaving when Claire goes full time to school?'

Anna looked almost dumbfounded. 'That's the last thing I want to do; you aren't thinking about leaving are you?'

'I'm very happy working for you and you know I love Claire like my own, but once she starts school you won't be needing a baby minder like you have done.'

'Oh but we do; you see Chris, I'm going to have another baby.'

It was the best and most unexpected news that she could have given Chris.

'We haven't told anyone yet but you are so much part of the family and we depend so much upon you that we wanted you to be the first to know. But we do need you to stay on with us for several more years it would seem. The baby is not due until December so I'm only just pregnant.'

If it was the most unexpected thing for Chris to have been told, Anna certainly caught Richard completely unawares when she said quite casually to him one evening that she was overdue with her period.

'How overdue?'

'Two weeks and long enough for me not to be just late.'

'How do you feel?'

'Not a little squeamish.'

'Do you mean that you feel sick or apprehensive?'

'Both. I'll go and see the doctor as soon as I can get an appointment because I expect he will want to keep a close eye on me this time.'

The pregnancy test was positive and Anna started feeling and being sick in the morning so there was no doubt that she was pregnant.

'Don't tell anyone yet but I do think we should mention it to Chris because after us it most affects her and I do want her to stay on and help with both our children.'

Richard was even more delighted by the news of this pregnancy than he had been by the first. Both had been unexpected but before Claire was conceived he had his fantasies of a large family. In the last year he was beginning to fear that Claire would be their only child. At the time that Anna was applying for maternity leave she had her permanent university lectureship confirmed. Things seemed to be working out really well. They calculated that the baby would be due around Claire's fourth birthday.

'How's that for perfect planning?' said Richard.

'It's not all that perfect; Claire wasn't due until the February if you remember.'

Anna was just beginning to get over the morning sickness phase when she wakened one June night with an awful pain and an awareness that she was bleeding. She woke Richard.

'Please help me quickly; I'm losing a lot of blood and I think there is something wrong with the baby.'

Richard rang the GP. He came over straight away knowing something about Anna's previous obstetric history. After examining her he decided that she would have to go into hospital because of the heavy bleeding. An ambulance was called but Richard could not go in with her because there was Claire to look after.

'If only we had some family round the corner or lived in a village,' he thought.

As soon as he considered that it was reasonable he telephoned the hospital. The sister told him that they were very sorry but Mrs Trevanion had lost the baby. She was going to have to go down to theatre because they thought she may have some retained placenta which was why she was bleeding so heavily. It was 5.30 am. He telephoned Mary and told her what had happened.

'Why ever didn't you ring me earlier? I could have come and stayed with Claire while you went in with Anna.'

'I didn't want to disturb you in the middle of the night.'

'What are friends for? I'll come over and get Claire up, give her breakfast and take her to playgroup and I'll still be in school in time.'

She was over to number nineteen very quickly.

'I'm so sorry about this Rick; give Anna my love. I'll pop in to see her later on today if she is up to having visitors.'

Anna had gone down to theatre when he arrived so he sat and waited. Mary would tell the Head where he was and he

111

would go in later in the day but he must see Anna first. She looked pale and drawn when he was allowed to go into the ward to see her and she was tearful.

He held her hand.

'How do you feel?' It seemed a stupid question because he knew how she must be feeling but he did not know what else to say.

'Weary, old. . . it's no good Richard. I can't go through this again. It's not meant for me to have children.'

'Don't talk about it now; you may feel differently about things when you are better. You have lost a lot of blood so you are bound to feel tired.'

But in his heart he knew that Anna would not allow herself to be pregnant again and that it would be grossly unfair for him to put any more pressure on her to have more children.

It was surprising how many members of staff thought it was important to tell Richard about the miscarriages which had occurred in their families and to reassure him that it had not stopped them having any more children. Mary heard them and she wished that they would be quiet. Anna had told her about the pregnancy soon after she returned home from her term in Cambridge. It had been the final factor in her decision to apply for a post which had been advertised in another London school. It would be near enough to her home to continue living there but it would end the almost daily contact which she had with Richard Trevanion and which she was finding more and more difficult to keep professional. She would never know how much her friendship with the Trevanions had made for difficulties in the marital relationship. What she did know was that for the sake of their marriage and her personal integrity she had to move.

She had delayed telling Richard about her application until she heard that she was required for interview and then she knew that she would have to give him an explanation for her absence from school that day. There was a look of genuine pain in his eyes.

'I've only just managed to survive one term without you being around. It doesn't bear thinking about how life here will be if you leave. I shall miss you terribly.'

'It's not all one-sided you know,' she said softly, 'and that's why I have got to move. Anyway, I have only been called for interview and I haven't been offered a job. I might have great difficulty in getting another job but I shall go on trying until I do.'

'Will you stay in London?'

'I don't want to move from that particular house just yet but if I can't get a post which is near enough then that will have to be the next decision I will have to make.'

But Mary had been offered the post which carried additional responsibilities and a higher salary, and she accepted it. She would move to her new school at the beginning of the autumn term. Over the following weekend she had called round to number nineteen to tell them both together. Two mornings later she was to receive the early morning call from Richard about Anna. At the end of that day she could understand Richard's extreme sadness and his comment that he felt doubly bereaved.

Once she was established permanently in her university lectureship Anna began to feel better. She took several weeks physically to recover from the miscarriage, but emotionally the damage was more long lasting. She and Richard had not talked again about any more children but the silent understanding between them was that she would not submit herself to another pregnancy. Claire was likely to remain an only child and Chris would have to reconsider what she wanted to do when Claire started to go to school full time a year hence. For Anna it was almost an uplifting relief. She had tried to meet Richard's wish to have another baby. It had not worked out and he seemed to be accepting that they were lucky to have Claire and that they should enjoy having one child. Adoption as an alternative was once vaguely talked about but both knew that for them it would not be a realistic proposition. Anna felt that she could now really concentrate on her scientific work and that her career would become her first priority. Perhaps she should encourage Richard to think about what he was going to do next. He had not been quite so settled in his work as he had been before Mary left. Anna knew there was a strong bond between the two of them but she loved and trusted them each so much that it would be impossible for her to appreciate how risky a relationship that could have become.

In the next year Anna received an invitation to go to Australia for a month's lecture tour. It was a great honour to receive so early in her career and she was very thrilled to be asked. The timing was good because Claire would be starting school in the September and Anna was due to be away for the latter half of October and November. She was hoping that while she was on the other side of the world she could spend a few days with Margaret, her friend in New Zealand whom she had first met in America and with whom she had maintained regular correspondence. Richard, with characteristic generosity, was happy at her success and ever willing to fill the parental gap when mother was not around. He was just a little envious of the trip round the world because the geographer in him had always the yearning to travel, and so far in his life there had not been much opportunity.

'If there is another time perhaps we could both go and take Claire,' suggested Anna.

'It would depend upon costs, whether or not I could have some sabbatical leave from teaching and would need a lot of organising, but who knows. . .'

Chris had resolved her future working life in an ideal way for the Trevanions. She had decided to be a registered child minder and to have several children each day while their parents were at work. When Claire started school she would be able to go back to Chris's house for tea with the other children and to wait until Anna or Richard came to collect her.

Richard was reluctant to make any changes in his work situation while Claire still needed to be taken and picked up from school. He was, in any case, very happy in this teaching post and had been from the time that he did his student teaching practice there. He was a popular and well respected member of staff and he would argue with good humour that there could not be two career people in one small family. But even he realised that he did need to make a move in the next year or two, otherwise he ran the risk of being there for life and, contented though he might be, that was not what he really wanted. However, if he tried to work out what he did want it was more difficult. There were factors to do with not wanting Claire to grow up in a big city coupled with his strong love of the countryside, yet a recognition that Anna had to be within reasonable travelling distance of the university. As there seemed no clear way forward at the moment he tended to let things be for the time being. He was also slightly influenced by the fact that Mary had not been quite so happy in her first year in the new school and he did not want this to happen to him also.

Anna's flight to Australia left Heathrow during the early evening so both Richard and Claire were able to go with her to the airport. They stayed with her until she went through to the departure lounge but then because it was dark and quite cold they went home rather than go out on the balcony to watch the plane take off. When it came to the point of actually leaving Anna always felt sad and she wondered if she would find it easier if they did not come to the airport with her. Once she got aboard the plane her excitement lifted her spirits and she would rationalise that she was not going to be away for long. Claire was always amazingly phlegmatic about Mummy's trips, but then she always had Richard there and that had been the ever constant factor in her life. This time the separation from Mummy was being cushioned by the knowledge that she was going to go and stay on her own with Granny in Cornwall for a whole week at half-term while Daddy spent some time decorating the sitting room.

☆ ☆ ☆

During the summer Richard had noticed that Mary's favourite opera was being performed on the three evenings during late October. This fact was of little significance to him until he realised that it was the week when Claire would be in Cornwall and he up the decorating ladder. In a moment of rashness, but also with the knowledge that the tickets would go quickly, he booked two seats in the stalls and waited until the Sunday evening of the half term week before he telephoned Mary.

'I've got two seat for Gluck's 'Orpheus and Euridice' for

Thursday night. Are you free and would you like to come with me?'

If he had written to her Mary might have refused but being caught unexpectedly by a telephone call and wanting very much to go she did not try to find a reason why not. They arranged to meet at the underground station and he insisted that they went out to a meal together before the performance.

When Mary arrived he was waiting for her and looked absolutely immaculate in his suit and also very handsome in the evening light. All the old but controlled emotions were stirred within her but she knew that they could be kept in check; she had had much practice at this over recent years. It was an evening which he had planned carefully. A table had been booked at a small French restaurant near to Covent Garden and he insisted that they had an extravagant meal with a bottle of wine. Over dinner they caught up on their news. Anna had written to each of them and they exchanged the information about her tour. Richard had told Anna that he was going to ask Mary if she would like to go to the opera. By being open and honest he never felt particularly guilty, but by now he was not so naïve that he did not realise that he might be creating future ripples in their relationship.

After their meal they strolled down to the opera house and found their seats in the stalls. He bought a programme and very nearly a large box of chocolates as well had not Mary said that they would not be able to eat another thing after their splendid dinner. Mary had loved this opera since she had first heard a record of Kathleen Ferrier singing *Che faro* many years ago and had been determined that she would see the opera at the earliest opportunity. That had come when she was a student in Scotland and she had stood in the gods feeling incredibly moved by the music and the dancing which opens the second act. Since then she had seen it once more in London several years ago and on this occasion she had had a seat. By the time she had realised that there was a production on in the half term week all the tickets had been sold. For Richard to telephone and tell her that he had tickets and wanted to take her was just too much of a wonderful opportunity for her to refuse. She could not

116

think of many things that she would like to do more than go to Orpheus with that particular person. Richard himself was not very musical but he enjoyed some opera because it was a spectacle as well. They sat enthralled in the first act as the beautiful music poured forth, so much so that when it came to the first interval they did not want to move but stayed quietly together in their seats. Mary told him about the first time that she had seen the opera and that the dances which she remembered so vividly would come at the beginning of the next act. In the second interval Mary was quiet and did not want to bother to go to the bar or to stretch her legs. Richard was happy just to be with her and had no wish to move out of the auditorium. He knew that the one piece that he was familiar with would be sung in the final act.

As the contralto began to sing the opening bars of *Che faro* he glanced sideways to Mary and noticed that there were tears on her cheeks. He took her hand and squeezed it gently. She did not move her hand away until she needed to find a hankerchief but after doing that she let him take her hand back into his. But the tears did not stop. Mary was clearly more upset than just being moved by a beautiful piece of music. He desperately wanted to put his arm round her but that was not the sort of thing to do in the stalls at Covent Garden. When the applause thundered out at the end of the piece he whispered

'Darling what is it?'

'It's nothing; its just so moving.'

By the time the lights went up at the end of the final act Mary had regained some sort of composure. They slipped out as quickly as the crowd would permit and Richard hailed a taxi, giving Mary's address as the destination.

'We can't go all the way by taxi.'

'We can and we are,' he said firmly. 'This is a special night and our half-term treat. He put his arm round her and held her close to him and still she wept.

'I'm sorry, I'm really disgracing myself.'

'Shush, it's all right.'

When they got inside her house Mary poked up the fire, which she had banked up before she left, while Richard carefully hung up his suit jacket and went to make some coffee. He brought back the tray and put it on the low table. Mary was standing by the fire, gazing into the flames and the tears were still flowing. He put his arms around her and held her tightly while gently kissing her tear stained cheeks.

'Tell me what it is.'

'It's the music; it's the absolute poignancy of that beautiful music and the impact of the words of "What is life to me without thee".'

'But I have never seen you to be so upset. When have I ever seen you cry before?'

'I keep a brave face on things but at times the facade crumbles and it has tonight.'

He guided her to the settee and sat with her. He poured her some coffee and handed her the cup. They talked together about things of no particular significance but they talked late into the evening, neither of them wanting it to come to an end.

'It's too late for you to go home tonight. Would you like to stay in the spare room here for the night?'

It was Mary who was always so strong and who behaved so correctly who was asking him to stay. There was no doubt in Richard's mind that he wanted to stay. He washed up the coffee cups while Mary sorted him out what he would need for the night including a pair of what had been Bill's pyjamas, then she went and ran herself a bath. After she had finished she called downstairs, 'The bathroom is all yours.'

He went up and on the landing Mary kissed him good night and thanked him for a lovely evening. He went to his room and got undressed, and then went to use the bathroom. When he came out he noticed that Mary's door was ajar but her light was out.

'Good night,' he called.

He did not hear if she replied.

He went into his room and found a book to read because he did not feel the slightest bit tired. He read for some time but he was not interested in what he was reading. He could only think of Mary and what had happened that evening. He knew that they loved each other and that it was the impossibility of their situation which had upset Mary. Her love of music and her emotional sensitivity had been so affected by the opera that she could not control her feelings and he had not wanted her to do so. He lay in the darkness for a while, then he got up and went into her room and knelt down by her bedside.

'Are you awake?'

'Yes.'

She gently ruffled his hair as he knelt beside her. He was aware of a softness and a warmth and he put his arm under the duvet and drew her nearer to him. She lifted up the side of the duvet and he slipped into bed beside her, their arms around each other. Both ceased to be sensible, responsible; they could not stem the strong physical need for each other's love any longer. They found each other's mouth, but the kissing was no longer gentle and comforting. Richard drew Mary's nightdress over her head and dropped it on the floor as she undid the buttons on his pyjama jacket. He pressed her breast hard against him then moved his lips down and kissed her nipples. He felt her undo his trouser button.

'Darling, darling Mary, I love you.'

'And I love you.'

Never had either of them made love with such urgency, with such passion and in such ecstasy. Only later as they lay in each others arms did more tears flow and this time it was from both of them because they knew that this overwhelming love for each other was not possible and that they could not again make love with each other.

They were still naked and in each other's arms when they woke up next morning. Once during the night Mary had been aware of Richard curled up into her back with his arm around her and his hand cupping her breast. It had felt very secure and she had drifted back to sleep without moving. But as the dawn broke things needed to be faced differently.

'I'll go and make some tea,' Richard volunteered. He found the discarded pyjamas and went downstairs. Mary went to the bathroom and when she came back she put on her nightdress and her dressing gown and then sat on the edge of the bed.

'Don't get up just yet; come back into bed and drink this tea.'

She got back into bed but kept her dressing gown on.

119

They drank their tea in silence neither of them knowing where to begin in what had to be said.

'You are not sorry about what happened last night?' he finally asked.

'No, how could I be? It was a most perfect and unique experience and I shall live with the memory of it for ever. But that doesn't ease the guilt I feel. You belong to somebody else. You are not free to love me and that is the end of it.'

'I cannot not see you. Anyway Anna would think it very odd if you suddenly stopped visiting us.'

'But that is what I am going to do. Until last night I thought I could keep a control on my emotions; now I know that I can't. Despite all my so called principles, my beliefs about the sanctity of marriage I'm as weak as the next. Once you held me and kissed me last night I found it impossible to contain my love for you. If you had not come to me last night I am sure that I should have come into your room. I just laid in bed and ached for you.'

'I could ask Anna for a divorce. . .'

'You couldn't. It is totally against everything which we believe in and I don't think I could live with my conscience or with you if you left Anna. You have also got Claire to think about.'

'Why is life so complicated? Why did Anna and I meet before you and I? Would things have been very different had we not rushed into a marriage when we were so young? I had this cosy feeling about marriage and family life and it's not like that at all.'

'I'm now into the second year of a job which I don't particularly enjoy and was only using as a stepping stone to the next move. The time has come for me to move from London and to sell my house. . .'

'. . . but this house is special.'

'I've never planned to end my days here. I always said that I would eventually reach the stage when I was ready to move and that time has now come.'

Richard was silent.

'How can I ever truly love Anna when I have known the sublime with you?'

'That is something you will have to work out. I'm not

going to find it easy to meet Anna since this has happened. She is my friend and she has trusted both of us and we have badly misplaced that trust.'

'I feel bad about that too.'

'Yes, I know you do.'

'I'm going down to Cornwall today to pick up Claire from Mum's. We could have gone down together and had a weekend by the sea.'

'And now we cannot. We dare not be on our own togther because we know that we cannot behave responsibly. Now we'll get up and I will make you some breakfast before you go home to clear up the decorating mess which you have left in the sitting room. I can't offer to help even because it would be unwise.'

She got out of bed.

'Mary would you do something for me?'

She turned and looked at him.

'I don't know.'

'I have never seen you without your clothes on and I would like to look at you. . . please Mary.'

He came round the bed and took off her dressing gown. She did not stop him. Then he slowly drew her nightdress over her head and laid it on the bed. She stood there, her lithe beautiful body pale in the early morning light; he gazed at it then raised his eyes to meet hers.

'It is exquisite and I shall love you for ever.'

He drew her to himself and kissed her.

'Thank you, my darling.'

Tears glistened in her eyes.

'Oh no,' she thought, 'I must not start weeping again,' and she rushed into the bathroom to wash. When she heard Richard going downstairs she emerged and went into the bedroom to dress. By the time she went downstairs he had gone.

☆ ☆ ☆

Anna's tour of Australia had been quite exhausting so she was glad to be spending a few days in New Zealand with Margaret. She had earned enough from the lectures, not only to pay her flight to Auckland, but also for a little

121

holiday for Richard, Claire and herself which she was planning as a surprise. They had not been able to afford for them all to come out to Australia, even with Anna's expenses being met by the Australian universities, but as a result of her being fairly abstemious while she had been away they should be able to have a week away somewhere special. She pondered the possibilities, thinking that perhaps they could go to Austria or to Switzerland during the Christmas holidays. Claire would love to see the snow if there was any by then. As soon as she got back she would go into a travel agent and make some enquiries about costs. She might even book it and not tell them keeping it as a very special Christmas present.

Although she and Margaret had only met briefly in America they had taken an instant liking to each other and had begun a friendship which was maintained across the world by regular correspondence. Anna had never made time for having many friends and apart from Mary and Margaret she did not really know anyone else well enough to consider them as personal friends. Margaret met her at the airport and they had a very happy few days touring the New Zealand sights. Several times Anna would remark to Margaret that Richard would have loved to have seen the hot springs or the examples of Maori culture and she resolved that one day they would both come and spend some time together exploring this beautiful country.

Her flight back to England was uneventful and twenty-one hours later when she landed at Heathrow it was a Saturday morning and there were Richard and Claire waiting to meet her. Claire chatted non-stop the whole way home about school, all her friends, going to Chris's house for her tea each day and staying on her own with Granny and Grandad in Cornwall. It made things easier for Richard who was feeling quite apprehensive about meeting Anna. He had tried to analyse the two kinds of love which he thought that he had experienced and was left feeling utterly confused and sad. He was very fond of Anna, proud of her achievement and somewhat protective of her. But in the eight years of their marriage he had changed from being an immature young lad to become an older, wiser man and he knew a great deal more about love.

He had not had any contact with Mary, nor she with him in the two weeks since they had gone out together, but he had thought endlessly about the situation, wondering if there could be any other way of dealing with it. He asked Anna a lot about her tour, partly because he was interested but mostly because he dreaded her asking him what he had done while she had been away. She admired the sitting room and commented that it must have taken many hours to make such a good job of it. She noticed the work that he had put into the garden before the weather broke and made any further gardening virtually impossible.

'Did you enjoy the opera?' she finally asked.

'It was a very good production.'

'It's not like you to choose opera for a night out.'

'No that's true; it was because I knew that it was Mary's favourite opera and it was more of a treat for her.'

'That was nice of you.'

She never said anything catty like 'you have never taken me to the opera,' or 'why did Mary need to be taken out for a treat?' It was alien to Anna to think evil of any situation and that made Richard continue to feel bad about things. But he felt terrible when she did tell him that she had earned enough on the tour for the three of them to have a short family holiday on the continent. Equally Anna could have been feeling guilty about the amount of time which she spent away from home leaving Richard with the entire domestic and parental responsibility. Treating them to a holiday was a way of making her feel better about things. In the end they spent Christmas at the rectory and then flew off to spend the New Year amongst the mountains and snow of the Alps.

It was not long after that Mary was appointed Head of the Geography Department in a large school in south Wales. She sold her beloved home in London and bought a cottage high up one of the valleys. She had come back to her native area and the place of her roots, and had turned her back on London and the two loves which she had known there. She wrote or telephoned the Trevanions sometimes, saw them occasionally and had her young goddaughter to stay regularly. As time went by the scars healed a little and the pain was less intense.

9

It was time for Richard to consider his career situation. He had been eight years in his first teaching post, which by all normal standards was far too long, but in his rather more unique situation was understandable. But he needed to do more than think about a move. Anna and he discussed this many times. She was too firmly established in her research department in London to really want to contemplate a move to another university, although, in the future, that might still be an option. She was willing to commute each day if Richard got a post out of London and she argued that as she was away quite often at conferences or scientific meetings it was entirely reasonable that they should consider primarily where it was best for Richard and Claire to be. They were all agreed that they should make their home in a more rural environment. So Richard began to look out for advertisements for suitable posts in pleasant parts of the country but fairly adjacent to London.

'How about this one?' said Anna after skimming through the *Times Educational Supplement.*

'It's Wiltshire, that is far too far out for you.'

'It probably isn't because there is a good rail connection and it's near to the motorway network which would be useful for me when I have to travel elsewhere in the country. Go and have a look at the area and the school and see what you think.'

He went for an informal visit to the school and liked what he saw. But more important was the possibility of living in one of the many pretty villages nearby. So he applied and was short-listed. It was a long time since he had been interviewed for his first job and then that had been by people whom he knew because it was the school where he had done his final teaching practice. He felt incredibly nervous as he walked into the school and even more so when he saw the other candidates sitting waiting. At the end of his interview he was convinced that he had no chance of being offered the post, but he was. He said that he would like to discuss it with his wife and would let them know his answer the following day.

He telephoned Anna at the university.

'Well done,' she said, 'you accept.'

'No, we've got to sort out how it will affect all of us. I have told them that I will let them know tomorrow.'

'I'll leave here early and pick up Claire and then we should all be home about the same time.'

Anna had already checked the travelling. The train service was reasonable and she always found it easy to work on a train. She would need to get permission from the university to live so far out but that was unlikely to be a problem. So Richard accepted the offer and after three weekends of house hunting they found a lovely stone house which reminded Anna so much of the cottages in Garside that she knew instantly that it would be the right home for them. It had four bedrooms and three large rooms downstairs.

'We can both have a study with all these rooms,' said Anna.

'Me too,' said Claire and they all laughed.

They moved in during the summer holidays and Richard started in his new post at the beginning of September. Claire went to the village school and they were able to arrange for her to go to the home of another little girl who lived nearby when she came out of school each day. There were two brothers and another sister in this family and their mother was very happy to have Claire and to give her tea when her parents were going to be late home. They also became a two car family, which for some families might have been a status symbol but for the Trevanions was a liability which kept Richard tinkering under a car bonnet for many hours of the weekend. It was always vital that Anna's car would start in the morning so

125

that she did not miss the train. They knew that the most important thing to be saving up for was a new car which would be more reliable.

So began a new era in their lives. Richard was much happier living where they did and Claire had freedom and friends in the village in a way that she had never done in London. But for Anna the days were longer, the travelling tiring and determined that she was that this decision was the right one for them as a family, she did feel a little remote from the university. She decided that she would see how it went through the winter months but if the weather got too bad and the trains delayed she may have to think about occasionally staying overnight in London.

When they had settled into the new house and had the usual invasion of Trevanion relatives for short visits to see where they were living, Anna suggested that they should invite Mary for a weekend.

'How about half term?'

'We don't know that our half terms will coincide.'

'You don't seem very keen. We haven't seen a lot of Mary in the last couple of years and certainly not since she moved to Wales. Now that we are living much nearer to each other it would be good to see more of her again. I know that she has had Claire to stay but I don't think she has ever suggested that we go to stay, although I'm sure we would always be very welcome if we did go.'

'We've all been moving jobs and houses,' Richard said. The conversation was getting difficult. 'You ring Mary and see what she says.'

Anna did telephone Mary and was very insistent that she came to stay for the weekend.

'I would have to go back on the Sunday evening because I have other arrangements made for the next day.'

Mary knew that there was no way out of it. Perhaps after two years time would have mellowed the feelings and she and Richard could get by. But she dreaded putting that to the test. Perhaps they should have been more honest and told Anna what had happened, but what might that have done to Anna? It did seem that she and Richard were getting on all right and Anna certainly appeared to be spending more time with him and Claire. But there would

126

be separations because so prestigious a scientist was becoming increasingly more in demand to lecture world-wide.

Mary arrived for lunch on Saturday.

'Aunty Mary is here,' called Claire running outside to meet her. 'Do you like my new house?'

Mary hugged her.

'It's lovely Claire and you must take me round and show me everything.'

She and Anna then hugged and kissed each other and she received a perfunctory kiss on the cheek from Richard. They immediately felt tense and each knew it. When they had met on the few occasions in the last two years there had not been a need to do this because Anna had not been standing there at the moment of arrival and they had not had to behave as was expected.

They all went for a walk in the afternoon. It was what they always did when they were together and the thing that they most enjoyed. October is a beautiful month and the colour of the trees was magnificent on that autumn afternoon. They went to look for some conkers and Mary had promised that she would help Claire make some furniture with them using pins and pieces of wool. Richard and Claire climbed to the top of a hill because they were sure that there were some chestnut trees up there. Anna and Mary walked together along the lower track.

'Do you remember our walk together in Cambridge? That was a lovely afternoon and I don't think we have had a walk together since then. We talked about careers and family life and I must have been only just pregnant but I did not know it at the time.'

'It was sad about losing that baby.'

'Mm. . . I was sorry for Richard because he really did want another child, in fact he would have liked as many children as his parents had, if not more! There can't be any more babies. . .'

'I thought that must be so because you haven't got pregnant again. The scientific world must have benefited from the situation.'

Anna laughed. 'Yes, that is one way of looking at it.'

They walked along for quite a way before Anna said, 'Mary, I wonder if I can ask you something rather personal and please tell me to mind my own business if I am intruding?'

'What is it?'

'Well, we used to see quite a lot of you and we don't seem to do so now. I know we have all moved and changed jobs but I get the impression sometimes that you just might be avoiding us.'

Mary was always a very honest person and she paused not quite knowing how to handle the question.

'When we were on our Cambridge walk do you remember talking about our relationships. . . ?'

'I remember commenting to you that Richard was very fond of you.'

'. . . and I of him, you and Claire. Later I came to realise that the affection between Richard and me was too strong and escape was the only way to deal with it.'

'Was that why you moved to Wales so suddenly?'

'Well it wasn't all that sudden, but it was a big factor in that decision.'

They walked along without saying anything to each other, then Anna broke the silence.

'I sometimes think that I am not the right wife for Richard. He is so home and family loving whereas I need to have a career and to use my brain. Don't misunderstand me because I wouldn't be without a husband and a daughter or the home that we have together, and when I am away it gives me a comfortable feeling that I've got that to come back to. But if I ever had to make a choice between career and home I just do not know what that decision would be. What I do know is that my career is the major part of my life now and, because I make that so, I must accept the risks that I run with other parts of my life.'

'I hope you don't see me as a risk, Anna because that is the very last thing that I want to be.'

'No, I don't think that I do. Richard and I get along well enough because we are good friends and he is such a compromiser but he has had to make most of the sacrifices. Was not seeing you another sacrifice?'

'He did the right thing.'

'The right thing does not necessarily augur well for happiness. I knew when I came back from Australia that something had changed and I have come to realise that deep down he is not very happy.'

'He is pleased about his new job and the house which you have bought.'

'Mary, I want to tell you something that I find difficult to talk about because I want you to understand. Since we lost that baby I have not found it easy to have a sexual relationship with Richard. At first he was very patient and kind and we hoped that given time things would get better. Instead what happened was that he seemed to lose interest and neither of us tries any more.'

'I'm not sure that I understand why you want to tell me this.'

'I don't really know either but I think it is that I'm confessing the reason for his unhappiness is entirely due to me being a failure as a wife. I suppose I may also be saying that he should have married you rather than me.'

'Well he didn't. He chose to marry you for all the right reasons and we all believe in the importance of the wedding vows which in this case are not going to be broken. I am convinced in predetermination. What has happened and will happen is all part of the overall scheme of things.'

Richard and Claire came racing down the hill, laughing as they gathered momentum and clutching a few conkers in the bag. He noticed that Mary and Anna were somewhat subdued but the rest of the weekend passed amicably and uneventfully. Mary left early on the Sunday evening, knowing that only for Claire the weekend had been really successful. She suspected that none of them would attempt to repeat the invitation for a long time but she hoped that Claire would still be able to come and visit her.

After she had gone Anna felt a need to say something to Richard. This was unusual because she normally pushed things out of her mind, believing that the least said the better. That evening she could not do that.

'I talked with Mary about her sudden decision to go

129

back to Wales.'

Richard immediately experienced great apprehension because he did not know how much Mary might have said.

'She told me that she was too fond of you to stay in London and that going to Wales was a sort of escape.' She paused and looked at him. 'Do you love her very much?'

It was a question to which he could not reply. He could not tell a lie and whatever answer he gave he would hurt Anna. Knowing him as well as she did, she knew he was struggling not to deceive her and yet his silence disconcerted her more than she had ever known. She left the room and went into the kitchen. Claire walked in a few minutes later and saw Anna crying.

'Why are you crying, Mummy?' She had never seen her mother in tears before and she was very troubled by it.

'I'll get Daddy.'

'No, don't do that Claire; it's nothing, I shall be all right in a minute.'

Nevertheless Claire went to find her father.

'Mummy is crying; did you make Mummy cry?'

'I think that I may have done.'

'But why did you make her cry? Mummy never cries and she is very sad and I don't like to see her sad.'

'I'll go and talk to her.'

Claire went along with him.

'Perhaps it would be better if I went to see Mummy on my own.'

Claire looked very disappointed about this but he was quite firm with her. A little while later she peeped through the crack in the door which had been left slightly ajar. Her parents had their arms around each other and Claire felt better that it was all over.

☆ ☆ ☆

In the following three years they became established in their new environment. Claire made many friends in the village, she joined the Brownies and when she was eight became a member of the church choir. It was not a choir which achieved great musical heights, but it was a group which practised once a week and made a more than

130

adequate attempt to lead the singing on Sundays. The younger children were in the choir only for the morning service and their presence was more appreciated for their angelic looks than their musical prowess. Neither of her parents was particularly musical so it was not to be expected that they would recognise a talent in Claire. In fact it had been Mary who had early noticed that Claire could sing and suggested to them that perhaps she should have some piano lessons. They had bought a second hand piano and had been very surprised at Claire's readiness to practise each day. She went to the piano teacher in the next village who quite early on said that Claire had some musical ability. She was also, much to her father's great pleasure, good at all ball games. As far as inheriting her mother's great intellect it was early days yet, but it did not seem to be much in evidence. She was a happy, gregarious and very entertaining child with whom to be.

Richard likewise became involved in village activities. He joined the cricket club and although he could have played a game at a much higher standard was content to be at village cricket level. He lent a hand coaching the colts team and in winter, although he was always a rugger man himself, he did referee matches for the village soccer team. The gardening club met once a month and if Anna got home in time to look after Claire he would go to these meetings. In July there was the horticultural show and he was persuaded to put in some entries the first year they were there. Although he knew it would not be tactful to have too much success when he was such a newcomer and comparative novice in showing he was well rewarded for his efforts with a second prize for his potatoes and a third with his roses.

Anna did not get involved in any of these activities because she just did not have the time. She went to the village church with them on Sundays when she was at home and she always tried to arrange things so that she could go to Claire's open evenings at school and to the various plays and concerts which Claire was in. But she had found the travelling each day to be tiring, and when she had the chance of a small room in one of the university halls of residence being made available to her for use when she had to stay in town, she decided to take it. She rarely stayed in it more than one or two nights a week but it meant that she could work late these evenings and then perhaps leave a little earlier the following day when she was going back home.

'We are not quite like other families,' observed Claire to her father one day.

'In what way are we different?' he asked.

'I am the only person in my class whose Mummy travels to London to work. Some of the Daddies go to London but not the Mummies.'

'Do you mind it being that way round?'

'No, I'm just saying. Alison Smith asked me today why my Mummy was away a lot and why it was always you that took me to Brownies or to choir.'

'Who takes Alison to Brownies?'

'Mostly her Daddy.'

'Well you are not all that much different are you then?'

'My Mummy is called Dr Trevanion but she is not a proper doctor.'

'You mean she is not a medical doctor but she is a real doctor in that she is a doctor of philosophy.'

'I think it is all very muddling because I know she is a scientist, not a phil whatever you said it was. Alison Smith said that she thought it was funny that you sewed the button on my coat when it came off.'

'Mummy would have done it if she had been there but she wasn't and I was. Is there anything else that Alison Smith objects to?'

'Alison is my best friend and she tells me what she thinks.'

'Doesn't Alison's mother work at the solicitor's office?'

'I don't know where she goes to work, but she works somewhere because some days Alison's Daddy cooks the dinner.'

Richard smiled at his daughter.

'I don't think there is all that much difference between your family and Alison's. As long as one of the parents does what has to be done then it doesn't matter which one it is.'

In fact Richard could turn his hand to any domestic task

132

that had to be done. They had Mrs Maidment from the village come in two days a week and she did all the cleaning and the washing and ironing. He did most of the cooking, although Anna would sometimes take over when she was at home at the weekend. He did a big shop at the supermarket every week. With reluctance he would do the decorating and, with great joy, the gardening. When it was necessary he would tinker with the cars but he really did not particularly enjoy having to do this. It was Richard who would have Claire on his knee for a cuddle and he whom Claire sought out when she had hurt herself. Anna was the parent who would patiently explain things to Claire, take great interest in what she was doing and encourage her to attempt new activities. But throughout her life Claire had always had her father around to look after her and inevitably he was the one she had always turned to with her problems. That was until one particular problem emerged which even resourceful Richard found was beyond his coping strategies.

Sooner or later Anna was going to be invited to spend the whole or part of an academic year in the States. Her international reputation was such that she really did need to have some time in one of the American universities. She talked with Richard about the possibility of them all going to the States for one year and he was moderately enthusiastic but not sure how he would organise a teaching post for himself or even if he wanted to do that. When the invitation came it was for one semester initially and they agreed that this was a preferable length of time but that only Anna would go. Tentatively they planned that Richard and Claire would fly out and join her for the Easter holidays and then there would be two ten week spells when they were separated. Claire was quite used to her mother being away on lecture tours but this would be a much more substantial absence.

'Do you think that Claire is old enough to be left for so long?'

'If she had been sent to boarding school she would have been away from her mother for that length of time and probably not have the treat of a trip to the States for her Easter holiday.'

'What about you, Richard? It's always you that is left holding the baby so to speak.'

'I particularly like the baby I'm left holding,' he said with a grin. 'What would you do if I said no, I'm fed up with being left at home while you go off. . .'

'I would not go.'

'And what would that do to your career? We have always known that you were likely to get this invitation and I'm quite relieved that it isn't for a full academic year or even longer than that. You know that it is important that you go and I'm glad they have invited you. Being a visiting professor to an American university can be only one step away from being appointed to a Chair in this country. Mind you, we shall have to consider carefully what Alison Smith's views might be upon the situation if you were to be called Professor Trevanion!'

Anna laughed. 'Alison has been quoted at us rather a lot just lately, although I think she has been less critical of our domestic arrangements since she has seen me wearing an apron and doing the washing up while you were mending the car. She seemed to think that we were both in the right domestic role.'

They celebrated Claire's eleventh birthday then had Christmas in their own home rather than down in Cornwall at the rectory. Shortly after this Anna packed the things which she was going to take to the States and with her customary last minute sadness at leaving home, she set off to fly to New York. Two days later both Richard and Claire returned to their respective schools and their usual daily routine was established again.

It was one Saturday evening in March that Richard found Claire crying. It was unusual for her to take herself off to her room and to be so upset.

'What is it, love?'

'I can't tell you,' she sobbed. 'It's too terrible to tell you.'

Richard felt very alarmed.

'Surely nothing is that bad that you can't share it with your old Dad?'

'I want Mummy. She is never here when I want her.'

'We could try to telephone her. . .'

'It's no use doing that; I want her here, now.'

Claire continued to cry and although he put his arms around her and comforted her as he had always done he felt very baffled by her behaviour.

'Tell me what it is and then I might be able to suggest something.'

'I can't talk about it to you.'

'Is there anyone whom you think you could talk to as Mummy is not here?'

'I don't know.'

Richard was at his wits' end to know what to suggest. He could not anticipate what the problems might be.

'Is it that you feel poorly; have you got a pain?'

'I think I am going to die.'

'Claire, darling, whatever makes you say that?'

'I'm bleeding.'

'Where are you bleeding?'

'I can't tell you.'

Richard thought desperately. Surely Claire could not have started her periods. She was only just eleven and seemingly not all that well developed. He did not know if she knew anything about menstruation. He and Anna had never discussed this so he did not know how much information she may have given Claire. He held her close to him.

'I know what we can do. I will telephone Mary and see if she can help us. You stay here while I go downstairs and give her a ring.'

'Please God may Mary be in,' he prayed as he ran down the stairs.

She was. Her calm voice was there at the end of the phone.

'She is very young to have started a period but girls are starting much younger now compared with how things were a generation back.'

She told him what he would need to get for her. 'Do you think Anna has left anything at home?'

'I shouldn't think so, and where does one get things like this on a Saturday evening?'

'I think the best thing would be for me to drive over and bring with me all that might be needed if Claire has started to menstruate. She may find it easier to talk about

135

it to another female in any case. Is that all right with you?'

'Yes, of course it is. Thank you, Mary.'

'I'll be about an hour, maybe a bit longer. Give Claire my love and tell her not to worry because we'll soon sort it out.'

Mary arrived about an hour and a half later as she had promised, and then she and Claire went off upstairs together. They were up there a long time and then Richard heard a bath being run. He built up the fire in the sitting room with logs and sat and waited. For the first time in his parental life he felt out of his depth.

Mary came down and with her most reassuring smile said that the matter had been dealt with. She and Claire had had a long talk about 'women's matters'. Then she said with more concern that it was hard for Claire to have started her periods without really knowing about them and while her mother was away. It was also tough for her that this had happened while she was still only eleven.

'You couldn't stay until tomorrow to help her get used to what has happened?'

'I suppose I could. It would be nice to have a sit by that lovely log fire.'

Richard made three mugs of drinking chocolate and Claire came down in her dressing gown and they all sat round the fire together.

'This is cosy,' said Claire. 'I like it when everyone sits down together by the fire.'

'Daddy has asked me to stay tonight and I said that I would like to. The only thing is that I haven't brought my nightdress. Do you think Mummy has a spare one in her drawer?'

Claire went to look and came down with a nightdress, a clean towel and a spare toothbrush.

'Are you going to sleep in the room that you stayed in when you came before?'

'Yes, if that is all right. I think I shall need to have an early night too.'

They talked for a little while longer and then Richard reminded Claire that even though it was a Saturday night it was time she went to bed. She kissed them both good night and went up to her room.

'I don't know what I would have done without you tonight. As soon as I suspected what might be the problem you were the only person whom I could think of who would help.'

She smiled at him.

'I think we have got it sorted out.'

'You would have been a super mother. . .'

'Ricky, don't say it. It's hard enough to be here knowing what has happened and not to feel just a little sad that Anna was not here when Claire needed her.'

'You filled the gap admirably.'

'It's not quite the same.'

As she went to leave the room to go to bed he put his arms around her.

'With Claire acting as a chaperone I cannot be anything other than well behaved but just let me give you a thank you kiss.'

When Richard got up next morning he looked into Claire's bedroom and found it empty. There was talking coming from the spare bedroom where Mary had slept and the door was ajar. He knocked and after a suitable pause went in. Claire had got into the bottom of Mary's bed and was sitting with the duvet draped around her. Both were wide awake and engrossed in a conversation.

'Would you girls like a cup of tea; I'm just going down to put the kettle on?'

When he came back with the tray Claire asked him if he was going to get into the bed as well.

'No, I shall sit on the chair,' he said very firmly.

Claire began to giggle.

'There were three in the bed and the little one said "Roll over" and they all rolled over and one fell out. . .'

It was obvious that she felt much better that morning and the events of the previous day had been taken in her stride.

'Will you stay and have dinner with us?' Richard asked Mary.

'Thank you, but no. I've got to get back. We've got a choir rehearsal this afternoon. It's our big night next Saturday so we are rehearsing today as well as our usual session on Thursday evening. Actually, Claire and I were just talking about it. I am going to do some shopping for Claire this week so that she has all she needs until Anna comes back home in the summer, and we were making an arrangement about picking up the goods. Claire said that she would like to come and hear us sing next weekend. Would you like to come as well?'

'Yes, of course I'd like to come. What is the choir singing?'

'Fauré's *Requiem*.'

'Oh, I don't think I know that do I?'

'Yes you do, some of it any way.'

Immediately both females began to sing Pie Jesu, one of the most familiar passages in the Requiem.

He laughed, 'I'm sure it will be very good for my education.'

When Claire was in the room with them they had always found that they could behave in a fairly relaxed and acceptable way. Both knew that it was fatal to indulge in an 'if only' way of thinking and they must always avoid getting themselves into situations which could potentially put their emotional control at risk. The years between the only occasion when they had made love and the present had done nothing to reduce the strong attraction which they felt to each other and they both knew that nothing ever would. It was for this reason that Mary had hesitated about extending the invitation to Richard as well as Claire, especially at a time when Anna was abroad.

'Can we stay the night with you?' asked Claire.

'That would be very nice,' replied Mary calmly. 'Come and have a meal with me beforehand and then if you stay over until Sunday we can all spend the day together. Now come on you two and clear the room so that I can get up!'

The following Saturday Richard and Claire drove over to Mary's house in the early afternoon. During the week Richard had written to Anna and told her about Claire having started to menstruate and that he had had to telephone Mary for help. He also added that they were going to stay with Mary so that they could go to her choir's performance of Faure's *Requiem*. There was no need for Richard to feel uncomfortable about this visit and he knew that Anna would be perfectly accepting of what they were doing, but he still had a niggling little twinge of conscience.

Mary had prepared what she called high tea. There was salad, home baked rolls and a chocolate cake.

'I wasn't sure what time you would arrive and as we have to be off punctually I thought it would be easier to have a cold meal.'

Richard and Claire washed up while Mary went to get ready. When she came down she was wearing a beautiful blue evening dress and she looked lovely. Richard just stood and gazed at her.

'Dad's gone all bog-eyed about you,' commented Claire with more truth in her statement than she would ever know.

'I didn't know it was such a formal occasion,' said Richard. 'I would have come in my dark suit had I realised.'

'It's only the choir who are dressing up. I doubt if many of the audience will even be wearing a tie.'

'Well at least I've got a tie and jacket on.'

Richard drove them down in his car and pulled up outside the front door of the hall to let Mary get out.

'I really do feel like a prima donna,' she said as she stepped out, gathering her long skirt up so that it did not trail in the puddles of rain water on the steps.

Richard went to park the car and then he and Claire found their seats. Throughout the performance he kept his eyes almost constantly on the soprano who was singing in the front row and, with a background of music of which he was only vaguely conscious, he allowed himself to indulge in a session of 'if only'. 'If only I could stop loving you as much as I do.'

'Do you like the music, Dad?' asked Claire when there was a pause.

'Yes, it's lovely; I'm glad I came,' he smiled down at her.

'I thought you looked a bit sad, that's all, and so I thought perhaps you were sorry that you had come.'

After the performance there were refreshments for the

choir and their families.

'You are my family for tonight,' said Mary as she insisted that they joined her and she introduced them to several of the choir members. Richard was always at ease at any social gathering and able to make conversation with almost anybody. He spent a long time chatting very amicably with one of the basses who farmed locally and they discussed the relative merits of Welsh blackfaced sheep against Devon longwools. He had a feeling that this farmer might have more than a fellow choir member's interest in Mary. On the way back Mary mentioned that she had noticed that he had been talking to Alun for a long time.

'He is a really nice chap. We were discussing sheep, actually. I think he may be carrying a torch for you.'

'Perhaps. His wife died at a very young age two years ago and he has only recently joined the choir again. I know he feels lonely and he farms on his own so he doesn't get a lot of company.'

After Claire had gone to bed Richard mentioned Alun again.

'Ricky, there is nothing between Alun and me. When I said that he might be interested in me that wasn't to say that I was reciprocating.'

'Where you are concerned I have never known such contradictory feelings. On the one hand I want you to marry and have children because you would be such a wonderful wife and mother, and on the other hand. . .' he paused.

'On the other hand you feel a little jealous.'

'Yes.'

'You must know how I have often felt, then, and how much I have chastised myself for being like that. Anyway, I'm getting too old to be having babies and I'm not planning to get married. And both you and I know that we cannot talk about this subject any more because it's – well – it's just too complicated for both of us.'

He nodded.

'I'm sorry. I broke the unwritten rule. But I shall never be able to stop loving you and maybe it's important that I tell you this just once in a while.'

The next day Mary took them to her family's farm. Her parents had retired now and her brother had taken over. With the help of his wife he worked incredibly long hours to make a reasonable living from this hill farm but he was a man who was contented with his life and would not want it any different.

'He was the only one of the three of us who did not leave the area to seek fame and fortune and he is the only one who could be described as being really happy. His two children will be just the same. They love the farm; it's a way of life that they have been born into and they have no ambition to move elsewhere or do anything other than farm here.'

'Do you envy them?'

She laughed.

'Not really; there are easier ways of making a living than being on a hillside in a force nine gale trying to find missing sheep which you suspect might have taken themselves off to lamb.'

'I wouldn't mind giving it a go.'

'Go on with you, the grass is always greener.'

As they drove home that evening, Claire was pensive for some time.

'Why do we always have shop-bought cake at home?' she suddenly asked.

'That's a funny question.'

'When we go to Mary's she always makes cake or bread or pies. I really liked that chocolate cake she made yesterday.'

'I'm not a very good cook when it comes to making cakes.'

'Why does Mummy never make cakes?'

'She is very busy at the university and she does not have much time for cooking.'

'Mary goes out to work and she still has time to make cakes.'

'Perhaps she does it because she likes baking; it's a sort of hobby.'

'Mummy doesn't seem to have any hobbies.'

'She is a very important scientist and not only does she do research but she writes books and papers for journals

141

and goes on lecture tours. She does not really have any spare time for hobbies.'

'Do you miss Mummy when she is away?'

'Yes, of course. Don't you?'

'It will be nice when we go to see her in America at Easter.'

10

On the Thursday before Easter Richard and Claire flew to America. They had only broken up from school the day before but most of the packing had been done the previous weekend and they had not left a lot to be done at the last minute. They went early to Heathrow because they were both excited about the relatively long flight and wanted to be at the airport in plenty of time. Claire had tried at school not to say too much about going to America because she did not want her friends to think that she was bragging. However, it was inevitable that Alison Smith would have a view to express on the matter of Claire's mother being abroad for so long.

'How much longer is your mother going to be away for?' she asked Claire in the playground one day.

'She will come back at the end of the summer term.'

'My dad thinks your dad is a saint to put up with your mum going away so much.'

'She has to go away; it's part of her job, and anyway we are going out to see her in the Easter holidays.'

'Where are you going to?'

'We are flying to America. We might even go to Disneyland while we are there.'

'Swanky, that's what you are Claire Trevanion.'

'I'm not; you asked me about it.'

After this little interchange Claire was not so sure that she liked Alison Smith enough to give her the title of best friend but she was very careful not to say anything to any of the other children.

They checked their luggage in as soon as they arrived and because they were amongst the first in the queue they had two seats next to each other, one of which was by the window and not overlooking the wing. They watched aeroplanes taking off for a while and then went to buy something to read on the journey.

After that they had a cup of coffee and then it was time to go through to the departure lounge. When the announcement came for them to board their plane Claire thought that this was the most exciting moment in her life. It was a massive aeroplane, much larger than the one she had flown on when they had gone to Europe. She and Richard each carried hand luggage which was stowed in the lockers for take off. In her bag was an Easter card which she had designed and painted for her mother. Not only was Claire musical, she was also artistic and she loved to draw and sketch animals. Perhaps being brought up with the Beatrix Potter books had given her an interest in this area but when she had shown Richard what she had made for Anna he had been most impressed with her ability. It was most important that the luggage was carefully put in the locker so that the precious card should not get damaged. As they moved down the runway Claire took hold of Richard's hand.

'I like it when the engines rev up but I also feel just a little bit scared too.'

Once they were airborne and were able to undo their safety belts they spent a lot of time looking out of the tiny window. Richard had always to resist the temptation not to give a geography lesson to his daughter but during this flight when they saw icebergs in the ocean beneath them both of them became enthusiastic. They read for a while, slept a little and partook of all the refreshment that was served to them. And just at the time when Claire was feeling very tired and ready for bed they began the descent to the airport.

Anna was there to meet them and they could tell, even from a distance, that she was as excited about their arrival as they were. She rushed across as soon as they had cleared customs and led the way to the car which she had hired. They were going to spend the first few days in the apartment which the university had provided for her and then they were going to do some travelling. But at that moment all Claire and Richard wanted to do was to go to bed and to fall asleep and Anna could understand this from her own experience of crossing the Atlantic. She drove and, although she was dying to talk to them both, they slept soundly all the way. Claire barely roused when they got to the apartment and they just helped her undress and get into bed. Richard and Anna had a little time together before Richard had to go to bed. Next morning he and Claire were awake ages before Anna and it took several days before they got their daily programme better synchronised.

The University of Virginia in Charlottesville owes much of its being to Thomas Jefferson whose house on the hill above the town was one of the first places that the family visited. They also went to the Rotunda and the Snake Walk, so called because of the way that the wall was curved, and then they called into the science department where Anna was based.

'Do you like being a visiting professor, Mummy?'

'Yes, the facilities here are good and I have to do far less teaching than I do at home which leaves me more time for research.'

'Are you still going to come back at the end of June?'

'Yes, of course I am. Six months is long enough for me to be away from home. In fact I think that I am going to find it hard when I take you back to the airport and know that I'm not coming with you.'

'You could if you wanted to.'

'No, I couldn't because I've signed a contract for six months and I have said that I shall be staying. In any case I do like it here but I miss my family and my home. It is the difficult thing about being in the academic world that sometimes you do have to sacrifice personal time.'

'There are two jobs that I'm never going to do,' said Claire.

'Oh I can guess what those are,' interjected Richard.

'I bet you can't.'

'Half a dollar if I'm right?'

'A dollar if you are wrong.'

'O.K. Would one of them be a school teacher and the other a university professor?'

'You have only got one right. I don't want to be a teacher or a university lecturer.'

'Well I was pretty close. Do I get paid anything. What do you think Mummy? Who do you think won this bet?

'I don't think either of you should be gambling with such high stakes.'

They all laughed and ended up by having ice creams which Anna paid for on the understanding that they would not place any more bets on which she had to adjudicate.

When Claire thought back to this time in Virginia she recalled it as being one of the few holidays when they had done so many things together as a family. Anna had only to go into the university for one morning while they were there and she did not go to her study to work on papers as she would have done had they been at home. In the second week they drove up into the mountains and enjoyed some long walks together. Claire did ask about going to Disneyland but when they showed her on the map just how far it was from where they were she realised that her small brag to Alison Smith would have to remain unfulfilled. For Richard it was something of a busman's holiday because wherever he went he was always absorbing facts geographical and taking photographs of things which might make good slides for teaching purposes. It was no exception in Virginia and there were many features which he climbed a long way to record. For Anna it was just the pleasure of having their company and the link with home but at the end of the two weeks she was raring to be back in the laboratory again and to be getting on with her work because there was not much more time left for her in the States. But the most treasured possession which Anna had was the Easter card which Claire had made for her and carried so carefully to the States. Anna put this on her wall at the university and often sat and looked at it and wondered how much she and Claire were missing out on their mother/daughter relationship by her choice of an academic career.

One evening towards the end of the holiday when Claire had gone off to bed Anna mentioned, almost in passing, that the Chair in Chrystallography was becoming

146

vacant at Oxford and she had had a preliminary enquiry to ask if she would be interested in applying.

'That is marvellous,' said Richard. 'You will apply, won't you?'

'Yes, I'm almost sure that I will. I'm reaching an age where if I'm going to get a Chair I ought to start casting the net around.'

'Anna dear, you are only 34.'

'For a scientist that is old. Do you know that the best work is always done in the early twenties and after that your scientific prowess declines rapidly? My best work may yet turn out to be the doctoral thesis which I completed in a hospital side ward waiting for Claire's birth.'

'So all the hundreds of papers which you have published since than are the works of an addled scientific brain?'

'That's a bit of an exaggeration. In actual fact I am moving much more into the study of the chrystallographical structure of human body stones such as those produced by the kidneys, and there will be a major opportunity to pursue this in Oxford.'

'It will also be nearer to home and not such a long journey.'

'True, and it would be even shorter if you ever wanted to move to a school in or near to Oxford.'

'That might be something for the future but at the moment I very much want to stay put. In comparison with what you have just told me my promotion to Head of Geography pales into insignificance, but that will be effective from next September.'

'You didn't tell me about it; that's very good.'

'In comparison with being a university professor it is hardly a career move which one is going to be shouting from the roof tops.'

'It isn't often that I detect a note of – well – resentment in what you say.'

'It's never resentment about your career, Anna, because I would never be clever enough to do what you do or, if I'm honest, ever want to lead the life you do. But just sometimes I feel as if I'm forever having to fit in with where you are planning to be. I know I'm not being quite fair about this because you did suggest we move to where we are to suit me and it has meant a lot of travelling for you. But there are so many times when you are the absent wife and mother and I can't go on filling that gap.'

'I'm really sorry about not having prepared Claire for what happened a month ago but it just never occurred to me that it could happen to her at such a young age. I was fourteen before I started and I presumed that was the age for most girls.'

'Well, that was one thing, but I'm sure as she gets into adolescence there will be other problems with which I cannot cope or which she will choose not to share with me. It was very fortunate that Mary was able to step into the breech. Have you had a talk to Claire about what happened?'

'Well, no I haven't; I really did not know how to bring the subject up or if there was any need to do so. Claire didn't say anything so I thought perhaps she would rather not talk about it. It's a fairly natural event in any case so there is no need to blow it up out of all proportion.'

Anna was thoughtful for a while then she asked Richard if he had thought any more about whether or not it might be a good thing for Claire to go to boarding school.

'I know when we talked about this a year ago you were very opposed but as you have anticipated problems in the teens do you think that it would be better for her to be in an environment where there are more females around?'

'If Claire went away to school I should feel totally bereft of family life. If she ever raises this as something she wants to do then I will consider it, but at the moment I'm very happy with the arrangement that she transfers to my school in September. In fact this will be easier for us both because we can travel together when we are finishing at the same time.'

Richard noticed that Anna did not say any more about the contact with Mary. He knew that she would never feel any resentment of Mary substituting for her as a mother. Whether or not she would tolerate her substituting as a wife was a completely different issue and one which was not on the agenda.

☆ ☆ ☆

It was a particularly warm summer in England that year. As soon as Richard and Claire got back from the States Richard was busy in the garden, planting seeds which he had delayed putting in until they returned. The grass needed cutting but once that was done and the flower borders forked over Richard felt that he had caught up on his gardening schedule. Mrs Maidment had spring cleaned the house while they were away and done the shopping ready for their return.

'We really have been lucky with the help we have always had,' Richard thought. He particularly liked Mrs Maidment because she was a quiet, unobtrusive person and utterly reliable. She appreciated that since her husband had had a stroke Richard always went round and did the heavy digging in his garden for him and helped him with the jobs which he now found difficult. She would always come and stay with Claire if ever Richard had to go out in the evening.

Richard also took his turn cutting the cricket pitch and getting the ground ready for the opening match of the season. The team had played well the year before and had been promoted in the league to a higher division so there was general and widespread enthusiasm in the village for cricket. There was even talk that this might be the year that they reached the village cricket final at Lords!

Claire was going back for her last term at the village school. She and all her friends would be transferring to the large comprehensive school where Richard taught and would travel in on the school bus each day. Following his discussion with Anna in the States about Claire going away to school Richard thought that perhaps he had been rather selfish in saying that he wanted her to remain at home. So one day soon after they got back he raised the matter with Claire.

'I'd hate to go away to school and leave all my friends here.'

'You would make new friends.'

'I don't want to go away to school.'

'That's good because I don't want you to either, but I

didn't want you to feel lonely at home just with me and Mummy when she is here.'

Richard later wrote and told Anna that he had talked to Claire about boarding school and that she did not want to go. He added that he hadn't put any pressure on her but he was glad that she didn't. When Anna wrote back he was surprised that she agreed and said that it had only been a suggestion which might make life easier for him.

Claire telephoned Mary soon after their return and said that she would have to come over and see her because she had brought her back a special present. They arranged that she would go over on the train the following Saturday and that Mary would bring her back in the car on Sunday.

'What about choir on Sunday?' asked Mary.

'They managed all right without me when I was away so one more Sunday is not going to make a lot of difference. Dad is playing cricket this Saturday and it is an away match so he is not going to be around.'

Richard put Claire on the train and Mary met her at the other end. It was the first train journey that Claire had done on her own and although it was only about three quarters of an hour she felt very grown up, particularly when the guard asked to see her ticket and called her madam.

One of the things which Claire most liked about Mary was that she always seemed to have time to talk about things. She was really interested in everything that they had done on holiday and asked how Anna was.

'She likes it in America but she misses Dad and me but she is not coming back until the end of June.'

Mary laughed.

'That seems a bit of a jumbled message. I'm sure she misses you both very much but she does have to do these tours if she is going to get to the top of her career.'

'I wonder why people want to get to the top of their careers? Sometimes it must make them unhappy. Look at Mummy; she says that she misses us yet she still does it.'

'Perhaps you appreciate her more when she comes back after being away.'

'I'm not complaining you know, but I wish Mummy would make cakes and things when she is at home.'

'When you go to your new school next term you will do home economics as one of your subjects and you will learn to bake, then you can make cakes.'

'Is that where you learned to make cakes?'

'No, I think I learned that from my mother. When we were all at home on the farm my mother used to have enormous baking sessions, particularly when there were extra men in to shear the sheep or pick potatoes. She had to provide 'drinkings' for them all and I used to have to carry the big baskets with the food and drink in down to where they were working.'

'Would you like to do that now?'

'In some ways, but being a farmer's wife is hard work.'

'Why are you not married, Mary?'

'The man I was engaged to be married to died.'

'I sometimes wish that you had married Dad and then you would have been my mother.'

'As well as Mummy?'

'Mummy is very nice and I love her but it seems that I don't see a lot of her and sometimes it feels as if I haven't got a Mummy.'

'Yes, I know how you must feel, Claire, but your Mummy is really a very clever person and her brain is going to help scientific research make progress. It would be an enormous waste of that brain if she were to stay at home and bake chocolate cakes which anybody can do, whereas only Mummy can work out the answers to some of those difficult scientific problems.'

'Umm, when you explain it like that I understand why she must go away and anyway there is always Dad around.'

'He is a lovely father and he is very proud of both of you.'

'Do you think he is lonely?'

'At times I think he must be, but he likes his job and he is a very good teacher. He enjoys playing cricket and doing his garden.'

'Granny said that he was such a good rugby player that he had a county trial but he gave it up when he was quite young.'

'Life is always full of compromises. You give up one thing and take on another. I'm sure Dad is very glad that he has the things which he has.'

When they got back the following day Richard had made tea for them and there in the middle of the table was the most impressive looking chocolate cake.

'I'm not having my daughter complaining that the only cake we have in this house is shop bought.'

'Did you make that cake, Dad?'

'What do you think?'

'You didn't.'

'I will have to confess that I did not make the cake. Yesterday there was a cake stall at the cricket match to raise funds for the club and so I bought it, but it is home made.'

It was a delicious cake and they all enjoyed a slice of it.

Anna was called back from the States during June to go to Oxford for an interview. The University of Virginia released her two weeks early and she landed back at Heathrow on June 19th and then went straight up to Oxford. All the other candidates were men, as had been expected, and most of them she knew by sight at least, but one man from Australia she had never seen or heard of even. On the basis of what she knew about the work of the other candidates she was sure that she was as well qualified as any of them but she always felt that as a woman candidate she did have to be that much better.

She knew that she interviewed well. She was tremendously impressed with the facilities which would go with the Chair and she realised that she had never wanted anything as much as she wanted that appointment. At the end of the first day there was going to be a further short list of two or three candidates who would go through to the final selection. Her name was on that list and she rang Richard to tell him.

'Well done.' He was his ever encouraging self. 'What is to be is to be, but there isn't anyone better qualified than you, is there?'

'There is one Australian that I don't know anything about.'

152

'If they have to choose between an unknown Australian and a famous female Brit there can only be one choice.'

'I hope you are right.'

Anna was appointed. She was absolutely delighted. As she drove the hire car which she had picked up at Heathrow back home that evening she felt as if she was on cloud nine. She was so looking forward to seeing Claire and Richard, to seeing the house which she had last seen in the depths of winter and to sharing with them the wonderful news that she had, at her first attempt, been appointed to a Chair in the most prestigious of universities. She wished that her mother had still been alive to share the moment with her but at the same time felt satisfied that she had achieved that which her mother would have wished.

In all the euphoria of the offer of the Chair, Anna had not prepared herself for the possible problems of returning home. She had been away for six months and Richard and Claire had adapted to her not being there to the extent that it was quite difficult for her to assume a role in the family. They had both become very integrated into village life and knew many more people than she did. They joined in activities in the village which she had never had time for, but in any case would not have wanted. While she had been away Mrs Maidment had assumed more responsibility for running the housekeeping, and while Anna welcomed this she began to feel almost superfluous at home.

The weekend after her return Richard was playing cricket on the Saturday and Claire had arranged to go out all day with the Guides. Anna had done her unpacking, got her papers sorted in her study and prepared to go back up to London on the Monday morning. She would need quite a long period of time to wind up her research in London and begin the transfer to Oxford. Nobody really envisaged that she would be taking up her new appointment until early in the following year, although she was keen to move as soon as was feasible. Richard and Claire had said all the right things about her new post but they did not really seem to share the thrill that she experienced when she thought about it.

As she made herself some lunch she felt almost a stranger in her own home and quite lonely. For the first time it really hit her quite forcibly about how far they had all drifted apart now. She had wanted what she had achieved but she knew she had paid the price in personal relationships. Yet, in a way, the lack of closeness gave her the personal space which she needed to continue pursuing her career. The price which she had paid did not seem to matter so much now. What did matter was to make an incredible success of being an Oxford don.

Richard scored a half century that day and helped his team to a comfortable win. They had a long celebration in the pub that evening and for once he did not have to hurry home to look after Claire. He rarely drank and when he did he got happy quite quickly. It was as well that he walked home that night and left his car in the car park until the following day. Claire was in bed when he got home but Anna was still up. She did not say a word but it was very obvious that she did not approve of his slightly inebriated condition. She was not too pleased to learn next morning that he had had to leave his car outside the pub all night.

Early in September Richard returned to school as Head of Department and Claire arrived at the school as one of the large first year intake. Having a surname which was unusual in this county it was soon realised that she was Mr Trevanion's daughter but there were several other members of staff who had their children in the school and it was never much of a problem in a school of this size. In school Claire related to him as a teacher and was even heard to refer to him as Sir because everyone else did. At home Richard was meticulous about not mentioning any staff room matters. But the fact that they now shared the same educational establishment gave them yet another common interest which Anna did not share and she often felt excluded when they were talking about things which had happened at school.

As the autumn days shortened and the journey to London became more tedious Anna opted to use her room in London more. She was also keen to get as much work as she had to do done as quickly as possible so she

154

did not want to waste valuable hours travelling on the train between Wiltshire and London. It finally resulted in her becoming a weekly commuter and only going home for the weekend.

'As soon as I have moved to Oxford it will be easier because it is so much nearer and I shall be able to drive over each day.'

Richard heard what was said but did not really think that the daily driving would last for long. One thing that he felt very sure about was that he was not again going to compromise his own situation. He liked living in the village and teaching at his present school. He had formed a network of friends and contacts in the area and Claire was very settled in this community. Long, long ago he realised that nothing, absolutely nothing, was going to deflect Anna from reaching the top. The trouble was that the top seemed to get higher and higher in the academic world. When he had first known her it was to get a first class degree, then a Ph.D., then a university lectureship, a readership, invitations to travel the world to lecture and then the Oxford Chair. She was now thirty-five, just half way to the three score years and ten and there was no knowing where her ambition was going to be driving her for the second half of her so-called allotted life span.

It was not the kind of marriage that he would have wished it to be and probably never had been, but whereas in the early years he was the one who always gave way and compromised so that the great ability in his wife should be allowed to flourish, he had reached the stage of being quite firmly of the opinion that enough was enough. The sacrifices had been very one sided and, whereas he did not feel the resentment which Anna had recently suggested he might be experiencing, he became firmly resolved that henceforth he was going to do what he wished to do. What always made such a resolve difficult was that he and Anna were good friends and she never seemed to be peevish if he dug his heels in about something. But being good friends is not enough in a marriage. There was never any acrimony but then there was an absence of any passion. Things were discussed in an analytical way but rarely with emotion, either of anger or of love. Perhaps Richard had slightly resented Anna going to America for six months. What was very clear to them both when she came back was that the pattern of their previous relationship, whereby they jogged along reasonably amicably together, was no longer operating.

Anna had always been a very self contained person. She had only made a few close relationships in her life and these, by comparison with other people's relationships, had a certain distance in them, but they were constant. Having made a friend Anna would always maintain that contact. So it was in her marriage and in motherhood. There was an unending commitment to both. She might not rate herself highly in either of these roles but they were an important part of her life. At times she found the intellectual gap between herself and Richard to be irritating. She could never really discuss her work with him because he had only the most rudimentary grasp of scientific principles. He was also only politely interested. He did not particularly enjoy scientific gatherings and when she had suggested in all sincerity that now Claire was old enough it might be useful for them all to go together to the summer meeting of the British Association for the Advancement of Science he had been quite dismissive of this being an interesting sort of holiday for the three of them. In previous years he might have been quite keen to go and probably would have enjoyed the input to the geographical section but it did not seem to be so now. Anna pondered about this. It was impossible that Richard could be harbouring any feelings of resentment of her success because it would be so alien to his character, unless he had changed. Could it be that what he was missing in other areas of his marriage were consciously, or subconsciously, being held against her academic achievements?

If only they could explore their feelings together about this but that for Anna was a non-starter. She knew that if she were really honest with herself she could not remember when she had last told Richard that she loved him; worse than that, she could not remember if she had ever told him.

Claire was a very mature eleven year old, not just

physically but also emotionally. No doubt that was due to the fact that so much of her early life was spent with adults and it was only when she went to school, and particularly when they moved to the village, that she spent a greater part of her day with children of her own age. She made several observations upon their family life and at times asked quite searching questions about their relationships. As a young child it had been quite easy to fob her off with a variety of answers but as she got older she was due for greater respect. It was one of these questions that put both her parents at quite considerable unease.

They were sitting at the table having Sunday lunch. It was only shortly after Claire had started at the comprehensive school and may have stemmed from a discussion that the children might have been having on the school bus. The three of them were having a relaxed conversation about nothing of any significance when Claire quite out of the blue asked, 'Why don't you two sleep together in the big bed?'

Richard's immediate response would have been to say, 'We do sometimes, but if Mummy is working late. . .'

Anna's answer would have been to say, 'Why do you ask this question?'

But both paused before saying anything and Claire immediately said, 'I don't want you spinning me tales because I know you have not slept in the big bed since Mummy came back from America. We were all talking about this at school and Alison Smith said that people who don't sleep together get divorced. Are you getting divorced?'

They both said no at the same time. Then Anna smiled and said, 'Well that must show that we are agreed on the subject.'

But Claire was not going to be deflected from her line of enquiry.

'If you are not going to get divorced, why are you not sleeping in the big bed?'

Richard suddenly felt annoyed with Claire.

'There are some things, Claire, which are none of your business and certainly none of Alison Smith's either. Where Mummy and I sleep is our affair and that's the end of the matter.'

She said no more but it was not the end of the matter because when they were on their own Anna raised it too.

'I suppose the main reason why we do not sleep together is that our sleeping habits have changed.'

'What utter rot,' he replied.

'Whatever the reasons, do you think we should try to keep up appearances at the weekends at least?'

'Just to satisfy the curiosity of Alison Smith?'

'It was for Claire's sake really. I just thought that we should try to be more like other parents.'

'We cannot be what we are not and we have all got to live with that.'

He walked out of the room and went into the garden and started to dig the lower vegetable patch with considerable vigour.

Claire, having decided that she wasn't going to speak to either of them ever again, had gone for a ride on her bicycle. Anna shrugged her shoulders and realised that there was no point in trying to pursue the subject any further so she retreated to her study and got on with some work. But she was aware of how much more irritable Richard had become and at times how miserable he seemed to be.

11

'There is nothing like Oxford' wrote Kilvert in 1876 and for Anna there could not have been a truer saying. She had felt some sadness and a slight betrayal of loyalty in leaving her own university but everyone said that they thought this was the right thing for her to do. The opportunities in her branch of research were going to be that much greater in Oxford, she was going to be given far more resources than ever she could expect in London and her accommodation was probably the most superior of anywhere in the academic world. If ever Anna needed an incentive to work then she was going to have it in Oxford. She knew from the very first day there that this was the place for her and that this was where she was going to spend the rest of her scientific life.

Her reputation had gone before her. She had published so much that she was the recognised authority on several areas of crystallography. The beginnings of her pioneering work on the crystallographic structure of body stones was inevitably to be of immense value to the medical profession and the human species at large. It was likely that she was going to get some major funding which would mean that she could build up a team of young, talented scientists to work under her. Anna had tremendous energy and dedication but she knew that she would have to work incredibly hard, at least at the beginning, to get the research established. As Richard had foreseen, she did not have time to travel home every evening, although the journey only took about an hour and a quarter, but elected to stay in her rooms in college and continue with what she was doing. There was also another side to her staying in Oxford. She wanted to get to know the other dons and to make the contacts which were important in establishing herself. This seemed to be the most important thing to be doing, although she realised that she ran the risk of becoming a lodger in her own home. It was not that she was deliberately trying to do this, but a case of not being able to modify the driving ambition to be an academic success.

Richard had given up the unequal struggle. He really thought that when Anna was appointed to the chair in Oxford she had reached her Mecca. As she began the transfer of her research from London to the new department he sensed that this was far from true. There was yet further unfulfilled ambition and he felt no longer able to accommodate it. The irritation which at times had surfaced during the last few weeks and the abruptness which he had most unusually shown in his dealings with Claire were symptomatic of his despondency. Sensing that Richard was behaving in ways which were not character- istic of him, Anna did suggest that perhaps he should have a few days away from home.

'What for?'

'Well you do seem a bit tired and fed up with things.'

'I'm all right.'

'Why don't you go down to Cornwall for a few days at Easter or go to stay with Mary in Wales? I mean go on your own, without Claire and me, and have a break from the family responsibilities.'

'I can't do that.'

'I don't see why not; well, think about it. Claire can spend part of the time here with me in Oxford or we can make arrangements with Mrs Maidment during the day and I will go back early each day, or I'll even take some annual leave. It would do you good to get right away for a few days and have some time which is yours.'

'I cannot go and stay with Mary and it would not be a break from family responsibilities to go and stay at the rectory, much as I love being down in Cornwall.'

'Richard, I know how you feel about Mary. I have known for years that had you had your time again it would have been Mary and not me whom you married. I know

160

you are both intensely loyal to our wedding vows but the fact of the matter is that we have a marriage now in name only, and you are more unhappy than you have ever been. I have my work and that fulfills me almost completely. I know that I would not be where I am now had I not been married to you and had all your support; now the time has come for me to make some sacrifices.'

'Let me be quite clear in my understanding of what you are saying. Are you suggesting that I go away for a week and stay with someone to whom you realise that I feel attracted and who, because she is a friend of yours, will not encourage those feelings because she believes it would be both disloyal to you and wrong in any case?'

'Put like that it sounds stark but I think that is what I am saying.'

'Are you thinking that if I do as you suggest I shall get it out of my system or that I will find the grass isn't any greener on the other side?'

'All I know is that in my peculiar way I value our marriage, I would be a foolish woman if I did not recognise the contribution which you have made to preserving that union, but it has now made you an unhappy man and perhaps I have been selfish and unfair to you. It would not be wise for you to go away by yourself when you are feeling low, so that was why I suggested the two places where I know you feel happiest. I don't want to push you into the arms of another woman but perhaps that is what you deserve when I'm not much of a wife to you.'

They left the discussion there but the following day Anna was tempted to telephone Mary and tell her what she had suggested. Mary was silent at the end of the phone and Anna realised that it had not been the most sensible thing to have done.

'I'm sorry, Mary. I really have made a mess of things. I am quite worried about Richard; I think he really is very depressed. I know that he loves to spend time with you. I do also know that he has been in love with you for many years and that you have both behaved most properly but, at the end of the day, doing the right thing has made three people quite miserable at times.'

161

'Was there any other way?'

'No, I suppose not but I'm the one who has done the best out of it. I had the husband, the child and the career.'

'I just find what you are suggesting to be so unrealistic that I cannot really believe that I am hearing you properly.'

'That's funny because that was virtually what Richard said. You must both think that I am incredibly naïve when all I think I am doing is trying to be generous and repay the debt which I owe him.'

By this stage Anna wished that she had not said anything and bitterly regretted having telephoned Mary. She confessed to Richard that evening that she had made matters worse by speaking to Mary.

'I do believe that you had the best of intentions in mind when you started talking to me about needing a little holiday but now I just cannot see a way out of the mess.'

'Since it is all out in the open one way could be obvious.'

With that remark Anna went to her study and focussed her mind on some calculations which she thought was the one thing she should not be able to mess up.

In the end Richard did what Anna had said would not be wise; he went away by himself. Anna had to go to an international symposium in Vienna at the end of March for five days. When she returned she found a note in her study from Richard saying that as Claire had gone to stay with his parents in Cornwall until the Easter weekend he was going away walking by himself and then would go down to Cornwall and pick up Claire. Anna felt quite odd when she realised that for the first time in her marrige she did not know where Richard was. She wondered if her parents-in-law did either, but thought it would be a little humiliating to have to telephone and ask. The note was dated that morning but it did not indicate where he was heading for or for how long he was going to be away, other than he would pick up Claire at the end of it. In the end she telephoned Claire in Cornwall to let her know that she was back and to see if she was all right. Claire was her usual extroverted self. Dad had put her on the coach in Bristol yesterday and Grandad had met her in Plymouth. It was going to be great because the cousins were coming to stay the following day and Dad had said that he would come down on Good Friday evening. She lowered her voice a little and then with a giggle said, 'I think he wants to miss Grandad's three hour service although Granny has said that none of us has to go if we don't want to.'

'Did Dad say where he was going walking?'

'Yes, I think he did. I think he said he was going to check out an area for a field trip.'

'Did he say where or leave an address?'

'I don't know. He might have been going to Pembroke-shire. Is that in west Wales? He said he was going to walk along the coastal footpath in west Wales.'

'Give my love to Granny and Grandad. I'll see you when you come back on Saturday.'

She knew that walking the Pembrokeshire coastal path was something which Richard had wanted to do for a long time. It had been her suggestion that he went away but when it had happened and without any prior warning she was slightly perturbed. On the other hand it gave her a clear week to get on with various important things which she wanted to finish.

After Richard had put Claire on the coach he went back home and packed his rucksack and walking boots into the car. He had told Mrs Maidment that he would be away until the following Saturday but that his wife would probably be there for some of the week when she returned from Vienna. He wrote the note for Anna and left it in her study and then next morning at 4 am he set off and drove west across the Severn Bridge. He was over halfway to St Davids before the dawn began to break and several people were probably still in bed when he arrived. The first thing he did was to treat himself to breakfast in a luxurious hotel and then he set out for a walk by the sea. It was a long time since he had felt so free of responsibility and able to enjoy the fact that he had only himself to think about. It was a cold morning but the sky was clear and he could see a long way. Below him the sea was rough as it pounded the rocks. Above him gulls circled screeching as they dived towards the water. He just walked and never once considered the fieldwork potential of the route he took. He had shed the role of geography master, husband, father. He was just Richard doing a thing which he loved. There were no ties on him; he could eat when he wanted to, stay where he chose and forget everything.

During the afternoon that feeling was wearing a little thin. It was all very well escaping, but supposing there was a crisis at home and nobody could get in touch with him? That would be a little irresponsible. So he bought a lot of postcards and sat in his car and wrote them to everybody. He said that he was staying near to St Davids in a beautiful farmhouse which overlooked the sea and that he was going for long walks each day, getting fit for the summer term. Since he was always fit this seemed a silly thing to put but he had to fill his card up with some information and he did find it difficult to think of appropriate things to say. He put the telephone number of the place he was staying on Anna's card and then he felt guilty no longer about having just gone off. He caught the last post that day, and having put first class stamps on the cards he was sure that they would be delivered the following morning.

Next morning Mary was surprised to receive a card from Richard which indicated that he was in west Wales. She had not spoken to him since the phone call which she had had from Anna which had indicated that he was feeling very low. She was a little troubled by the card. It was not like him to send cards; he had always been one of the world's worst correspondents. What he had written lacked any of the usual witty comments associated with Richard and she felt for the sadness which seemed to be conveyed. She thought about it on and off during the day and in the evening she telephoned Anna.

Anna had had a card as well and was relieved to have been given a phone number. She did not intend to use it unless it was really necessary but throughout her married life she had always left a number where she could be contacted in emergencies and this was a habit which she thought was important for them all.

'Is Richard really depressed, or is he just tired and feeling a bit fed up with things?'

164

'To be honest, I don't know. I think he is fed up with things and my being away so much and leaving him with the greater share of the family responsibility has finally caught up with us. I can assure you that I feel bad about that. That was why I was trying to get him to go away in the first place. He finds it difficult to talk to me about what is wrong but something is making matters much worse. You don't think you could telephone him and talk with him; he always finds it easy to discuss things with you. I am a bit worried because I have never known him go off quite like this before. I wonder if he is ill?'

Anna insisted that she gave the telephone number to Mary. When she thought about it later she realised that she did not want to have the sole responsibility of being concerned about Richard. She did also trust Mary's judgement and knew that in her dealings with people Mary was infinitely more skilled than she.

When Richard woke on his second morning at the farmhouse he could hear the wind blowing. The previous day had been cold again but it had been fairly calm. He got up and drew back the bedroom curtains. From the window he had the most fantastic view across the fields to the sea beyond. It was not raining but there was a strong wind blowing and there were white horses racing across the sea. He loved days like this because they made him feel exhilarated. He realised that the room he had been given was probably the best in the house. It was enormous with two large windows looking towards the sea. He had slept for the first time in his life in a four poster bed. But the room had all modern conveniences in that it was centrally heated and there was an en suite bathroom which in the past had probably been the dressing room. He reflected on the fact that in days gone by it was probable that a large jug of hot water had been brought up and possibly even a hip bath provided for the inhabitant. There was still an open fireplace in the room and he thought how lovely it would be to have a fire in the bedroom. When they had been ill in bed as children their mother would light the fire in the rectory bedroom. He could remember lying in bed once when he had chicken pox watching the flames flickering in the half light and thinking that that was the best part of being ill. That, and his mother bringing up his meals on a tray and stopping to talk with him while he ate. He could recall her always finding time to read him a story. Having only had one child, but at times finding her almost a full time occupation, he realised how hard his mother must have always worked and still did, because she had a house full this week as well as the parish activities of Easter week.

'Stop feeling guilty,' he said to himself. 'Mum loves having her grandchildren to stay and particularly when she has the complete responsibility of them. She was very happy to pack you off for a geographical reconnoitre, or that was what she was led to believe it was.'

He went downstairs. There were only two other guests staying because the season had hardly started yet, and they were moving on that day. Sometimes, at the height of the season, there were as many as fourteen people staying there but it was much more pleasant for him to be the only person as he would be for the rest of the week.

If he was feeling low, as Anna had thought, it did nothing to affect his appetite. Breakfast at home had long ago become a rushed bowl of cereal or a piece of toast grabbed and eaten in the car as he drove to school. Here he ate everything which was provided and relished having a mixed grill as well as cereal and masses of toast and home made marmalade. Although the weather was not particularly good he was going to take a packed lunch with him and be out for the day.

'Which way will you be heading today, Mr Trevanion?' asked Mrs Williams when she cleared the plates from the table.

'I thought I would walk along to the end of the headland and then as the tide goes out this afternoon walk back along the beach.'

'You ought to make sure that the tide has turned before you go down on to the rocks at the headland, especially when the wind is as strong as it is this morning, but I don't expect I need to warn a Cornishman about treating the sea with respect,' she said with a smile.

'One can never be too careful and I'm glad to have your advice. The wind may drop as the tide turns. Anyway, I

166

plan to be back in time to have some of your scones for tea.'

He had had scones when he had come back the day before, feeling ravenous after a day in the fresh air, and it had not affected his appetite for the dinner which was served at 7 pm. That might have been because he had gone out into the milking parlour and helped Mr Williams milk his herd of Friesians and the additional activity had increased his appetite.

After breakfast he packed his small knapsack. Mrs Williams gave him a flask of soup as well as a package of sandwiches and pies. She obviously believed in the philosophy that an army marched on its stomach. He wondered whether or not to bother taking his camera because the light was not good but in the end put it in, together with his Ordnance Survey map and an additional pullover in case it really did get a lot colder. He set off along the track, at times having to bend forward into the wind. He did not meet a soul as walked but then it was not surprising in rough weather like this. It took him nearly three hours to reach the end of the headland but the view from the top was magnificent. Great waves were crashing on to the rocks below and spray was flying high into the air. He took some photographs because it was not often that the sea was as dramatic as it was that day. Then he found a fairly sheltered place behind an outcrop and sat down to have his lunch. The soup was home made and delicious and as he was on his own he dipped his sandwiches into it.

'The joys of being away from the necessity of having to set a good example,' he thought.

He did not sit for long because it was cold. He noted that the tide was beginning to go out but it would be a little while before he could get down to the beach from where he was. He did a little more exploring and then turned back to the path which went down from the cliff top to the sand and rocks below. It seemed safe enough now to climb down. When he got down on the beach he was surprised at how much more sheltered it was than the cliff top. He walked along the high water mark gathering shells and other pieces of stone which took his interest and then, as the sea had gone out quite a long way, he walked out across the sand to the water's edge. Oyster catchers were feeding and he noticed several shags skimming close to the surface of the sea and occasionally diving into the swell to catch fish. He turned towards the farm which he could just make out in the distance at the other side of the bay.

As he walked across the sands, which at times was quite hard going because they were soft and his boots sank down, he was aware that there was somebody else walking on the beach on the far side.

'Another hardy outdoor person,' he thought, 'perhaps it's a local fisherman come down to dig for bait.' But the person was walking quite quickly and after a while he realised that the person was coming towards him. It was difficult to ascertain who it was because an anorak hood was tightly tied round a chin and hands were deeply plunged into trouser pockets. He was amazed when he heard a voice call his name above the strong wind and the person waved. He quickened his pace and the person began to run towards him. In absolute joy he knew who it was and he held out his arms as she ran towards him. When she reached him he held her tightly and buried his face, which was wet with the spray, into her shoulder.

'Darling Mary, how did you find me?'

'You left enough clues for even an amateur to pick up the trail.'

'It is just so good to see you.'

'Is it all right for me to intrude on your retreat if only for a little while?'

He didn't bother to answer her. Instead he found her mouth and kissed her with all the passion that had been so frustrated for so long.

They walked back across the sands hand in hand. Mary told him about being disconcerted about his postcard and how she had telephoned Anna the previous evening and she too had been worried. Anna had given her the telephone number and had suggested that she should ring him.

'But I couldn't do that; the phone is so impersonal, so I drove down to St Davids and then telephoned Mrs Williams to try to book some accommodation. She said there was only one other gentleman staying. When I arrived I told her that the gentleman was my reason for coming and she was able to tell me which direction you had said you would be coming back from. So I came down on to the beach to meet you.'

'Did you say that you had booked in to stay at the farm?'

'I gather that you are staying until Friday morning so I have booked myself in until then.'

He stopped walking and turned Mary to face him.

'I love you and it is so good to be here with you.'

'And I love you, so much so that I have been very presumptive; I said to Mrs Williams that there was no need to prepare another room. . . if you will have me I'm going to share that splendid four poster bed with you tonight.'

'How do you know I have a four poster bed?'

'I saw it when Mrs Williams took me upstairs to put my things in there.'

'What do you suppose she thinks about our relationship?'

'I've no idea; I did not say that I was Mrs Trevanion. I just said that I was Mary Swaine and that I would like to share a room with you.'

'You brazen hussy!'

'I know, I surprised myself by the calm way that I was able to do this. But I had to be honest and she might have put me in another part of the house from which it would have been very tricky to try to creep into each other's rooms. I don't think this is the first time that she will have had this happen.'

They walked the rest of the way back with their arms around each other. When Mrs Williams saw them together she felt reassured that she had done the right thing in showing an unannounced lady into her guest's room. She had been having visitors to stay for many, many years and there had been few whom she had liked as much as Mr Trevanion. When an equally attractive woman had turned up saying that they would like a double room she had had an initial slight apprehension but had decided that it really was no business of hers. It was clear that they knew each other very well indeed but they did not have the same

169

surname. However, in this day and age several women preferred to keep their maiden name. It could well be something like that.

She warned Mr Williams that it was likely that he would be milking on his own that night!

After having a tray of tea and scones by the fire in the guests' sitting room Richard took Mary upstairs to their room. There, to his absolute delight, he found that Mrs Williams had lit the fire in the bedroom. He had commented on the fireplace on his first day and told her about his memories of fires in the bedroom as a child. As they had opened the door they had seen the flickering of the flames in the half light and it made the room look very cosy. They did not switch on the light but went across to the fireplace, kicked off their shoes and knelt down on the thick rug in front of the fire warming their hands. They turned to each other and had their first kiss in complete privacy and with no inhibitions. For them both the setting, the joy of of being together and the deep love which they continued to feel for each other made this a precious moment in their lives.

Richard gently drew Mary down on to the rug and stretched out beside her. She snuggled close to him and slid her hands beneath his shirt, pressing them against his bare back. She desperately wanted to feel the contact of his body and as he began to remove her jumper and then unbutton the front of her shirt she responded frantically to his searching tongue. Together, and sometimes quite clumsily, they removed each other's clothes and then lay together in the warm firelight.

'Shall we make love here or get into the four poster?'

'Here in the firelight, please, now; I can't wait until we get into bed. . .'

'It's much more romantic by the fire. . .'

It was quite dark outside when they next spoke to each other and the fire had got quite low.

'It's a good job that our window is not overlooked or somebody might have seen some interesting antics going on in the firelight.'

'Even so, I think we had better draw the curtains before we switch on the light.'

Richard went across to the window and drew the curtains. Then he switched on a small bedside lamp and put some more coal and wood on the fire. Mary went into the bathroom and began to run a bath, adding some bath foam as the water ran which filled the tub with lovely fluffy bubbles. Richard came and sat on the edge of the bath as Mary immersed herself in the foam then he took the soap and gently began to wash her, letting his hand linger as it slid across the breasts which he had lathered.

'This is my idea of heaven,' said Mary.

'Mine would be to come in the bath with you.'

'It would be a bit of a tight squeeze. . .'

'. . . but great fun.'

She sat up to make room for him and then with much giggling they proceeded to soap each other, interspersed with equally soapy kisses.

'It must be nearly time for dinner and I am really hungry.'

They were both dresssed and quite respectable again when they heard the gong for dinner. Mrs Williams always had a lady from the village to help serve the evening meal while she dished up in the kitchen. She was an excellent cook but tonight Mary and Richard would have eaten anything which was put before them. Later, when she brought them some coffee to have in the sitting room, Richard thanked her for lighting the bedroom fire and said how lovely it was to have it burning.

'I was worried that the chimney might smoke or it might blow back with all the wind, but there was not the slightest problem. As you had said how much you liked it when you were a boy, I thought it would be a treat for you on a rough night like this.'

'You really are spoiling us.'

'It's a pleasure when it's appreciated and I do want you to have a good holiday here.'

Mary and Richard went up to their room early.

'I'm dying to get into that four poster bed,' said Mary. 'I've never been in one before. Did you draw the curtains round?'

'No I wasn't sure if they were functional or just for show.'

It was not long before they climbed into the grand bed and snuggled down together.

There was so much to say and yet so much that did not need to be said.

'Ricky, I came because I cannot bear to see you becoming so unhappy.'

'I'm certainly not unhappy right now. I don't think I can look back on a moment in my life when I feel as contented as I do lying in your arms in this great big bed.'

'You and Anna have tried to make your marriage into something good but the stresses within it are becoming very overt, even Claire is referring to them when she comes to stay with me.'

'I don't in any way want to criticise Anna because she continues to be a person of great integrity and one who never thinks or says anything ill of anyone. I am also fond of her and admire her greatly. What I find difficult to come to terms with and now almost unable to cope with is her driving ambition to get to the top. I was convinced that when she got the Chair at Oxford that was it, but it isn't. She has far more ambitions yet to be fulfilled and I have lost the will to both support her and to encourage her. I want a home, a family, a job I like doing and peace to potter along in. She must find me an incredible stick-in-the mud.'

'What we may never know is how much our relationship has caused Anna to throw herself so much into her work.'

Richard was quiet as he reflected upon what Mary had said.

'We deliberately kept apart; we didn't let our affection develop.'

'But we were not successful in hiding the fact that we did love each other and Anna has known this for a long time. She trusted us because she knew we all believed that a marriage is for life.'

'I cannot hold to that any longer. It is making too many people miserable. It's all very well being sanctimonious about making vows for ever but that makes no allowances for changes in the situation. Anna is not happy, you are not, I am not and Claire is feeling the effects of everyone's unhappiness.'

They woke on the Wednesday morning knowing that they had two more days together before Richard would have to leave to go down to Cornwall to pick up Claire. The wind was still blowing and when Richard drew back the curtains he could see that it was raining quite hard.

'The weather is not good; how about spending the day in bed?'

'What a lovely idea, but who is going to explain that to Mrs Williams?'

'Perhaps it would be easier to get up, but not just yet.'

'Do things seem different in the cold light of day?'

Richard looked at Mary.

'That is an odd thing to say.'

'I wondered if you might be having second thoughts about what has happened.'

'What a funny lass you are. After spending the most memorable night sharing a bed with my dearest friend she asks me if I am thinking differently about things.'

'We can spend two more days together and then we have to go back and pick up where we left off.'

'I don't think we can. I certainly cannot. I know that with you I find what must be the nearest thing to perfect happiness and I'm not going to give that up again.'

'I'm not making any demands upon you; I need you as much as you need me, perhaps even more so but I am not asking anything of you. 'You are not free to live with me; the most we can have is the odd few days together.'

'I don't think that is enough for us both. We have tried to keep apart and the pain it has caused has been very great. I want to be with you all the time, not just for snatched weekends.'

'Ricky, my darling. You know that I love you and that I want to share all your life. The matter that we are ducking talking about is that you are a married man and not able to do what we want.'

'If I am not free to marry you would you ever consider living with me?'

'I don't know; I just do not know. For both of us that means abandoning so many principles in which we have always said that we believe. And nobody can do that on the spur of the moment.'

173

'It would not be on the spur of the moment. For something approaching twelve years I have reflected upon the dilemma. Until yesterday I could not be sure that you would take any risks. Now I know that you love me enough to flout the conventions of society. . .'

'. . . or to lay aside everything that we have held to as practising Christians.'

They lay in each other's arms with the rain lashing down on the window outside.

'Let's just enjoy the time we have together now and later give some more thought to the future. Whatever that future holds there are certainly going to be problems and pain in it.'

'That sounds terribly dismal.'

'No, just the reality of life.'

They got dressed and down for breakfast in about five minutes when they suddenly realised what the time was. Mrs Williams never rang the gong for breakfast, believing that if people were on holiday and wanted to have a lie in it did not really matter to her when she cooked the meal. She always had plenty of other jobs with which to be getting on. Despite the weather they decided that they would take a packed lunch and go walking for the day. It was something to do with them both being geographers that every opportunity to be out in the countryside was seized upon. They also knew that they had lovely warm accommodation to come back to if they got wet through, although that was unlikely because they both had oilskins and strong walking boots.

As it was the morning remained wet, but in the afternoon the weather improved and the sun came out. They had had their picnic lunch sitting in the shelter of an overhanging ledge but it had not been much protection from the elements and they had got cold when they stopped walking. Later when the rain stopped they were able to take off their waterproof trousers which made walking easier, so they were able to move more quickly and to get their circulation going.

'Do you remember the first time that we spent a day together when we went to Scotland to prepare for the field trip?'

174

'It was at this time of the year but it wasn't so cold, or perhaps it is that we are getting older and we feel the low temperatures more!'

'Come off it, we are still well on the right side of forty; we are not all that geriatric yet.'

'You know, I was a little bit anxious when we set off in Joe's car because I did not think that I knew you very well, and I was sure that as you were a specialist in physical geography and at least two years senior to me I should not know enough to be able to contribute.'

'And I was worried because there was I having to walk across rough terrain with this fanatical rugby player who was bound to be incredibly fit and I was sure that I would not be able to keep up with the pace.'

'Do you know what it was that made me first feel very relaxed with you?'

'Tell me.'

'It was the way you drove the car. There are all these sick jokes about women drivers and then when it was your turn to take the wheel you were really superb in that you didn't hang around but your anticipation and control was really good. I felt safe with you then. . . and I suppose I have never lost that feeling.'

'You rarely drive with me.'

'I didn't mean just driving; I think I meant that I'd trust you with anything that I said or did.'

As the following day was Maundy Thursday they decided that they would come back from their walk earlier and then get changed and go to the evening service in St David's Cathedral. The small cathedral, so magnificently situated at the western tip of Wales, supported a fine choir, mostly drawn from the local community. There was not a particularly large congregation at this mid-week service but the singing was beautiful. Richard had rarely had the opportunity to go to church with Mary and as she knelt beside him, or as she stood beside him singing in her lovely soprano voice, he found difficulty in differentiating who it was he was worshipping. Perhaps it was that the love of one led to a closer relationship with the other. He held her hand at any time in the service when they were sitting, and as he walked behind her to the altar to receive communion he momentarily put his hand round her waist to guide her. She half turned and gave him a smile. When he knelt to receive the bread and wine he found himself praying, 'Oh God, what are we to do?'

Mrs Williams had not minded serving dinner later that night, especially as they were the only guests who were staying, but if there had been other people there she said she would have put their meal in the oven to keep hot for them. They sat longer in front of the sitting room fire drinking their coffee and when she came to take the tray away Mrs Williams stayed and talked to them about farming in this part of Wales and how they had had to resort to the tourist trade to make the farm viable. By the time they went up to their room it was getting quite late.

'I'm beginning to feel really sad because this is our last night.'

'It's only our last night together staying here in Wales; it's only our last night until we can sort out what we are going to do.'

'What are we going to do?'

'Come on, let's get undressed and get into bed and talk about it.'

All the inhibitions which Mary thought she had about taking her clothes off when Richard was with her had disappeared at least two days ago. They were both totally relaxed and comfortable with each other, no matter what they were doing.

'I know that the first thing that I have got to do is talk to Anna.'

'What will you tell her?'

'What she already knows – that I love you and that I want to live with you at least for part of the time.'

'Don't you think that might be an untenable compromise?'

'Mary, I asked you two days ago if you would live with me. Have you thought any more about it? You said that it couldn't be a snap decision but, well, have you given it any thought?'

'I am struggling very hard with this. I love you so much and want to be with you as much as is possible. I've no qualms any more about what people might think, other than Anna and Claire.'

'Don't you think they might come to understand?'

'Anna needs you as much as I do and she has a greater right to you. You are her husband.'

'We got married when we were very young and it may have been a mistake.'

'Who is to judge that? I've told you before about believing in predestination and that there is a reason for everything. It could be argued that it was predestined that you would meet Anna before me and that you and she were to marry. . .'

'. . . but that is allowing man no free will; I can't believe that you subscribe to such fundamentalist thinking.'

She laughed.

'No, you are right. I'm totally confused about everything but what I have learned from the last decade is that I am not going to fall out of love with you, nor you with me, and I don't think we have been entirely selfish in this because we have tried to avoid being with each other.'

'I shall talk to Anna about getting a divorce.'

'But none of us believes in divorce.'

'Then we are all going to have to compromise our beliefs.'

'That is easier said than done.'

'We are going round in circles and we are not going to get any further tonight. We can always have this conversation driving along in a car but it isn't often that I am lying in bed naked with the woman I love and right now I don't want to waste time talking.'

She drew him to her as he began to kiss her. She just ached for this man to make love to her and as her body pressed against his she felt him respond to her need and her love for him.

12

All the way down to Cornwall Richard thought about what he could do. He wondered if he should discuss the problem with his father, yet he was sure that his father, as the priest who had married Anna and him, would argue the case for 'keeping unto each other so long as both shall live'.

'It would be so much easier if we all had no Faith, no respect for each other and had made no marriage vows.'

There was also Claire to think about. She was now twelve, and although she was a very independent youngster she did need to have a secure base. He knew that she loved Mary, probably as much as she did Anna, but that might change if she were to know that her father and Mary were lovers. She seemed to have coped well with her somewhat unusual upbringing but he had always ensured that she had a home and that there was always somebody there.

There were jobs to be thought about too. Both he and Mary were Heads of Department in their respective schools, which were about fifty miles apart. Anna was now fully established in her new appointment in Oxford, which was a further seventy miles east, and she was keen for the family to move to Oxford; Richard was equally determined that he would not.

He knew that he would have to talk to Anna but he could not anticipate how she would respond. It had been she who had suggested that he went away in the first place, it was she who had mentioned staying at Mary's home as a possible place, but had she done this with complete naïveté about the risks that might ensue? She was a woman of great intelligence, one of the country's youngest professors, and yet in her understanding of human nature there might be an unrealistic deficiency.

Claire had had a very happy week in Cornwall. She enjoyed it more when the cousins were there and they seemed to be allowed much more freedom in the rectory than Richard could ever remember that he and his siblings had had. When he had once mentioned this to his mother she had smiled and said that, at the end of the day, the responsibility for the grandchildren's behaviour was with their parents, and she could spoil them for a week and then let them go home to be sorted out! He stayed the night and then he and Claire returned to Wiltshire for the rest of Easter weekend and to be with Anna, whom they had not seen for a fortnight. They had telephoned Anna on the Friday evening. She had just come in, having spent most of the week in Oxford, but she expected to be at home for a few days. She enquired if they had both enjoyed their respective holidays and asked Richard if Mary had been in touch. That was the question which Richard knew would be coming and which he was not sure how to respond to on the telephone. He just said that she had and he would tell her about things when they got back.

Richard and Claire reached home during the afternoon. Anna had been out to do the shopping and Mrs Maidment had done some baking for them. She had made them a simnel cake with eleven marzipan balls on the top.

'Do you think Mrs Maidment got muddled and miscounted her little balls?' asked Claire.

'No, she has the right number. There are supposed to be eleven to represent the disciples who were left after one of them had betrayed Jesus. I only know that because Gran used to make us a big simnel cake every Easter and she always made that number of little balls for the top.'

'I don't think she made a cake this year.'

'As there is only going to be her and Grandad at home tomorrow she probably thought it was better for their figures not to be eating cake.'

'The rectory is a big house for them when they are on their own.'

'Yes it is, but it goes with the job. I'm not sure that the next incumbent will want a house as big as that and the diocese may be forced to consider selling it and providing a much smaller house for the rector.'

'It would be a pity because big houses are fun.'

'They are also expensive to maintain and hard work to run.'

'Dad, you really are getting to be an old stick-in-the-mud.'

It was chilly that evening and although the central heating was on Richard lit the fire in the sitting room.

'I wouldn't have bothered,' said Anna, 'but it is nice to have a fire once in a while, even if it does make extra work.'

Anna showed signs of preparing to go to her study to work after Claire had gone up to bed.

'Do you have to work tonight?'

'Not if there are other things to be done.'

'I think we must talk.'

'I see.'

Richard hesitated and Anna waited. She had some idea about what might be coming but she was not going to help him.

'Mary did get in touch with me as you suggested, but not in the way that you thought she was going to. She did not phone me but came down to St Davids to find me.'

'That would not be difficult since you had sent the telephone number of the place where you were staying.'

'I only sent it to you. I did not give it to Mary or to anyone else in the family when I wrote the postcards to them.'

'Did Mary coming down help to make things better?'

He paused before replying; it seemed such a loaded question.

'In one way it did make things better and in another it made things worse.'

Anna remained silent.

'Mary stayed at the farm with me until I left yesterday to go and collect Claire. We shared a room.'

'Did Mary sleep with you?'

'Yes.'

'Have you and Mary slept together before?'

'Once, seven or eight years ago, and that was the reason why Mary moved back to Wales. We have tried not to let this thing develop, believe me, we really have.'

Anna looked pale and she was quite clearly shaken by what she had heard.

'What do you want to do?'

'I don't know. No, that is not true, I do know what I would like to do but that is not going to be possible.'

'You want to marry Mary.'

'Yes, but I'm not free to marry her.'

'I know that I must be partly responsible for this because I have not been a very good wife to you in that I have not enjoyed the physical side of our relationship, not really since Claire was born. But I do love you in every other sense of the word and I do not want to be divorced from you. I think Claire would find it difficult if we were to part but she is old enough to understand.'

'Has the fact that you knew I loved Mary contributed to you working so hard at your career?'

'I don't know. It is something deep inside me which makes me work hard. I certainly don't think there was any conscious sublimation of energy or whatever the jargon for this might be. But I did trust you and Mary and never believed that you would become lovers. That is the hardest thing to cope with – the personal acknowledgement that I have failed you in bed and you have gone elsewhere.'

'That sounds a bit crude.'

'I'm sorry, I didn't mean it to be. I thought of Mary as one of my best friends and I really am finding this very hard to contend with. What does Mary want?'

'She doesn't want anyone to be hurt and she doesn't want us to get divorced. She has tried to be faithful to your friendship, and in a way you have not made it easy for her because you continued to invite her over and even suggested that I went to stay with her.'

'I was trying to make you feel happier.'

'Anna, I don't know about our future but what I do know is that I love Mary and that she loves me and that we will have to spend time together. You are away from home a lot and we could see each other surreptitiously but I'm not very good at being dishonest and you would find out sooner or later.'

'I don't know what is worse, to be told that you are going to spend the weekend with Mary or for me to find out accidentally. Oh God, what a mess it all is.'

'I'm sorry.'

'Stop saying you are sorry. Are you apologising for falling in love with another woman or are you saying that you are sorry I find it such a mess?'

'You do find me a bit of a disappointment as a husband. I don't match up to your colleagues when it comes to intellectual discussion. I have little ambition other than once I would have liked to play rugby for England and that went out of the window at a very early age.'

'Had you not married me, that ambition might have been realised.'

'Who knows what might have been? If I had not married you I would never have applied for a teaching post in London and then I would not have met Mary.'

There was nothing more to be said at that point in time. Next morning was Easter Day and for the festivals in the church Anna would usually go with them. The choir was going to perform a special anthem that morning and Claire was going to sing one of the solo parts. They had rehearsed this anthem for several weeks and had had an extra rehearsal the previous evening, mostly because Claire had been away and the choir master thought it would be good for all the choir to have a final run through the music for the following day.

When Anna came into the kitchen next morning she looked awful.

'You didn't sleep much I suppose?'

'No, did you?'

'Not really.'

'I don't think I am going to come to church this morning. I know Claire is singing a solo but I just do not think I can face the world.'

'She will be terribly disappointed. It would have been the first time for ages that you would have been able to go and hear her sing. If I were to stay at home would you be able to go?'

182

'Don't be silly; it's not a problem about being with you – it's – well, I think I might start to weep.'

'What will you tell Claire?'

'I will probably say that I do not feel well, which is true.'

'Perhaps you should go back to bed and try to get some sleep.'

'Maybe that is the best thing to do. Will you explain to Claire?'

'Yes, of course. She is likely to want to come and see you.'

'That will be all right; if I'm in bed it will be so unusual that she is bound to think that I am ill.'

'Anna, I am sorry about causing all this pain. . .'

'Stop apologising, will you; it makes it worse.'

The church bells were ringing and Richard had to shout upstairs to see if Claire was ready.

'Coming,' she called.

'Have you got any collection?'

'No, can you lend me some?'

'Lend or give?'

'Give, I expect. Is Mummy ready?'

'She is not feeling well this morning so she has gone back to bed.'

'She won't hear the anthem then. I'll go up and see her.'

'Claire, it is getting late. I am going to start walking down to the church. If you go up to see Mummy you are going to have to really get your skates on.'

She rushed upstairs to her mother's study and Richard set out for church. He was half way there when he heard someone running up the road behind him.

'Dad, wait for me.'

He turned and watched Claire racing up the road, her coat unbuttoned and flying in the wind and one of her socks half way down her leg.

'Mummy was asleep so I didn't say anything. Is she being sick or something?'

'No, I think she is just tired. If you race about like this you will have no puff left to sing your solo!'

'Don't worry, it's not for ages yet but I had better run on and get into my choir things or I shall be getting a rocket from you-know-who.'

With that she started to run down the road, trying to pull up her socks as she went.

He adored this child of his and there was nothing that he would not do to ensure that she was happy. But at some point she was going to have to be told what she probably knew already and tried not to believe, and that was that her parents' marriage was under extreme stress. How would she react to the knowledge that her father loved her godmother more than he loved her mother? Richard felt terrible as he reflected upon the situation. He wished that he did not have to go through the church porch and take part in an Easter Day service. It was always one of the most joyous celebrations in the church year and he had never felt less like going. He slipped into a short pew on his own hoping that nobody would need to join him because he felt very much in need of being alone. As the choir processed in to the church Claire turned to smile at him as she went down the aisle; he gave her a wink and she grinned back. They were soon all singing the opening hymn, 'Jesus Christ is Risen Today'.

In a small but packed church high up in a Welsh valley another congregation was singing the same hymn. One member of that congregation was there alone thinking back to only the previous Thursday when she had last been in church and had felt so much nearer to God than she did at the moment. She would have dearly liked not to go to church that morning but had she missed the service she would have been inundated for the rest of the day by very well meaning neighbours who would be concerned for her health. She had not heard from Richard since she got back. She could not stop thinking about him and wondering if he had spoken with Anna. She had tried hard to pray; it had not been easy.

Richard and Claire cooked the lunch together and Anna got up to have some with them. She did not eat much but she seemed better. In the afternoon they went for a walk and behaved as any other family, although both Anna and Richard were ill at ease with each other. On the Monday Richard had promised that he would help with getting the pitch ready for the cricket season and Claire was going for a cycle ride with some of her friends. Anna planned to use the time to get on with some work.

'Nothing really changes very much,' she thought, but in her heart she knew that a lot had changed. Whatever suspicions about Richard and Mary she could have had in the past she chose to blank out of her mind completely, always believing the best about anyone. Now she could do that no longer because she had been told by Richard the truth about that relationship. She wondered if she might be able to convince herself that if she did not have any domestic ties at all she would be able to concentrate a hundred per cent upon her research. But what about Claire in all this? She knew that Claire was close to Mary but could she actually bear for Mary to take over her daughter as well as her husband? She doubted very much that she could.

'If I'm not careful I am going to let this interfere with my work. I must put it to the back of my mind and concentrate on the research which my team is doing. It won't be the end of the world, I suppose, if Richard goes to spend the odd weekend with Mary, or will it?'

That was a question that she determined not to try to answer.

While Richard cut the grass he decided that he would not commit himself to playing for the first eleven this season. It tied him too much at the weekends. He would play for the seconds when they were short and he was available. When he had done his fair share of the tasks he went home. Anna was in her study and Claire was still out. He sat down and wrote a long letter to Mary. For somebody who had the reputation for being a poor letter writer he was surprised at how easy he found it to convey all that he felt and to describe what had happened since he had left Mary at the farmhouse in St Davids. His letter to Mary crossed with one from her to him. She made no attempt to disguise her writing or to try to conceal from Anna the fact that she had written to Richard. As it was, the post came after Anna had gone to Oxford so she did not see it. Richard did telephone Mary when he was alone. They did not find it easy to speak to each other on the phone. He tried to arrange to see her but it would depend upon Anna being available to look after Claire or taking Claire with him. It was not going to be easy to organise a much more complicated life. Perhaps he would have to tell Claire about him and Mary but first he must check this out with Anna. He found that he was missing Mary terribly and he was not sure that he was going to be able to cope with only seeing her occasionally. Sooner, rather than later, he was going to have to force the issue of his and Anna's future life and not let things just drift along as it seemed they were beginning to do. The question was how to do it.

Richard had a busy term ahead of him when he returned to school. Apart from all the final preparations for pupils taking public examinations he was heavily involved in coaching cricket. He had always enjoyed the summer term, even though it was a hectic one, but this year he went back to school feeling very lacking in enthusiasm for the job. Claire, on the other hand, was very excited when the first day of term came. She mostly chose to go on the school bus with her friends, rather than travel with her father in the car, and on that first morning she was there early at the bus stop. This was the term that she was going to start playing tennis seriously and with Wimbledon firmly in her mind she had determined that this was the sport in which she was going to excel. She had a natural aptitude for all ball games and had shown promise playing hockey and netball during the winter, but it was the summer games that she was really looking forward to and it was nearly all to do with the attraction of the tennis courts.

Anna took very little leave from her research and although, as professor, she was required to give the occasional lectures to the undergraduate students, the Oxford terms were so short she never thought in terms as did the rest of the family. She had only one trip abroad arranged for that summer and it was to a scientific conference in Japan which would be for a week in June. When this had been arranged she had toyed with the idea of extending her time in the Far East and going to New Zealand to see Margaret. After the events at Easter she decided that the week at the conference was a long as she would wish to be away. There was also the further factor of still being involved in establishing her research team and wanting to be closely associated with this in the early months.

The dilemma for her was how much time should she be spending at home. When she was in Oxford and very immersed in her work the so-called domestic problems faded into the background. She realised now that what she had originally thought would be a very convenient arrangement, in that the family would all move to be near to Oxford, would not now happen. She would still have the drive of seventy miles each way or she would stay up in her rooms and only go home at the weekends. What was the more important demand upon her time? What was she trying to achieve by being at home more? Was she thinking about Claire's needs or was she trying too late to shore up a deteriorating marriage? Had she been totally selfish or did she have a responsibility to use the talents which she had been given? Rather than mull over these unanswerable questions Anna found it easier to put all her energy into her work and let things at home drift along. That had been her pattern of operating for many years but it was not likely to be a strategy which would work for much longer. She was not making allowances for the fact that Richard had changed.

'We are going to have to tell Claire,' said Richard to Anna when she came home that weekend.

'What do you propose to tell her?'

'She must suspect that all is not well between us because she does ask difficult questions at times.'

'That doesn't answer my question; what is she to be told?'

'I think that she needs to know that I. . . that we. . . that Mary and I. . .'

'. . . she knows all that. She has been involved in this triangle of relationships all her life.'

'Things are different now.'

'Well are they? All that is different is that you have told me about what has happened.'

'Don't you believe me when I tell you that until the week before Easter Mary and I did not let things happen?'

'Yes I do believe you. . .'

'What is different is that they are going to go on happening and that it will affect Claire very much.'

'Are you going to go away with Mary again?'

'I don't know but I do have to spend time with her and Claire has to be given credit for being adult enough to realise that the visiting is not just being sociable geographers.'

'I've dreaded this moment. I hoped if we ignored what had occurred the problem might go away. . .'

'. . . for an intelligent woman you say the most incredible things at times.'

'I'm only intelligent about things scientific; I'm out of my depth in this sort of thing. I don't know what to say, I don't know what to do and I desperately wish that nothing had changed the way life was before. But you could say to me that I did not invest enough effort into preserving the status quo.'

'If you would prefer it I will talk to Claire when I am on my own with her.'

'What will you say?'

'I will tell her that I have fallen in love with Mary and that I have made you very unhappy by doing so.'

It was important that Richard chose very carefully the moment for telling Claire and as there was no immediate rush to do so he could wait until the time seemed right. One evening Claire had stayed late at school to play tennis and had arranged with Richard that she would travel home with him. In a car it is often easier to have a difficult conversation. The passenger and driver are sitting side by side and not looking at each other; there is no possibility for one of them to walk out of the conversation, unless the car stops and often the sound of the engine takes the edge off the harshness of some dialogue. As they drove home that evening Richard began to talk about him and Mary.

'When I went to Pembrokeshire before Easter I spent some time with Mary. She and I stayed at the same farmhouse.'

'You told me and Gran that you were going to have some time on your own and that you were doing some preparations for a field class.'

'That was true. I did not know that Mary was going to come.'

'She must have known where to find you.'

'Mummy had my telephone number and she gave it to

Mary.'

'What's this all about? It's no big deal if you and Mary end up in a farmhouse in Wales is it?'

It was harder than Richard had thought it would be.

'What I am trying to say is that Mary and I are very fond of each other. . .'

'I know that; everybody knows that.'

'We love each other and I am going to spend more time with Mary.'

Claire was suddenly very quiet. What perhaps she had suspected and had not wanted to know she had now been told. Had she heard correctly? Had her father said that he loved Mary? She did not think she wanted to know about this. She turned her head and looked out of the car window.

'Claire, I really am sorry that I am having to tell you about this but I decided that you do need to know.'

'Does Mummy know?'

'Yes.'

'What is going to happen?'

'I don't know yet. Mummy is very sad about things.'

'Is that why she said she was ill and didn't come to hear the anthem when she had promised that she would?'

'Yes, that was part of the reason, but she was feeling very tired.'

There was a long pause.

'What is going to happen to me?' Richard pulled into a layby and switched off the engine.

'Claire, darling, nothing is going to happen to you. If I go to see Mary in Wales you can come just as you always have or you can stay with Mummy if you want to.'

He put his arms around her and she began to cry.

'I'm sorry Claire; I didn't want to make you sad but I thought you ought to know. Perhaps I was wrong.'

'Does Gran knows?'

'No nobody else knows.'

'What shall I say to people?'

'Do you need to say anything?'

'I suppose not. What shall I say to Mummy?'

'I'll leave that to you, Claire.'

'Are you going to get divorced?'

'I don't think so.'

'What are you going to do?'

'I don't know. I am going to stay with Mary next weekend; will you come too?'

Claire did not answer and he did not push the issue. He started the engine and they drove the rest of the way home in silence. As he glanced sideways at the tear-stained little face he felt wretched that he had caused her so much grief. Would it have been better if he had not said anything to Claire? Was she really too young to be burdened with adult problems? Would it have been easier had he not said anything to either Anna or Claire? When they got home Claire went to her room to do her homework and he got some tea ready. She came when he called her but she did not eat very much and it was in silence. She helped clear up and then she went back to her homework.

Richard drove to Wales the following Friday evening on his own. Claire had said very little to him since the conversation in the car and his attempts to communicate with her had been met with monosyllabic replies. Anna had detected that there was an atmosphere between them and had assumed that Richard had done the telling which he seemed so insistent should be done. He told her that he was going to Wales the following weekend and that he was very happy for Claire to go with him if she would like to but Anna said that she would be home for most of the weekend. Claire said that she would stay at home and that she did not want to go to Oxford with her mother on the Saturday.

'I'm only going for the morning,' said Anna.

'I've got things I want to do at home,' replied Claire.

Anna found it extremely difficult to analyse her feelings about Richard going to see Mary. It had not been very many weeks ago when she herself had suggested that he did this self-same thing, but then she had not known as much as she now did. It was completely alien to Anna's nature to be sarcastic but she did have to struggle very hard to remain rational and to be civil with Richard.

'What do other women do when their husbands so blatantly go off to visit another woman?' she thought and then, because that seemed such a degrading view to hold about Richard and Mary, she tried to dismiss the thought from her mind.

'I know I am feeling jealous and angry and I don't like myself for being like this. I must not do or say anything which will make matters worse or influence Claire.'

In the end Anna did not go to Oxford on the Saturday but stayed at home and worked in her study. She and Claire had their meals together but neither of them mentioned Richard or the reason for his absence.

He reached Mary's house just after nine o'clock. It was a beautiful warm early summer evening and she was in the garden when he arrived. He was not sure if it was the done thing for him to kiss her in full view of the neighbours but Mary had no qualms about doing so.

'They have seen you here before and I only gave you a sisterly kiss,' she said when he commented upon the neighbours' likely interest.

'Now that we are inside is it all right if I behave in a very unbrotherly way?'

She laughed.

'If your car remains parked outside for the weekend there may be some interest in the nature of the relationship and supposition that it is more than familial. Don't worry about it.'

It was five weeks since they had seen each other and for each of them it had been a difficult time, not just because they had been apart but because each of them was struggling to come to terms with the effect that their relationship was having upon Anna and Claire. Opportunities to speak to each other on the telephone were few and Richard had not really been able to share with Mary how things were at home since he had told Anna. Over supper he told her. The worst thing had been that Anna did not rant and rave but had been genuinely upset and had taken a large part of the blame for what had happened onto her own shoulders. She did not want the marriage to end but recognised that it was probably impossible to retrieve their earlier happiness.

'And what about you in all this, Ricky?'

'I feel bad about making Anna and Claire unhappy but I cannot contemplate a future in which you do not feature greatly. I love you in a way that I have never loved anyone

191

and because of that I am very determined that we are going to make some life together.'

'No doubts, no second thoughts?'

'None. What about you?'

'It's so much easier for me; I'm not in the middle, but I can't let you go now. After all it was I who came chasing after you to St Davids!'

It was a weekend of sharing the preparation of meals, doing the washing up together, pottering in the garden, going for walks in the Black Mountains and retiring early to bed. They did not go to church and avoided situations where they would meet people, solely because they had so little time together that they could not bear to have to share it with others. It was a very happy two days but the latter part of it was overshadowed by the fact that it was coming to an end.

'Next month is when Anna goes to Japan. Would you like to come and stay with us?'

'I don't think that would be kind to Anna, for me to wait until her back is turned and then come to Wiltshire; it is a bit different if you come here. Do you think Claire would like to come as well?'

'I'm not sure. She has taken this harder than I thought she would. She is so fond of you that I did not anticipate that she would behave in this way.'

'Give her time. She is moving into adolescence now and having to come to terms with many aspects of sexuality. Perhaps it might help if I were to telephone her sometime, or maybe write to her.'

A few days later Mary telephoned Claire and they had a long conversation together. When she came off the phone Claire looked much happier. Richard did not question her nor did she volunteer any information, but she subsequently became much more amicable with him. Later Mary was to tell him that Claire had said that she would come over to Wales to stay when next he visited Mary.

Anna left for Japan on the Wednesday, knowing that the following weekend both Richard and Claire were going to stay at Mary's house. They left as soon as school finished on the Friday afternoon and were at Mary's house before six o'clock.

192

'Come on,' said Mary 'I've made us a picnic supper. Lets go down to Rhossili Bay for a swim.'

Despite it being a warm evening there were few people on the beach and none in the sea.

'They are all wise, the water will be cold.'

It was. They paddled first of all and then when their bodies got slightly more acclimatised to the cold they went further out. Richard believed in rushing in so that he did not have time to think how cold it was. Mary preferred to go very slowly and gradually adjust to the low temperature. Claire could not decide which way was better but in the end kept with Mary. None of them stayed in long and then they had a game of 'catch' to get warmed up.

'I've remembered to put some matches in the basket so if we gather up some drift wood we can light a fire. It will keep the midges at bay if it doesn't do anything else.'

Claire and Mary gathered the wood while Richard blew on the little flames in his pile of kindling and got the fire going. They spread their wet swimming things on some stones near the fire. Mary had had a spare costume for Claire, but Richard had had to go in the sea in his pants. Then they sat on the up wind side of their fire, which was proving to be rather smoky, and had their picnic. Mary told Claire about the time that she and Richard had taken her to the sea and she had found the crab which she had been very loath to leave on the beach and how they had had to travel back to London with lots of pieces of seaweed in the car.

'I can't remember that at all; how old would I have been?'

'You were not three and children are not supposed to remember things which happened to them before that age.'

'Did Mummy come?'

'No she had gone to America for a conference.'

'Same old story.'

'Don't be like that, Claire.'

'I'm sorry.'

She did not say any more and after a while she wandered up the beach picking up shells.

'I think I had better go after her and see if she is all right,' said Richard.

'I wouldn't if I were you. She will be much better if she is left on her own for a while. She will come back when she is ready.'

Mary was right. Claire had found some echinoderms and she brought them back to show them. Mary was quite knowledgeable about these shells and the three of them went along the high water mark together searching for some more. It was quite late when they left the shore and drove home.

While Claire was having a bath Mary made them all a hot drink and then she took Claire's up to her. She waited until Claire came out of the bathroom and then she sat on the end of the bed while Claire drank her hot chocolate.

'It was a nice evening on the beach, Mary. Thank you for suggesting it. When I went for that walk on my own I was thinking that some of the best times I have had have been with you and Dad, although I have had fun when I've been down to stay with Gran and Grandad.'

'I could say the same. That day when we took you to the south coast which we were recounting to you this evening was a really happy day. We built a massive sandcastle and miles of water courses linking it with the sea.'

'Dad told me about you and him.'

'Yes, I know he did. It has not been easy for you and we both understand that.'

'It's not that I don't like you. . .'

'I know that, Claire; it is that you are concerned about Mummy and her being upset about things.'

'. . . and what is going to happen to me. If Dad and Mummy split up, where am I going to live?'

'I don't think any of us knows the answer to any of those questions but there is one thing which I want to say and can say. Whenever Dad comes here to see me I want you to know that I would always want you to come as well. You have always been a very special person to me and that is not just because you are my godchild.'

'Are you and Dad going to sleep together tonight?'

'Yes.'

Claire was silent.

'Is that the worst part of it for you, Claire?'

'I don't know. When my friends at school used to talk about what they knew adults did in bed I used to be scared in case they asked me about things at home. I can't remember Mummy and Dad sleeping together for ages and ages. I don't know what is worse, them not sleeping together or you two. . . doing it.'

Mary moved up the side of the bed and put her arms around Claire and held her tightly. She felt Claire relax against her and then she kissed her and said good night.

'Have you got something to read in bed?'

'I'm not going to read; I'm going to lie down and think about things.'

'Think? Not worry?'

'Just think. Good night.'

When Mary went downstairs she left the door of Claire's room ajar; when she came back up to go to bed the door was closed. She bathed and got into bed waiting for Richard to join her. He had asked if everything was all right with Claire and had been told that it was getting easier for her but he must be patient. When he came up he sat on the edge of the bed.

'Do you think we should sleep together when Claire is here?'

'She asked me if we were going to and I said yes.'

He smiled down at her. 'You are a wonderful person; have I ever told you that?'

'Hurry up and come to bed.'

It was a warm night but neither of them would have worn night clothes had it not been. As Richard got into bed and put his arms around Mary he whispered to her that he loved her.

'You don't have to speak quite so quietly. The walls here are fairly substantial and I like to hear what you are saying!'

'Do you find it difficult having Claire here as well?'

'Ricky, you know that I love Claire dearly and whatever future we have together must involve Claire. I'm saying that, not because she is your daughter but because I want it that way. However, Claire may have difficulty in accepting that we are lovers and she must be free to make her own choices.'

'You are so good at understanding the mind of a child.'

'She is nearly a teenager, you must remember that she is growing up.'

They woke in the morning to find that it was quite late.

195

Claire had apparently been up for some time and had been for a walk through the village. They had a big breakfast and then went for a long walk in the hills. That evening they had a barbecue in the garden.

Next morning Richard and Mary were up, dressed and having some toast and coffee when Claire came down.

'Hi folks,' she said. 'What's on the agenda for today? Don't tell me – it's church, church and more church.'

They all laughed.

'What would you like to do?'

'Let's give church a miss.'

'OK. What's the alternative?'

'Is there time for us to go down to St Davids?'

'Yes, but why? It's quite a long drive from here.'

'Well, if not today, will you take me there sometime?'

'Of course we will, but is there any particular reason?'

'I'd just like to see it.'

Mary intervened.

'If we get ready and leave soon we have plenty of time to go there today. We'll take my car and I will drive because you have a bit of driving to do when we get back and you have to drive home.'

While Claire had some breakfast, Mary packed up the food and Richard went round tidying up, making beds and loading what they might need into the car. Within fifteen minutes they were on the road.

It was a glorious day in St Davids, so different to how the weather had been during Easter week. It was also much more crowded, with many more summer visitors thronging the place. They took their picnic out on to cliff walk and stretched out in the sun.

'Is it as you expected it to be, Claire?'

'No, I thought it would be different. I didn't think there would be so many people here.'

They went for a walk by the sea. When Claire had wandered far out of earshot Richard asked Mary if she had any idea why Claire had wanted specifically to come here. She said that she had not but it had seemed to be very important to Claire.

'Perhaps we shall never know and it doesn't really matter if we don't; we have had a lovely day out.'

☆ ☆ ☆

Anna had not particularly enjoyed her trip to Japan and was surprised by this because it was the first time that she had been there. Usually when she went to a new country she found the experience stimulating, regardless of the quality of input to the conference.

'Perhaps the overseas travel is beginning to pall with anno domini,' she thought, 'or maybe I'm wanting to put some roots down in Oxford.'

But she knew the value of maintaining contact with the international scientific scene was immense and that she would continue to travel as was needed. She landed at Heathrow on the Thursday evening and went straight to Oxford to deal with her post and any other urgent matters. Later in the evening she telephoned home and spoke to Richard. Claire had gone to her Guide meeting and had not yet come home.

'Isn't she a bit late?' queried Anna.

'Well, now you mention it, I suppose that she is, but the evenings are very light and she does like to talk with her friends; I think she finds life at home with me rather dull, you know.'

'Are you having a dig at me?'

'No, of course not. I'm just stating a fact and offering an explanation for Claire not being here. She will be sorry to have missed you.'

'I shall be home tomorrow night.'

'How was Japan?'

'It was quite a good conference, but it is nice to be back.'

13

As a family Anna, Richard and Claire had had few holidays together. In the early years they went to Cornwall because it was all they could afford and they were fortunate that their relatives lived in a beautiful county with miles of coastline. Anna had taken them to Europe after her Australian journey and they had had two weeks in America while Anna was working out there. As Anna became more and more immersed in her career she did not feel the need to take long holidays. She could never just relax on the beach and do nothing. When they had been in Cornwall and had gone to the beach for the day, Anna would always take one of her scientific journals to read. She would join in games of cricket on the sands for a little while but never really enjoyed it. She did like being out in the fresh air and had always been prepared to go rambling or for an energetic walk, but that had the purpose of getting fit or being good for one, and was not deemed to be time wasting. Time was a tremendously important factor in life and its organisation and use had to be carefully monitored.

Every year as the summer holidays approached they had some sort of discussion about whether or not they should go away, and more often than not it ended up with Richard and Claire going to Cornwall and Anna joining them for perhaps a long weekend. This year the discussion did not happen. Anna was clearly going to be too busy in Oxford to want to go away.

'Mary and I are going to rent a cottage at Gairloch for two weeks during the summer,' Richard suddenly told Anna one evening.

'That presumably is in Scotland.'

'Yes, it's way up the west coast. We would like to take Claire as well but she might not want to come.'

'Have you asked her?'

'No, I wanted to tell you first.'

'I do worry about Claire in all of this.'

'We all do, but she isn't the first child to go through this sort of experience. She is struggling hard with divided loyalties.'

'We don't make it any easier for her by our attitude. I find that I cannot bring myself to have any communication with Mary although we have been friends for a long time.'

'Surely that is very understandable.'

'I am trying not to be angry, not to be jealous and not to resent bitterly what is happening and I am not having much success. At the end of the day I fear that I shall lose all three of you. . .'

'. . . you won't lose Claire; she is your daughter and she loves you too much, and I hope that whatever is going to be for us that we will always retain some sort of amicable relationship.'

'Don't you think that is completely unrealistic? Even I, who used to pride myself on being able to manage most situations, find that I am totally bewildered by what seems to be happening, and that my behaviour is unpredictable. Do you think that I like the idea of you going to Scotland for two weeks with Mary? I hate it, but I would not want to spend a fortnight isolated in that part of the country when I have other things that I need to be getting on with.'

'That has been the problem for us for many years. You have so little time to spare for the needs of us as a family.'

'If I had do you think that would have prevented you falling in love with another woman?'

'That is an impossible question.'

'I'm sorry. I do try to be. . . well I suppose the word is understanding. . . but it may be asking the impossible of me.'

Claire was going to the Guides summer camp for the first week that Richard and Mary would be in Scotland but she said that she would like to come up for the second week. Anna agreed to pick Claire up when she returned from camp, help her sort out her washing and to re-pack her things and then to put her on the train. Claire was now twelve and well able to care for herself on the journey and she would be met at the other end.

Richard and Mary set off on the Friday afternoon driving north in Mary's car, which was always a newer and more reliable vehicle than Richard ever owned. They spent the night in a small hotel near Carlisle and then set off early to complete the journey to Gairloch. It was nearly six o'clock when they arrived at the cottage, which was ideally situated overlooking the beach of Loch Gairloch. They unloaded their luggage and all the food supplies which they had brought with them and prepared some supper. Then they went for a walk along the shore. Being so far north the evenings stayed light much longer than they did in the south, and although it was after nine o'clock when they set out the sun had a long way to descend before it set. The sea was as calm as a mill pond and only the tiniest of waves were gently breaking on the shore. They had the beach to themselves and the gulls, which either screeched in the air above them or bobbed up and down on the almost still water. As the evening shadows began to lengthen they looked across the Minch to the Isle of Lewis on the distant horizon and watched as the sun began to dip down and cast a golden streak across the water.

'This must be the nearest place to Heaven that we have been in,' said Richard with his arm round Mary's shoulder. She smiled up at him.

'I feel that wherever I am with you but this is most incredibly beautiful. I think I could quite happily retire up here.'

'Think what it is like in winter when there is a force nine gale blowing and the rain is coming down in torrents.'

'Well perhaps I'll re-phrase that and suggest that I have a summer retreat up here and go back south for the winter months.'

'Shall we walk over to those rocks at the end of this bay and sit on them and watch the sun go down? You're not feeling chilly are you, darling?'

'No, I'm fine, thank you.'

They walked, on hand in hand, carrying their shoes so that they could wade at the water's edge. By the time they reached the rocks the sun was a large golden ball on the horizon just beginning to go down behind a belt of mist which separated the sea and sky. They climbed on to the rock and sat with their arms round each other, watching as the sun very quickly disappeared out of sight.

'Shall we start walking back?' Richard asked.

'In a minute or two. I've got something that I want to tell you and this seems to be the perfect setting for doing so.'

'I'm intrigued.'

'Ricky, my darling, I'm going to have a baby.'

'You are what – a baby, a baby – Mary? Oh that is wonderful but are you all right? When is the baby due; you are certain about this?'

'I am about four months pregnant and the baby is due around Christmas week. I have been to see the doctor, I've had a positive pregnancy test and when we get back from our holiday I'm due to go to the hospital to have a scan. It has also been suggested that as I am, what they call, an elderly primigravida I should have an amniocentesis test but I wanted to discuss this with you because I am not keen to have this done. I think this baby was conceived in a certain farmhouse in Wales.'

Richard knelt up on the rock and kissed Mary.

'If that was when the baby was conceived then there can be no doubt that it was a love child. If it happened on that rug in front of that bedroom fire then it is an absolutely certain fact. But have you been feeling sick and getting tired?'

'No, not at all. In fact I don't remember ever feeling better. I have been sensible about not lifting heavy things but I have exercised regularly, been swimming and generally living a normal life. I didn't want to tell you until I really was sure and when the risk of an early miscarriage was past.'

It was beginning to get dark so they started to walk back to their cottage. Richard was walking on air. He could not remember feeling so happy for a very long time, but his brain was actively working out what he was going to do. He would need to move in with Mary to look after her and everything else would have to be organised around that decision. As he thought along these lines Mary said that she did not want this pregnancy to make any more pressure for the Trevanion family. She had had plenty of time to think about how she would manage. When she went back to school she would be putting in for maternity leave and this would carry her through to the end of the school year.

'I'm coming to live with you. You need to have the baby's father around to look after you both. I can easily drive back to school each day; it's less than an hour's journey.'

'What about Claire and Anna?'

'I have not thought that through yet. The time has probably come to sell the home in Wiltshire and for Anna to get somewhere in Oxford which is what she really wants. Claire can decide where she would like to live but I hope she stays with us because Anna is away from home so much.'

'Ricky, you do realise that this baby will be born out of wedlock. That does not matter now to me, but how about you and what will your parents think? It will be particularly hard for your father because he married you and Anna and it was after him that you repeated those very solemn wedding vows.'

'How they react, how Anna behaves and what Claire thinks are small issues in this situation. This is a baby which has been conceived by two people who love each other very dearly and it is a much wanted child. Given time all those people whom you mention will adjust to the situation. Have you told your parents?'

'No of course not, silly; apart from the medical profession you are the first to know. My parents will, I think, take it all in their stride. I am, after all, thirty-nine so I believe they think that I am old enough to know what I am doing. They may be a little sad that I am not married. . .'

'. . . but we will as soon as we can.'

'That is a more complicated issue than getting pregnant!' she replied with a smile.

When they got back they made a drink while they waited for the immersion heater to warm the water.

'I shall never be able to sleep tonight,' said Richard. 'I'm much too excited.'

'That will be very unusual. After our early start this morning and all the fresh air this evening I doubt if you will be able to stay awake long enough to kiss me good night.'

'Try me and let's see who is right.'

In bed that night they could hear the sound of the sea. As they lay there Richard ran his hand over Mary's abdomen and commented on how much bigger it was.

'I never even noticed that your slim, flat tummy might not have been as sylph-like as it was.'

'It is quite a long time since we have been able to sleep together and when you last were in bed with me I was only a very few weeks pregnant.'

'You didn't let it stop us making love.'

'No, and I don't think it should at any stage in the pregnancy. Ricky, there is an aspect about this pregnancy that just troubles me a little. It could be construed that I got pregnant to hook you...'

'... but you didn't do that.'

'That is true and we both know that, but there could be a less charitable interpretation made. It could be said that we should have taken contraceptive precautions. For me that would not have been right. I veer towards the teaching of the Roman Catholic church in this matter although I guess that church, or any other for that matter, would not be too enthused about my single parent status!'

'You are not really a single parent; you have just conceived out of wedlock. This baby is going to have two parents and a half-sister, four grandparents, six uncles, and aunts and their spouses and, at the last reckoning, five cousins.'

'You don't feel trapped?'

'I do and I love it!'

'I'm not asking you to leave Anna; I'm not asking you to support me in any way. All I am doing is sharing with you the baby that belongs to both of us.'

He held her very tightly to him.

'I don't know what I have done to deserve such unselfish love from so wonderful a person. I do love you so much.'

The next morning they went to an early service in the little chapel and then they drove across the moor by Loch Tolladh and headed north along a very minor road to the west of Loch Ewe. When the track finally petered out they put on their walking boots and set off round the headland overlooking the Minch. It was quite rough walking.

'Is this going to be too much for you, Mary?'

'Are you mollycoddling me?'

'I don't want you to get overtired.'

'It is good for the baby if I exercise regularly. I am sure that this baby will be born addicted to walking judging by the amount that the parents do!'

They must have walked for about five miles when they came to a small sandy cove and here they stopped for lunch. They were both hot with walking and were glad to take off their boots and thick socks and to let the sand run between their toes.

'I wonder when man last inhabited this small corner of Scotland?'

'I doubt if many people come this way because it has been something of a trek, but isn't it worth all the effort? The view, the peace and just us two.'

'Are you recovered enough from the walk to go for a swim?'

'Yes, of course.'

'There is nobody within miles of us. We don't need to bother with swimming costumes.'

They ran naked hand in hand across the sand and plunged into the water. It was a sea warmed by the Gulf Stream but for Mary the entry into the water was much faster than her normal rate.

'You never know when somebody with binoculars might be actively bird watching and come from behind the rocks.'

'Would you mind?'

'All this skinny-dipping is hardly the behaviour of a sedate middle-aged couple!'

'Next time I shall take you swimming in the moonlight.'

'That sounds very romantic.'

'So is this,' Richard replied as he swam to her and put his arms around her and kissed her. 'Do you think we could make love in the water?'

She laughed.

'It could pose problems. Perhaps you should postpone it for the beach after the swim that you are proposing on a moonlit night!'

They ate their lunch and then stretched out in the sun to rest.

'You had better be careful about not getting burned,' said Mary. 'I'm fairly dark so I don't usually burn easily but you are so fair.'

He put on his shirt and let Mary rub some sun tan lotion on to his exposed parts.

'I'm finding this very erotic.'

'Are you objecting to my assistance?'

'No I'm just warning you.'

She screwed the lid back on to the tube and then she knelt beside his outstretched body and leant across and kissed him.

'I don't think I can ever have too much of you. You need never warn me that you are attracted to me or apologise for being aroused by me.'

He pulled her gently on top of him and drew her close.

'I hope those bird watchers are not behind the rocks because I feel very attracted to you at this moment.'

So passed the first week of their holiday. The weather was typical of the west Highlands with variations of temperature, amounts of sunshine and rainfall. Only on one morning was the rainfall too heavy for walking but within a couple of hours it had cleared up enough to go out. The sheer joy of being together, of learning more about each other and of spending that time in a most beautiful part of the world was as much as they wanted. But at the end of the week they were both looking forward to Claire joining them for the second week and what they knew they would lose in privacy in their relationship would be countermanded by Claire's company and amusing conversation.

Claire had enjoyed her train journey north, particularly as Anna had given her the money to have dinner on the train. She had never done this before and when the waiter from the restaurant car came round she took a seat for the first sitting, fearing that they might not have enough food left for a second sitting. She contemplated the menu for a long time and the waiter gave her some help in sorting out what she would like. She found the most difficult thing was to drink her soup when the train was going fast but she noticed that everyone else seemed to have the same trouble. She marvelled at how the waiters could carry trays of food and serve it as the train lurched round bends at incredible speeds. Not only did she have a good meal, it also broke the journey up for her, because it was a very long way to travel. She was glad when she arrived and found Richard and Mary on the platform waiting for her.

She had lots to tell them about the Guide camp and some things that she thought perhaps she should not mention. It was a fairly long drive to the cottage but Mary had prepared a special meal to welcome Claire and once they got back it soon was ready. They went down to the beach for a breath of sea air before Claire went to bed.

During the second week they chose more gregarious activities. They hired a boat and went fishing with herring traces and caught enough for Mary to souse for supper. One day they drove up to Ullapool and caught the ferry across to Stornaway on the Isle of Lewis. It was a long day's outing but they all loved the trip. They went to some Highland games and watched the men tossing the caber and taking part in bagpipe contests. One evening they went to a ceilidh which had probably been arranged mostly for the benefit of the tourists, but nevertheless was fun. When they stayed in for an evening they all played either Scrabble or Monopoly, both games being provided in the cottage. At the end of the week Claire rated this as one of the best holidays that she had had, and when Richard asked her if she had felt lonely without her friends she said not at all. They did not tell her about Mary's pregnancy. There were other people who needed to be informed first. They were careful not to let any hints be dropped but Richard found it hard not to be protective of Mary and she had to warn him about being too attentive. Claire seemed able to cope with the fact that Mary and her father shared a bedroom and to all intents and purposes acted as a married couple.

Anna found the situation very much harder than she had imagined she would. The most difficult thing had been putting a very excited Claire on to the train knowing that she was going to join a couple who were enjoying all the things which once were hers to enjoy and which she had chosen not to do because she wanted to have this academic career. But once Claire had left and she had gone back to her research laboratories she, as usual, let the domestic issues recede to the back of her mind. Some very significant results were being obtained by her research team and she was in charge of a programme of work which was poineering completely new methods of investigation of the medical problems caused by body stones. They were so near to achieving a very significant breakthrough in this area and she did not want anything to distract her from work at this point of time. While the family had been away she had stayed all the time in Oxford. It was so much easier to be living virtually on top of the laboratory thus making it possible to return during the evening or at the weekend to check equipment and to record results. She planned to work throughout the long vacation and had no intention of taking any leave when the research was at such an exciting stage.

She did go home the weekend that Richard and Claire returned from Scotland. As they had all driven down in Mary's car she came back to Wiltshire to drop them off. It was the first time that Anna and Mary had met since Richard had told Anna about his relationship with Mary and it was not easy for either of them. Had they not liked each other it might have been less of an ordeal but because they had been such good friends it was so much more fraught. Mary, who was always the most honest of people, hoped that Anna would not notice that she was putting on weight, yet she knew that Anna would have to be told soon about the pregnancy and that it was a bit unfair that it always had to be Richard who shouldered the reponsibility. But Mary knew that she could not face the telling, at least not just at that moment. She stayed and had a cup of tea with them but it was all very strained and the warmth of their earlier family encounters had gone.

Claire also seemed to sense the tension and she said that she was going to see Alison and went down to the village. Mary left soon afterwards. Anna had tactfully made herself scarce. Mary did not feel able to do anything other than give Richard a fleeting kiss in the hallway before they went out to the car. He did not embrace her again and it was not the way that they would have wished to end their holiday.

'I'll give you a ring as soon as I can. Now that we are on holiday it will be relatively easy to see each other. I know that I have a lot of sorting out to do.'

Anna had gone to her study, and since Claire was visiting Alison it seemed as good a time as any to tell her about the baby. Richard knocked on her door and heard a rather surprised voice say, 'Come in.'

'You don't usually knock when you come in.'

'I thought you might be busy and maybe not want to be disturbed.'

'I have got a lot to do but I don't mind you disturbing me, as you put it.'

He sat down on the spare chair in the room.

'What I am going to say I know you are not going to like and if you have a lot to do tonight it might be better if I wait until you are less busy.'

'That's not likely to be in the foreseeable future so we might as well get it over now.'

'What I have to tell you is that Mary is expecting a baby, my baby.'

Anna twiddled her pen between her fingers and looked out of the window. It was some time before she said anything and Richard remained quiet. Then she turned and looked at him.

'I am at a complete loss for words. What does one say to one's husband in situations like this? I suppose it was inevitable because you did want more children. . .'

'. . . it wasn't a planned baby but you are right in saying that it is a very much wanted baby.'

'I suppose that is the end of our marriage.'

'I want to be with Mary and look after her now that she is pregnant, especially as she is rather old to be expecting her first baby.'

'Are you planning to move?'

'That's what we need to talk about. I could move over to Wales and travel back to school daily because the journey is no longer than you do to Oxford each day. We have to think about Claire and what to do about this house.'

'We shall have no further need of this house if you are going to live with Mary so I suppose we should sell it and I will buy somewhere in Oxford, but Claire will be upset because she likes living in the village and she has all her friends and interests centred here. Does she know about this baby?'

'No, of course not. Nobody else knows apart from Mary and me and the doctors. I wouldn't dream of telling Claire until we had had a chance to talk things over.'

'I just feel completely numb and, strangely, quite calm. We have got to agree whether or not we give Claire a choice about her future. I don't want to lose her but my work takes me away from time to time and she may prefer to be living with you. . .'

'. . . and coming to stay with you. Whatever she does she is going to have to leave the village and change schools.'

'Would boarding school be best for her? So many children from broken marriages go away to school.'

'Broken marriage sounds dreadful. Is that really what we have?'

'Well I don't think there is any other way of referring to a marriage which the husband has abandoned in order to live with the mother of his child.'

Anna now was feeling angry and terribly hurt. She knew that there was no way that the marriage she and Richard had could be maintained. She was about to lose her husband, her home and possibly her only child. The only thing which remained for her was her work; it was the only area of her life where she felt she had had any success.

'If you don't get out of my study I think I might hit you.'

'Anna don't say that, please let us try to remain good friends as we have always been.'

'Richard, get out! I want to be on my own.'

He went. He had never known Anna to be so angry. It was a much greater shock to her than he had anticipated. He felt distressed but was also equally determined that he was going to live with Mary. He looked in the fridge to see what there was for an evening meal. Mrs Maidment had obviously done some shopping for them and left one of her bacon and egg pies. He set the table and got the meal ready and waited for Claire to come home. Anna did not appear so he went up and asked her if she would like him to bring her up some supper on a tray.

'No, thank you all the same. I will come down. I am sorry I behaved as I did.'

Claire came back while they were eating the meal and

joined them.

'I did have some tea with Alison but I can eat some more.' Anna asked about the holiday in Scotland and Claire, without much enthusiasm, described what she had done. She was obviously trying to protect her mother from the knowledge that they had had a good time at Gairloch.

'Claire, we have got to make some important decisions which involve you.'

'Are you going to split up?'

'Dad is going to go and live with Mary.'

'I don't think that is fair.'

Richard thought he ought to do some explaining and not leave it to Anna.

'The reason that I am going to live with Mary is that she is going to have a baby; it will be your half brother or sister.'

Claire stared at him and then she looked at her mother who avoided the eye contact. Then she got up from the table, knocking her chair over as she went.

'I hate you both, I hate you.'

'Claire, come back,' called Richard.

'Let her go; it's a shock for her although she has suspected that this is going to happen for a long time. But that doesn't make it any easier when it does.'

'You won't really believe this Anna but I am desperately sorry to cause so much hurt to you and Claire.'

'I expect we shall weather it, just give us time.'

Richard got up and began to clear the table. As he did so Anna could not help feeling the slightest bit sorry for him. He had had so many years of doing the menial tasks and perhaps neither she nor Claire had really appreciated just how much he had done to make their lives as good as they had been. Now that they were losing that input they were realising, too late, how important he was to them. She got up to help him and in silence they washed the dishes and then put them away.

'What shall we, or rather what will you, tell your parents?'

'I will go down to Cornwall and see them. It will make them sad, I know. They are very fond of you and extremely proud of their daughter-in-law.'

'Proud of her academic achievements rather than her as a daughter-in-law.'

'I don't think so.'

Claire stayed in her room until late in the evening and then came down to find her parents, most unusually, sitting talking with each other.

'What have you decided to do with me?'

'We want to know what you think is the best thing.'

'To go on as we are.'

Richard began to think that they were going to go round and round in circles and that nothing was going to be resolved so he said very firmly that he wanted Claire to move with him to live with Mary and that she should go and stay with Anna as often as she and Anna wanted.

'Think about it,' he said 'but we shall be selling this house and none of us will be able to live here.'

Claire had been thinking about it for the last three hours. She hated the idea of her parents separating but she had to admit that life with Dad and Mary was often more fun than life at home with him and Mummy and that he seemed much happier when he was with Mary. What was more, she had never once felt in the way or been made to think that she was a nuisance and sometimes she felt she was second to her mother's work.

Richard went to Cornwall on his own. He told his parents that he was leaving Anna and going to live with Mary who was expecting his child. The way he put it was to take all the blame on to his own shoulders and to exonerate Anna completely. That his mother would not have.

'It takes two to make or break a relationship and I have watched, from a distance, for many years and thought how hard you have tried to make it work. Anna has had, and will continue to have, great academic success, but it is because you have protected her from the responsibilities in the home which perhaps she should more readily have assumed had she wanted to keep your love. You know that we both like Mary very much.'

'Dad, you're not saying much.'

'The dilemma for me as a priest is that I believe vows are exchanged for life. I am sad that two people have tried to keep those vows but have ended up causing hurt and suffering to each other. As a father I cannot condemn you for having fallen in love with another person, and I do respect you for taking on the full responsibility of Mary and your child. I do also believe in a loving and caring Heavenly Father who understands and forgives when his children have tried and yet not succeeded in what they set out to do. It goes without saying that we shall love and welcome to our home Mary and our new grandchild and that we shall also continue to love and welcome Anna whenever she wishes to come and see us.'

Richard was quite moved as he listened to his father speaking but he knew that he no longer shared his faith to the extent that he might once have done.

'I'm sorry for all the hurt I may have caused through this but I have never loved anyone as I love Mary.'

'We've know that for a long time,' said his mother, 'right from the first weekend when she came to stay and she acted as godmother at Claire's baptism.'

'You never said anything.'

'It was not the sort of thing to mention was it? We can only look on as parents and give advice if we are asked for it. Mary is a lovely person and Claire likes her very much. Claire, incidently, has often spoken about you and Mary when she was down here.'

'It seems that it isn't quite the terrible shock that it could have been.'

'No, you could say that we did pick up some early warning messages,' replied his mother with a smile. Then she got up and came across and put her arms around him and he saw that her eyes were filled with tears.

From Cornwall he drove to Wales. Mary was due to go to the hospital for her scan the next day and he had said that he would like to go with her. Her appointment was for ten o'clock but they expected that they would have a long wait. Mary had been told that she must come with a full bladder but when she got there they gave her a jug of water and a glass with instructions that she was to drink all that fluid as well. At the moment that it was deemed to be full enough a nurse came out and called, 'Mrs Swaine, we are ready for you now.'

'They call every one Mrs here,' Mary explained to Richard, 'I didn't book in as a married woman!'

Richard sat in the waiting area with the other expectant

mothers and a few fathers. He would have liked to have gone in with Mary but he presumed that fathers were not allowed into the radiography unit. A little while later the nurse who had escorted Mary away came back into the waiting area and came across to him.

'Mr Swaine, the radiographer wonders if you would like to come in while they are scanning your wife?'

It would have been too complicated to explain that his name was not Swaine and that Mary was not his wife. He followed her into the room where Mary was lying on the bed looking at the screen.

'We think the scan is showing something exciting and we thought you would like to see this together,' said the senior radiographer who had been called in to check the scanning. Mary smiled up at him. 'Be prepared for a shock.'

'What is this all about?'

'Let me show you on the screen.'

The radiographer pointed to a rounded area and explained that that was the head and the curved bit was the spine.

'But look here, behind the baby there is another head and an arm. Your wife is carrying twins.'

'Twins, that is great news, but will it be all right for Mary since she is a bit older than most mothers having their first pregnancy?'

'Everything looks fine from the scan but the consultant will see you both shortly. Are there twins in your family?'

'I have twin sisters.'

'Right, Mrs Swaine, we have finished with you now. The toilets are just down the corridor. I'm sorry we had to make you drink so much but we did get a very good scan picture as a result.'

Mary shot off at great speed, grinning all over her face. Richard waited for her to come back and then they were shown into a little examination cubicle to wait for the consultant.

'Are you in a state of shock, darling?'

'I'm very happy about it even if it does come as a shock. Having waited to my great age to have one baby, it's really rather splendid to be expecting two. That must be why I seem to be getting much bigger than either of my sister-in-laws did at this stage in their pregnancy.'

The consultant felt Mary's tummy and confirmed the scan results that it was a twin pregnancy. All Mary's other test results were fine and he saw no reason why she should not have a normal delivery. He asked her if she was working, and when he heard that she taught and was on her feet a lot he did suggest that she should start her maternity leave by mid-October so that she was able to rest more in the last two months.

Richard took Mary's arm and guided her carefully to the car park.

'Just because I am expecting two babies there is no reason to wrap me up in cotton wool you know. I am feeling very well and I am always a very fit person. Being pregnant suits me.'

'My experience has been of Anna being unwell in pregnancy and you will have to forgive me if I want to cosset you.'

'I like the sound of that, of being cosseted I mean.'

During the rest of the summer holidays there were many changes that had to be made. The house in Wiltshire was put on the market and a couple who were keen gardeners, and were immediately attracted by the garden which Richard had so lovingly created, made an offer which was accepted. Anna found a spacious flat in the centre of Oxford, within close walking distance to her laboratories, and Richard offered to help her to move into it. She found it particularly hard to face dividing up the contents of their home but Richard was insistent that she had the larger share because he would be acquiring the use of things which already belonged to Mary.

They were both determined that they would remain civil to each other and perhaps in the future would revert to being good friends again. At this time Anna was still struggling hard not to feel aggrieved by what was happening and this had to be worked through.

Claire was to live with Richard and Mary and change schools at the beginning of the autumn term. They were all agreed that it would not be an ideal arrangement if she were to go to the one that Mary currently taught in, so she transferred to another comprehensive which was in the opposite direction. She would go up to Oxford and spend time with Anna at weekends and in the holidays. Mary and Richard knew that sometime before the babies were born they would need to acquire a larger house but in the immediate future they could all live in Mary's cottage. Richard would drive across the Severn bridge each day to carry on teaching in Wiltshire but the sensible thing would be for him to begin to look for a post in Wales.

By the second week in September schools had gone back. Claire had been sad to leave her friends in the village and the change of schools was for her the worst part of the upheaval. She and Richard moved in with Mary just before the term started and on the first day Mary drove her to the new school.

'What shall I say to people about why I am here?'

'Could you say that your Dad has come to live in Wales and you have moved with him?'

'What shall I say about Mummy?'

'You could tell them that she works in Oxford and that you go and stay with her.'

'What shall I say about you?'

Mary smiled at her.'

'With a bit of luck you might be able to get by for quite a long time without having to explain me as well. If you do. . . well I always think the best thing is to be honest. . . but perhaps to be economical with how much information is given.'

She dropped Claire at the front gate of the school and felt desperately sorry for the rather forlorn figure who walked into the entrance. In all the upheaval Claire was the one who really was having the roughest deal.

14

Anna moved into her new flat towards the end of September. The exchange of contracts had been delayed by a particularly zealous solicitor who had been meticulous in checking every aspect of this purchase. She would want to make some changes to the decor but would leave this until the following year when she had had time to get the feel of the place and decide what she would most like. However, it was important that her study was immediately operational so she engaged a carpenter to build extensive book shelves and to make work tops for her computer and printer. Then she had an electrician put in more power sockets and additional lighting. Finally she decided that she might as well have the room decorated and carpeted before she moved in all her material and books. When it was completed she felt very satisfied. This was the third, and she hoped final, time that she had made a work base at home and she rectified the mistakes in design that had been made in the first two when money had been in shorter supply.

The flat was spacious but everything was streamlined and efficient. It had gas fired central heating which as soon as it was switched on quickly warmed the entire place. In addition to her study, which was perhaps the most pleasant room in the flat, she had a sitting room, a dining room and a large kitchen. On the floor above she had three bedrooms and a bathroom. From the rooms on the upper floor she could look across the Oxford skyline and hear the sound of Big Tom tolling the hour. She knew that this would be a place which would inspire her to work.

She also needed to have plenty of room because she

hoped that various members of the family would come to visit her. After everyone had been made aware of the fact that Richard was going to live with Mary, Anna had been overwhelmed with letters and messages from Richard's parents and his brothers and sisters saying that they hoped that all their relationships would continue as they had been. Since this was the only family which Anna now had, she had felt very touched by their warmth and she gladly responded to them. She would have Claire coming to stay with her regularly and she hoped that Claire would feel that this was her home as much as the one she lived in with Richard and Mary. Once Anna was established in this flat she was able to feel more positive about the events of the last year. So often in the past she had felt enormous pressure by needing to get a vital piece of work completed, but knowing that she should be giving some time to family matters. Now she was absolved of that responsibility. Her time was nearly all her own and she could do what she had to do when it most suited her to do it. She came to realise that she had not lost as much as she had initially thought, and she had gained much more than she had allowed herself to realise.

Two weekends after she had moved in Claire came up on the train to stay. They spent some time exploring Oxford together, for although Anna had been there for nearly nine months she had not allowed herself time to wander around. They went to a special restaurant for a meal and Anna showed Claire round the laboratories. So far Claire had shown no particular aptitude for things scientific and, as yet, there was no indication that she had inherited any of her mother's formidable intellect. She was actually not very interested in the laboratories and much preferred seeing the squirrels which abounded in the Parks. Also, although the flat was very pleasant, for Claire it did not have the feel of home. It was extremely tidy and Claire, who had inherited some of her father's tendencies to be a little untidy, found it a slight strain to be so organised. Anna asked about how things were in Wales and how Mary was feeling; she was infinitely relieved that it was not she who was expecting twins.

Claire travelled back on the train on the Sunday afternoon. She was still feeling that she did not really belong anywhere and she missed the house in Wiltshire and her own bedroom. When the train drew into the station there were Mary and Dad waiting for her and she could see them anxiously peering into carriage windows until they got a sight of her and then they both waved. It was good to see them. As they walked out of the station they told her that they had something to show her. There was about another hour before it got dark and they would have to drive about eight miles.

'What are we going to see?'

'It's a surprise; you've got to wait until we get there.'

'It is something for me?'

'It won't be a surprise if we give you any clues.'

'I shall watch the milometer and then I shall know when we are nearly there. You said it was eight miles.'

'I said about eight miles. When we are nearly there do you want to close your eyes?'

'I'm not a little girl any more; no I don't!'

They had turned off the main road and had been driving along a quiet lane. They came into a small village and Richard parked the car near the green in the centre.

'Now we are going to walk a little.'

'Is this all a joke of some sort?'

Mary intervened.

'Stop teasing, Richard. Claire, what we are bringing you to see is a house which we have viewed this weekend and which we thought was lovely. The owners know that we are going to come back with you so that you can have a look at it and see what you think.'

They walked through the gate and paused to look at the large garden. The front door opened and a man with a young boy came out to meet them. He suggested that they show Claire round themselves. It had been a farmhouse in the past but all the land had been sold off separately many years ago and there was only about an acre of garden that went with the house. The ceilings were low and there were beams everywhere. Some of the floors were quite uneven. In the living room there was an enormous inglenook fireplace and in the kitchen an Aga range which heated the water and provided two ovens for cooking, as well as warming that end of the house. Upstairs there were five bedrooms, most of which had beams and creaky floor boards. Claire could see from the window sills just how thick the outside walls were and she thought how cosy the house felt. She paused to look from the window of one of the rooms. There was an uninterrupted view across the fields to the mountains beyond. This was the bedroom of the young boy who had met them when they had first arrived. He came up while they were looking at it.

'This is my room,' he said 'I think it is the nicest bedroom.' Then he turned to Claire. 'If you come here why don't you choose this for your room. You can see the mountains from this room; sometimes they have snow on them.'

On the way home Claire was asked what she thought about the house.

'It's a smashing house and we would have plenty of room for the babies.'

It was the first time that Claire had actually mentioned the expected twins in her conversation. She had been told about them soon after Richard and Mary knew but there had seemed to be a reluctance to talk about them and the matter had not been pushed.

'That was why we looked at a house with five bedrooms. We can also have a guest room and you could have your friends from Wiltshire to stay, that is if you wanted to of course.'

This was the house they bought and by mid-November they moved in. Mary had given up teaching at the end of October and had been able to oversee the final negotiations and to plan the move without unduly exerting herself. They actually moved on a Friday and Richard was able to take the day off to help. Some of the furniture from the Wiltshire house had been in store, including the things from Claire's bedroom. When she came home from school on that Friday evening Claire found that all her things had been arranged in the bedroom with the view to the mountains. For the first time in several weeks she felt that she belonged somewhere again.

They spent the weekend getting straight. Carpets were laid and pictures hung. Some curtains fitted but others looked either too long or the design did not match the wallpaper, but nobody minded and it was fun improvising. On the Monday morning Richard and Claire set off to their respective schools with strict instructions to Mary that she was not to do too much.

'Stop fussing,' said Mary with a laugh, 'when I feel tired I shall put my feet up on the Aga and have a sleep.'

Claire found the best thing about Mary being at home was that there was always somebody there when she came in, the house was warm and there was the smell of supper being cooked. If she felt ravenous, as she did most days, there was a piece of home made cake to keep her going until the main meal which they had as soon as Richard got back. Mary was interested in what she had been doing and always had time to talk with her. She helped her with her music and now that Claire had started to play the flute as well as the piano, Mary would accompany her when she practised. It was the sort of home life which Claire had so rarely had and which she now found she so much enjoyed. It also contrasted quite starkly with Anna's home in Oxford and Claire began to feel that her visits to see her mother were less and less enjoyable and for both of them were a duty. Perhaps sometime her mother would be able to come and see them in Wales.

The opportunity for that came towards the end of Claire's first term at the school in Wales. There was to be a parents' evening.

'Who would like to come to my open evening?' asked Claire at supper.

'Well I for one,' said Richard.

'What about you Mary?' asked Claire.

'I was wondering if Anna would like to come down and go to the school.'

'Why don't you all come?'

'Why not indeed?' said Richard. 'Look I'll ring Mummy and ask her what she thinks about it.'

He was pleasantly surprised at how amenable Anna was to this suggestion and when he told her that Claire wanted all of them to go together she agreed that it was the right thing.

'Of course it is not long before Mary is due to deliver so we may not all get there.'

Anna declined the invitation to stay at the farmhouse overnight.

'I would find that too difficult to cope with as yet, but there may come a time when I feel about to do it.'

In the end only Richard and Mary were able to go. Anna had to go to an urgent meeting in London concerning some research funding for her department. She telephoned Claire and said that she was really sorry but she would like to come to the next one.

'It's a good job I have two mothers,' remarked Claire when she was on her own with Richard, 'at least that guarantees that I have somebody at my school events.'

She would not admit to being hurt again that her mother had not been able to support her.

Claire had had her thirteenth birthday at the beginning of December and, in deference to the fact that she was now a teenager, this had been celebrated with a supper party to which she invited several of her friends from school. She had told them that Mary was her stepmother and left them to assume that Mary and Richard were married.

Although Mary was in an advanced stage of her pregnancy she prepared a splendid buffet supper and then she and Richard discreetly withdrew from the disco which the youngsters had in the sitting room until 10 o'clock.

'One advantage of not having fitted carpets in there yet is that we don't have to worry about the damage that the younger generation might be doing to our furnishings,' Richard commented.

'It's no use being houseproud if you have a family; a home is for living in. They are having a lovely time even if the volume of noise from that record player must be doing permanent damage to their ear drums!'

'If she had been born in June we could have had this party in the garden or even let them have a barn dance in the old barn. I wonder why it is that all my children are to have December birthdays? Even the baby which we lost after Claire was due to be born in December.'

'Perhaps you thought you could get away with giving a joint Christmas and birthday present and it was all very carefully planned!'

'It might even be something to do with me being more

221

randy in the spring time.'

'Oh, I hadn't particularly noticed that there was a seasonal variation. . .'

'Who's being cheeky now?'

It had been calculated that the exact expected date of delivery was December 27th but everyone knew that the babies might arrive at any time during the month. Richard was very firm in insisting that Mary had some regular help in the house and although Mary, initially, resisted the idea she realised towards the end of her pregnancy that she was getting very tired and needed to rest much more than she had ever had to do before. She also knew that when the babies were born she would have to spend nearly all her time dealing with their needs. They advertised in the village shop window and ended up with a very likeable young woman who was wanting to have a few hours work each day now that her children had started school. She was equally willing to do cleaning, shopping, washing and ironing and to help bath babies. The only problem which she said she might have is that sometimes in the school holidays she might have to bring her youngest boy to work with her.

'I really don't see that as a problem,' said Mary with a smile, 'particularly as you can do so many of the household tasks.'

Mary and Richard would clearly have to spend Christmas at the farmhouse and were very happy to do so. But it was going to be the first Christmas that Anna was on her own and Richard had many qualms about this which he did not share with anyone. They asked Claire where she would like to be and she said that she would stay at home and by home she meant with them. Richard finally telephoned Anna and was very surprised to be told that she had been invited by his parents to spend Christmas in Cornwall at the rectory. She had not decided if she would accept the invitation but she had been touched by her parents-in-law kindness to her. After hearing that he felt much more at peace with himself and the world in general.

Mary went into labour two days before Christmas and Richard drove her to the hospital. He stayed with her through what, for the so-called elderly primigravida, was a relatively short labour and witnessed for the first time in his life the birth of not one baby but two. They had twin sons, both of whom cried lustily at birth and each weighed in at nearly six pounds. Mary was very relaxed throughout the delivery and they both hugged each other with joy when it was all over.

'What are we going to call them? Why did we think that we were going to have girls? We seem to have thought of lots of possible girls' names.'

Richard had been thoughtful.

'I did just wonder if you would like to call one of them William? It is a name that I like very much and it would sort of perpetuate Bill's memory.'

There were tears in Mary's eyes as she replied.

'I would like that very much. You don't mind your son being named after the man to whom I was engaged?'

'I think Bill and I would have got on well together had we had the chance to meet and I would be very happy to have a boy named after him.'

The other boy they decided to call Thomas because it was a name they both liked but it also had family connections. They had already agreed that the children would be registered as Trevanion.

The first person that Richard telephoned was Claire.

'You have got two little brothers,' he said.

It was difficult over the phone to ascertain what her reaction was but he thought she seemed pleased.

'I'll come home shortly and bring you back to the hospital to have a little peep at them.'

Then he rang his parents. They sent their very genuine congratulations and their love and said that they looked forward to seeing the babies as soon as it was practicable. They also said that they would tell Anna when she arrived the following morning to stay with them for two days.

'It's a strange coincidence, Claire but you, like William and Thomas spent your first Christmas in hospital. When Mummy and I came in to see you on Christmas morning you had been transferred from the incubator to a tiny cot for the first time.'

'Do you ever miss Mummy?'

'There are some things that I am sad about.'

223

'Like what?'

'Well at times like Christmas for example. You had to choose which parent you wanted to be with and as things have turned out you are landed with just spending Christmas with your old Dad. If you had gone with Mummy you could have been in Cornwall.'

'It's not quite the same as being at home is it?'

'Do you feel that this is home?'

'Yes, I think so. Anyway, I like being with my old Dad. He has been a good old Dad to me.'

'Are you going to mind sharing him with two other young lads?'

'It depends. As long as it is fair shares, I expect it will be all right. I'm not sure how much I am going to like these babies, especially if they cry all night and are sick over everywhere, but they might improve as they get older.'

Richard gave her a hug.

'After all these years and the amount of time that we have spent together, you know that you can never be anything other than very special to me.'

It was Christmas Eve. They did the final preparations for Christmas, then they took two little stockings filled with small parcels into the hospital. Mary had insisted that both babies remained in her room with her even though it meant that she did not get much sleep. Claire fastened the stockings to the end of each cot.

'Some children are lucky; Father Christmas has called early in this hospital. Tomorrow I will help you both unwrap your presents.'

Mary and the twins came home from hospital on New Year's Eve and life immediately became a round of feeding, bathing and nappy changing. Mary was breast feeding both babies and as she became more proficient she was able to put both babies to her breasts simultaneously. She had to remember to alternate the sides and in the end had to write down if it had been William or Thomas who had had the left side at the last feed.

'Does it matter?' asked Richard.

'Only so far as each boy needs to learn to feed either side and just in case the supply of milk one side is better than the other.

The twins were hungry feeders and they had to have supplementary bottles to satisfy them. For the first month that they were home they did not sleep well at night and Richard and Mary seemed to be up for hours on end changing nappies and giving extra bottles. It was a particularly tiring time for Richard because he still had the drive to Wiltshire to make each day and in that January the weather was bad. There were frequent falls of snow in the mountains and sometimes this extended to the lowlands. Maggie Jones who came in during the daytime was a great asset. She was always calm and would do any job that needed to be done. She gave one twin a bottle while Mary fed the other and together they coped with bathing the babies and getting their washing done. Mary was very determined that she should make time for Claire and that the babies should not completely monopolise her energy. When Claire came in from school Mary always tried not to be doing things with William and Thomas. As it was this was the time of day that they were quite happy and contented and prepared to sleep. Their restless time came much later, just as their parents were dropping with fatigue and ready to go to sleep. From about 11 pm until 2 or 3 am neither of the babies showed any inclination to sleep and certainly were not willing to lie in their cots. They cried relentlessly until they were picked up and then were very contented until one of their parents tried to put them down again whereupon there was a wail which disturbed the other.

'Who was it said that she felt it was a great blessing to be having twins?' asked an exhausted Richard at 3 am one morning. 'This is more like hell on earth!'

'Do you still want that large family?'

'I planned to have one child every three years, not one followed by two thirteen years later.'

'Look love, you go and sleep in the spare room. You have got to teach tomorrow and I can go to bed during the day when Maggie is here.'

'I'm never going to start sleeping in the spare room. It will get easier. Surely at the end of six weeks they will settle down?'

And, miraculously, at the end of six weeks they did! They were both given a feed at 11pm and went through

225

until nearly 5 am. Richard also began to develop an ability to sleep through their cries.

As the spring term progressed Richard seriously scanned the journals for suitable jobs in Wales. One evening Mary made the suggestion that was so obvious that he had never thought of it.

'Why don't you apply for my job?'

Her maternity leave was nearly ended and everyone had known that Mary Swaine would not be returning to teaching, at least not in the foreseeable future. The job could now be advertised.

'You are a hard act to follow; I seem to have spent my life doing just that.'

'No, I'm serious, Ricky. Why don't you get an application form and details about the post. They would be very pleased to appoint somebody who could offer sport as a second subject. There is plenty of strength already in music which I did as my second subject so that would not be a loss.'

'It would be very attractive to be teaching at a school which is only three miles away. I could almost walk there each day. I could certainly jog in if I felt so inclined.'

He applied. The night before the interview Thomas was very disagreeable with life so Mary took him downstairs and slept with him in the sitting room so that Richard could get some rest. Even so Richard felt only half awake as he made his way to the school.

'I must concentrate and try to interview well. It is so important that I get this post.'

☆ ☆ ☆

'I see from your application form that you played rugby for London University; you were awarded your "Purple",' said the governor who was chairing the selection panel, 'do you still play rugby?'

'I have not been able to play all the rugby that I would have liked to have done due to early family commitments but I coach the first fifteen in my present school and I train hard so that I keep fit.'

'You have also played for Cornwall when you were a younger man,' the governor continued. 'They play a very

226

good standard of rugby down there. Now this school has a very good record in rugby. We have already produced one national player in recent years and we want there to be others. Would you be offering your services to coaching rugby if you were to be appointed?'

'They hardly asked me a thing about geography or how I would manage the teaching within the department of which I would be head. It was all rugby; that was all they talked about.' Richard was responding to Mary's question about how the interview had gone when he got home.

She roared with laughter.

'You must have had Mr Llewellyn-Hughes on the panel. He lives, breathes and dreams rugby. He has a debenture seat at Arms Park and he is there for every international match that is played. Rumour has it that he celebrates for the whole weekend whatever the result.'

'The Headmaster did not say too much about things geographical either but he did ask me about taking school trips away for activities.'

'When are they going to let you know the decision?'

'They have. On the basis of my prowess on the rugby field and my knowledge of taking school parties away for educational visits, I have been appointed to be Head of Geography Department to succeed the very eminent young lady who last held that position.'

'Oh, Ricky that is super. Well done.'

'Do you think that there may be those who think that the appointment has some flavour of nepotism?'

'Certainly not. It was your rugby skills that clinched the job for you, not that I'm implying you are deficient in skills geographical.'

'You know there might come a time when we think about job sharing.'

'No thank you. I want to be a full time mother and housewife and I think the time has come for you to be relieved of those tasks so that you can develop your career and personal interests. I have had fifteen years of it and I'm not sure that I would ever want to go back. Being a home-maker is what I have always wanted to do eventually.'

Richard took her in his arms and kissed her.

'I love you. Don't ever forget that will you?'

227

'Not so long as you keep reminding me.'

Claire came through the door.

'Ugh, you two are getting sloppy again.'

'We are celebrating that your Dad has got a new job.'

'That's great, Dad. Of course it's not such a good school as mine but for a simple chap like you. . .'

'Wait till I get my hands on you.'

Amidst much laughter Richard shot out of the room after Claire as she leapt up the stairs two at a time. There was a general pandemonium which, although it wakened the twins did not distress them in the slightest. They were clearly going to enjoy a fair amount of rough house in their lives.

15

Snow had fallen through the night. When Anna drew back her curtains on the Sunday morning she looked across a beautiful skyline of ancient buildings enhanced by the layer of snow which seemed to emphasise the magnificence of the roofs and domes. She was planning to call into the laboratory first thing because there were some test results which needed to be checked daily and she had volunteered to do them over this weekend so that her junior staff could have the weekend off. She stopped for a quick cup of coffee and then walked down to the college. There were very few people about and hardly any traffic had been down the High. The snow seemed to be muffling any sound and there was an incredible silence and feeling of peace. Anna did her work in the laboratory and then went out across the quadrangle.

'Good morning Professor Trevanion,' said one of the undergraduate students in her department. He was dressed in a track suit and obviously was out for an early morning run.

'Hello Mark. Where are you going to train this morning?'

'I thought I might run through the Parks. I just love being out in the snow.'

'Yes it is a splendid morning.'

Anna decided that she would enjoy walking back through Christ Church Meadow. There was only one other set of foot prints in the snow, but it was still very early in the day. She detoured to the river bank and stopped to admire the view across the water to the snow encrusted banks. There would soon be hardy rowers out on the river but at that time, with the exception of some noisy ducks, the water was deserted.

For the first time in many months Anna realised that she was feeling happy with her life again. She had recovered from the impact of Richard moving in with Mary and of Claire deciding to make her home primarily with her father. Her work was going extremely well. She had written two major scientific books which were standard texts for university students and more recently the first results of her work on the crystallographic structure of human bladder stones had been published in *The Lancet*. Those who were closely associated with this work believed that she was on the brink of a major breakthrough and she herself was excited by the preliminary findings. So important did she feel this work to be that she now realised the shedding of the domestic ties had freed her to concentrate exclusively upon her research. She reflected on the fact that had she still been at the home in Wiltshire that day she would have had to cook a meal and spend time with Claire and Richard. As it was, the day ahead was entirely hers to use as she wished. When she got back to the flat she might have some breakfast and then she would go to her study and continue writing the current paper. She turned for home with a sense of well-being and of purpose.

As winter gave way to spring Anna never ceased to marvel at her good fortune to be living in such an attractive city. She worked very hard but she also allowed herself time to relax and go walking. Occasionally she would go to the theatre but this was one thing that she did find hard to do on her own. Claire's visits seemed to be less frequent but when she came they enjoyed their time together. She did suggest to Claire that during the summer they might go away for a short holiday together to somewhere exotic. Claire said that she would think about it but did not seem too enthusiastic and Anna did not push the idea. She tried to remember if she had resisted going away on holiday with her mother and did not think she had. The situation had been different because her mother was the only parent she had ever known, so there was no alternative.

Anna knew that at some stage soon she would have to go to Wales because she had promised Claire that she would attend a school function. She had never been to Claire's new school and realised that Claire felt a little aggrieved by this fact. She knew too that she ought to try to visit Richard and Mary and meet the twins. After they had been born she had written a note of congratulations which Mary had answered with a warm invitation to come down to the farmhouse whenever and if ever she could. For Claire's sake it was important that she bore no animosity to either Richard or Mary. She had heard of a similar situation where a colleague's marriage had ended in divorce when his wife had established a relationship with his best friend. Once the hurt had eased he had been invited to stay with them so that he could see his children, and it had ended up with them always spending Christmas together and he going away for holidays with them all. Anna had commented to him that it all sounded very civilised but there must be some snags. He said that initially the only thing that he had found hard was seeing his former wife going into another man's bedroom, but now it did not matter and he regarded them as close and dear friends. Anna hoped that she could be equally charitable but doubted it. She did wonder if Richard would ever mention the issue of divorce. Although they had earlier all been opposed to it, since the twins had been born there did seem more reason to reconsider the situation. For her it did not matter; she knew she would never marry again. She much preferred to have personal space and was contented to be alone. On the odd occasion that she needed to have a partner or people to accompany her to functions she could always make a request to somebody in the family.

Anna had a conference in San Francisco in April and she travelled there with her Research Fellow. They were jointly presenting a paper on one aspect of the project. The American media were particularly interested in the fact that it was two women who held these important academic positions in Oxford and they were interviewed several times on television. When Anna got back to Oxford there was a letter waiting for her from London University. In recognition of her outstanding contribution to science, particularly in the field of crystallography, they would like to award her, as a former student and lecturer in that University, with an Honorary Degree. Of all the awards that Anna had had in her academic career, nothing had given her so much pleasure as did that letter. She wrote back and said that would be greatly honoured to receive the degree.

The conferment of the honorary degrees would be made at the post-graduate degree awarding ceremony in June, which would be held at Senate House. It was hoped that royal duties would allow the University Chancellor personally to make the presentations. Two seats would be reserved for Professor Trevanion's guests. Anna knew that she would like to invite Richard and Claire to come and decided to write to Richard and asked him if it would be possible.

It was the first time that Anna had asked Richard to do anything for her in the year since he had left her and gone to live with Mary. He had only seen her infrequently and she was still promising to come to Wales but as yet had not been able to manage it. However, he recognised that this was an important award and that Anna might be opening the door to better communications between them all by making this request.

'Would you like to go?' he asked Claire.

'I don't know.'

'That seems to be your stock answer at the moment.'

'I'll think about it.'

'That's the alternative stock answer.'

'They are both the right answers. I don't know and I will give some thought to the matter.'

'Well, Mummy wants to know as soon as possible, because if we can't go I expect she will want to give the tickets to somebody else.'

Mary suggested that he did not hassle Claire for an immediate answer. There was no rush because the tickets were reserved for Anna's guests, whoever they were. He knew she was right so he dropped a note back to Anna saying that he and Claire would try to come. A few days later Anna sent the tickets saying that it would be lovely if they could both be there and she did not want to invite anyone else if they could not manage it. She would look out for them at Senate House. There was a reception for the recipients of honorary degrees and their guests with the

Chancellor.

On the morning of the degree ceremony Anna travelled to London by train. She had been invited, with the other three recipients of honorary degrees, to a rehearsal of the conferment and to try on the academic regalia which had been hired for them. They were also being entertained to lunch before the afternoon's proceedings. She had not heard definitely that Richard and Claire were coming.

After lunch she went into the hall which was fast filling with guests, most of whom were proud parents who had come to see their children being awarded their higher degrees. Anna knew that the two seats which had been reserved for her guests were in the front row. They had a very elaborately inscribed card upon each chair which stated 'Guest of Professor Trevanion.' It was time for her to go to the robing room and prepare for the ceremony. The Chancellor's procession would be the last one to enter the hall and the Honorary Graduands were to process in the front of this one. She could hear the band of the Grenadier Guards playing in the hall. Then there was a tremendous fanfare of trumpets as the final procession entered the hall and slowly made its way to the platform. As she passed the front row she glanced sideways and saw that there were only two seats which were unoccupied. They had not come.

On a tennis court in a school in Wales a very important match was in progress. An exceptionally talented young thirteen year old was playing for the first time for the school's senior team. Nobody could remember a pupil from the junior school ever having played for the first team before and a much larger crowd than usual had gathered at the court side. Among the group was a proud father and an enthusiastic supporter with a double pushchair in which were seated two identical babies. On the door mat of Professor Trevanion's flat in Oxford was a letter which had been delivered after she had left for London. It said that they knew that she would understand what were their priorities that day.